DIE AROUND SUNDOWN

ALSO BY MARK PRYOR

The Bookseller

The Crypt Thief

The Blood Promise

The Button Man

The Reluctant Matador

The Paris Librarian

The Sorbonne Affair

The Book Artist

The French Widow

Hollow Man

Dominic

DIE AROUND SUNDOWN

Mark Pryor

MINOTAUR
BOOKS
NEW YORK

First published in the United States by Minotaur Books, an imprint of St. Martin's Publishing Group

www.minotaurbooks.com

Designed by Omar Chapa

Library of Congress Cataloging-in-Publication Data

Names: Pryor, Mark, 1967– author.
Title: Die around sundown / Mark Pryor.
Description: First edition. | New York : Minotaur Books, 2022.
Identifiers: LCCN 2022005969 | ISBN 9781250824820 (hardcover) |
    ISBN 9781250824837 (ebook)
Classification: LCC PS3616.R976 D54 2022 | DDC 813/.6—dc23
LC record available at https://lccn.loc.gov/2022005969

First Edition: 2022

10   9   8   7   6   5   4   3   2   1

This book is dedicated to all fellow sufferers of misophonia. May you find a place of peace, quiet, and solitude to enjoy Henri's adventures.

DIE AROUND SUNDOWN

CHAPTER ONE

Monday, July 15, 1940

I stepped out of the Police Préfecture, pausing to light up a cigarette, and set off to walk to the scene of the robbery by myself, which went against protocol these days. Albert Durand was supposed to partner me, but his asthma was acting up and he didn't fancy the walk in the heat. Nor did he want to suffer the new views of Paris we were all being subjected to, especially after yesterday, Bastille Day, which was normally a day to celebrate France. For me, at least, it was a day to sit behind my desk and try very hard not to be ashamed of her. Even today, as I left the building, I kept my eyes on the cobbles under my feet, unable to meet her gaze. From time to time I had to look up, of course, and every time I did there they were, the garish, bloodred banners and black swastikas with which the Germans had stained

every important building in the city. All I could do was light
another cigarette, keep my head down, and walk.

Also, I knew Durand would grumble about me smoking,
which I can do without. He'd read reports that doctors were now
saying smoking could give you cancer or blacken your lungs,
but given how many people smoked, and for how many years, I
doubted it. In any case, you'd think that when your city is over-
run by uniformed savages from the east, people would have
more to worry about than someone else sucking in a lungful of
peace, relaxation, and (maybe) slow death.

Durand was useless as a partner, anyway, slow on the up-
take and more likely to get me in trouble than out of it. Since the
Germans had taken Paris not even a month ago there'd been
tension between the people who used to wield authority (us
cops) and the conquering force who now did. Not only had the
bastards taken our precious city, they'd knocked us down in
the pecking order of things. I'm not afraid to bang a few heads
now and again, but in general I find my mouth to be more effec-
tive than my nightstick. But plenty of other cops had taken
the power dilution personally and our chief, Roger Langeron,
wanted an immediate stop to street *flics* and detectives talking
back to the Germans and getting slapped about for their trou-
bles. Two-men teams were thus mandated, on the theory that
at least one of the two would have a cool head. Thing is, Durand
isn't a hothead and I only like to goad the people I work for, so
it's a pointless pairing.

Heading southwest, I crossed Pont Saint-Michel and passed
two grim-faced nurses who glanced my way—they were middle-
aged German women and we called them *les boniches*, "maids,"
for the large white bonnets they wore as part of their starched

uniforms. The Germans love their uniforms . . . Durand told me yesterday that to preserve their image as dignified conquerors, the bastards weren't even allowed to loosen their ties in public. What a joke.

At least those maids get shade from the summer sun, I supposed as I refused to acknowledge their existence.

I stayed on the sunny side of the street myself. Not because I wanted to get sweaty but because the Boche in their wool uniforms stuck to the shady side and the fewer of those cabbage-munchers I encountered, the better for my mood.

Still, it was impossible to ignore the signs of them. Often literally—on rue Grégoire-de-Tours I stopped to read a notice on the front door of one of the forty brothels throughout Paris the Germans had requisitioned. There was a notice with some drivel written in German, and one below it in French: NO ENTRY FOR CIVILIANS OR FOREIGNERS.

And just like that, we weren't even allowed to screw our own women.

I'd heard of the rules *les Fritz* have for their own men in these places: no alcohol allowed, no civilians inside, prophylactics always, and the most ridiculous of all, a soldier was required to note the reference number of the girl he'd been serviced by, after the act. All in the name of efficiency, no doubt, but compare that to the French brothels—no one went inside unless they were drunk or drinking, which meant that condom use was occasional, and only if the girl put it on for you. And no goddamned reference numbers; they had real names like Chantal and Princess and GlouGlou. (Well, no one is christened "Gobbler," but how nice she got to choose a name to match her skills.)

I crossed boulevard Saint-Germain and started down rue de Rennes, slowing as I passed the open doors of a bakery, the smell of fresh bread and sweet pastries drawing me in like a siren. I stopped in my tracks when a baby-faced German got to the door first and held it open for me, an anxious grin on his face.

"Suddenly, I'm not hungry anymore." I said it slowly so he'd understand, and I watched the grin drop from his face, enjoying every second of his discomfort, and then kept walking. I turned my mind to what little I knew about the robbery: the victim was a famous psychoanalyst who lived in a beautiful house and was well-connected. I touched my jacket pocket to make sure my trusty notebook and pencil were ready to flesh out those meager details, but by the time I got to the three-story house I was just glad to step out of the heat. Even gladder when I saw the lady of the house had put a tray on the foyer's circular table with glasses of cold water for . . . the cops who were already there. Which I was not expecting.

There were two, and my heart sank at the sight of them. One in particular. I didn't much mind Marcel Rapace, I'd only come across him and his drooping mustache a couple of times and we'd never had a beef. Not so with Georges Guyat, with whom everyone at the Préfecture had had the whole cow. His nickname was GiGi, and not just for his initials—he had the long face and big eyes of a horse, but one that hadn't been fed in a month. His trench coat, which he wore no matter the weather, hung off his thin, sloping shoulders and no one, I suspect not even his mother, had ever seen him smile.

Of course, the other thing that made my heart sink was that they were murder detectives.

"What are you doing here?" GiGi asked. Being a fine

detective myself, I recognized the sneer he barely bothered to conceal.

"I was told there was a robbery."

"There was. And then a murder. Or the other way around, it doesn't much matter. Either way no one needs a bumpkin from the robbery division."

I moved past him into the living room of the grand house and looked around at the velvets and silks for furniture fabric, the paintings of horse races and pheasant hunts on the stretched canvases, and took in the smell of polish and gentility all around. Which, I thought, I wouldn't recognize if I was a real bumpkin.

"Where is that accent from?" Rapace asked. I couldn't tell if he was sucking up to GiGi or genuinely curious. I gave him the benefit of the doubt.

"Pyrénées." I looked around. "So, what happened here?"

"Nothing you need to know about." GiGi looked past me as a woman entered the room. She looked to be about sixty, with wavy, graying hair parted neatly down the middle and a long pearl necklace she worried at with her fingers. She had thin lips and a rather prominent nose, but her most interesting feature was her wide-set and intelligent eyes. She looked past the other two detectives, directly at me, and her eyes were a lot steadier than her hands.

"And who might you be?" she asked.

"I am Henri Lefort, madame." I gave her a small bow, which was rather out of character for me. It would make more sense later, though.

"I am Marie Bonaparte," she said, her eyes never leaving my face. "And this is my home."

"It's very beautiful," I said, not knowing what else to say.

"Thank you." She looked at GiGi. "Why do I need a third detective?"

"You don't," he said curtly. He unwrapped a stick of gum and I felt my blood pressure instantly rise. The few times I'd been around him he chewed gum like a cow, with maximum force and maximum noise. I cursed the Americans for bringing the damned substance to France. I hated that sound more than any other in the world, and I hate a *lot* of sounds. "Especially not this farmhand." He didn't try to be nice, even when we were with our clients.

"Farmhand?" Bonaparte raised an eyebrow.

"He's from the mountains," GiGi said snidely, popping in the gum. "Maybe a shepherd."

"I'm from Castet in the Pyrénées," I told her. "And don't chew that anywhere near me, if you want to keep your teeth."

"Try it," GiGi said, and smacked his lips to rile me.

"You don't like each other?" Bonaparte asked. She seemed almost amused.

"No one likes him," I said, and she glanced at Rapace for confirmation or denial. He just shrugged, giving her the former.

"Well, since you're here you might as well help." She tilted her head just slightly, still looking at me.

GiGi harrumphed, but he already knew what had just dawned on me—our client was Princess Marie Bonaparte, from the family of Emperor Napoléon Bonaparte himself. Which meant that her wealth, power, and influence outranked his surly attitude and disdain for all humanity, and by some margin. If she wanted me there, I stayed.

"We are leaving for Africa, my husband and I," Bonaparte told me. "Yesterday we sent three servants to pack what we need, and when they didn't return, I came to see why. I found all three." Her voice wobbled a little and she looked down. "In different parts of the house."

"All dead," GiGi piped up, utterly oblivious to her feelings. "Two shot in the chest, one in the back."

"And if a robbery was reported," I said, "not only were they . . . well, some of your belongings are missing?"

"Some jewelry. Quite a lot, I suppose." She glanced at GiGi. "As I told Monsieur Guyat, I saw a man leaving as I came in. Well, I heard him upstairs, and when I ran to the back of the house, he was downstairs already, he went out the back and ran through the garden. Hopped the wall and was gone."

"Anyone you recognized?" I asked, hopeful. So often it was tradesmen or even servants employed by the homeowners who robbed them blind.

"No. But he left some suitcases behind, I assume to put stolen items into."

"Can I see?" I asked.

"A suitcase expert, are you?" GiGi asked. His jaw worked the gum like it was a wrestling match. "That sounds about right, actually."

We all ignored him and Bonaparte led us out of the living room, into the grand foyer, and then up a flight of wide stairs to the second floor. There, in the middle of the long hallway, were three suitcases stacked on top of each other. I circled and inspected them, something bothering me.

"Are these yours?" I asked.

"No, none of them."

Rapace and GiGi had lost interest in the suitcases, assuming they ever had any in the first place.

"Mind if we check the rooms?" GiGi asked, and received a nod from the princess in reply. The way he said it, though, it was as if he was looking for something to do, to entertain himself, rather than for investigative purposes. But, to be entirely fair, he had a pretty good clearance rate so maybe he was being nosy for the right reasons.

"Did you say two men were shot in the chest and one in the back?" I asked.

She shook her head. "I didn't, but your detective friend did." She gave me a small smile to let me know she was joking about the *friend* part.

"He may be a crocodile dressed as a human, but if he said it, it's probably true." It was there in my mind, the knowledge that something was wrong, and I wasn't seeing it. And then I did.

The hair stood up on the back of my neck, and I shouted down the hallway at my two colleagues. "GiGi, Rapace, stop!"

I pulled my gun from my shoulder holster and started toward them. A servant doesn't confront a robber and get shot in the back. No, he gets shot in the back by the robber's compadre. Likewise, one burglar can't carry three full suitcases, that takes two men. And those deductions told me that the feet Princess Marie Bonaparte heard on this floor likely weren't the same pair that carried a man across her back garden.

Which, in turn, meant that one burglar got away, but the other one was still in the house.

I strode toward GiGi, who'd opened a bedroom door on the left side of the hallway. He stood there, waiting for me with his gun in his hand, too. Rapace stood in a doorway a little farther down and across the hall, looking unsure, but also holding his pistol.

"Just wait," I told him.

Turns out, he didn't wait. He tried clearing that bedroom alone, as we were clearing ours, but where ours was empty, his wasn't. The bang almost split my eardrums in the confined space and I ran into the hallway with my ears ringing, just as a man in dark clothing stepped out, smoke still curling up from the barrel of his gun. I raised mine before his eyes focused on me and fired three times, the last as he was already falling. I turned at the sound of a squeal behind me, and saw Princess Marie Bonaparte standing with her hand over her mouth, eyes wide with shock.

I left her to GiGi and ran into the room where Marcel Rapace lay, propped against an oversize armoire, his legs spread wide, his white shirt now red with blood and his eyes staring blankly at the wall opposite him. I could see that the bullet had gone right through his heart so I didn't bother checking for a pulse, I just sat on my haunches next to him, fighting the anger and choking back the tears that I was surprised to feel stinging my eyes.

CHAPTER TWO

Within minutes, hordes of French police and German soldiers descended on the house. The two sets of uniforms generally tried staying out of each other's way, but the crossing of paths was inevitable and, from where I sat watching, excruciating. My once noble and proud force had become a crew of kowtowing bellhops to the German army. At one point, a weasely little SS officer showed up in his black uniform and overly polished boots and I saw one young *flic* throw the bastard a "heil Hitler" salute, at least he did until he caught my eye, and my glare, and dropped his arm to his side.

There were too many people milling around for my liking, but none of the people more senior than me would let me leave, so I went out into the garden for a cigarette. I was about to light up when Princess Marie appeared behind me.

"I'm sorry, there's no smoking on my property." She said it nicely, but the ache in my lungs didn't much appreciate her politeness. "Why don't you come sit with me inside for a moment? I have some things I want to ask you."

I shrugged and followed her into the house. We went through the glass conservatory, past the many uniforms in the main living room, and went through a heavy door into what she called her "own parlor." We sat in red velvet wing-backed armchairs that faced each other beside an ornate fireplace.

"First, I want to thank you for saving my life, Detective."

"I think that's putting a little too much—"

"Not at all," she interrupted. "If you hadn't realized that man was there, he'd have killed both of your colleagues and then me." She grimaced. "I saw with my own eyes how ruthless he was."

"In that case, you are very welcome." I looked around at the wood wainscoting and the delicate silks of the other furniture. "I've never been in a royal house before. Nor met a real princess, let alone one related to Napoléon. What's the connection exactly?"

"I am his great-grand niece. My paternal grandfather was Prince Pierre-Napoléon Bonaparte, and his father was Lucien, the emperor's little brother."

"The great warrior himself."

"Oh, do you think so?"

"Don't you?"

"I think of him as one of the greatest mass murderers the world has ever seen."

I raised an eyebrow but didn't say anything. This woman was . . . different.

"You're impressed by the connection to him?" she asked.

"Mildly. I'm impressed by wealth, but I'm not much of a royalist."

"Well, we can agree on that," she said. "On a different subject, or maybe the same one since the Germans are obviously not impressed by my title either—I've received notification that they wish to take over my house. What can I do about that?"

I thought about it for a second, then said, "I'd recommend moving. I'm sure they're a tidy bunch but not much fun to be around."

"I'm serious. You're a policeman, you're supposed to protect my rights, so tell me what I can do about it."

"Madame, in my honest and considered opinion, absolutely nothing. If they want your house, then the best you can hope for is time to pack a few things and move out."

"It's a disgrace," she said. "We're moving anyway, as you know, but I didn't expect them to take my house while I'm gone."

"You better let them know about the no-smoking rule."

She looked hard at me, her eyes narrowing a little. "You're a glib sort of man, aren't you?"

"I worry about things I need to worry about, about things I can control." I shrugged. "For the rest of it all, I try to get on the best I can."

"You misunderstand, it wasn't a criticism, merely an observation."

"In that case, yes, I am a glib sort of man."

That made her smile. "How long have you been a policeman?" she asked.

"Fifteen years or so."

"And before that?"

"I wandered around a bit. I was in the army for the 1914 war."

"I'd wondered about that." She cleared her throat. "Do you know who Sigmund Freud was?"

I nodded. "Of course. One of those mind doctors, a psycho-something."

She smiled. "If we're being precise, he was a psychoanalyst."

"I see." I didn't, and I didn't much care.

"We were friends," she said. "I helped him get out of Austria. He spent a day right here in this house before heading to London."

"You knew him through your husband?"

"My husband?"

"Yes, someone told me he was also a . . . psychoanalyst."

"Prince George?" She laughed gently. "He most certainly is not."

"So why did . . ." I thought about it for a second, then almost blushed. I'd been told a famous head doctor lived at the house, but not who that person was. "Ah, *you're* the . . . psychoanalyst."

"Correct." She cocked her head sideways. "I was Sigmund's patient, then his student, and then we became friends. He would have enjoyed talking to you. You're an interesting study."

"Me? No, not really."

"You are." She picked up a pencil and started tapping it absentmindedly on her chair. The sound was irritating at first, and within seconds it was all I could hear. My mind works that way, I can't explain it and I don't like it one bit—if someone makes a repetitive sound, even breathing loudly, I go from annoyed to angry in seconds. I extract myself from those situations whenever possible, but sometimes it's not.

"Do you mind," I said as politely as I could, "not doing that?"

"Doing what?"

"The pencil. Tapping it like that."

Then she surprised me. Most people, when I ask them to stop doing something annoying, do it more, trying to be funny. At which point I either explode or walk out. Yes, I know it's petty, but I can't help how certain sounds make me feel, I just can't. So I was happy when she just gave me a big smile and put the pencil down.

"You know, I was working on several interesting projects with Sigmund before he became ill," she said. "One of them was crime related."

"How so?"

"We called it 'aspect association.' The basic idea is that you match aspects of a crime with those of a person's personality, and that tells you something about the criminal you're looking for."

"That doesn't seem . . ." I struggled for the right word.

"Ladylike?" She fixed me with an icy glare. "No one has ever called me that, and no one ever will."

I felt like a chastened schoolboy. "My apologies. Tell me more."

"Very well." The ice in her eyes melted away. "I imagine in its simplest form you're already doing it, just without giving the practice a name. For example, if a robbery scene is a wild mess, then the person you're looking for is likely a stranger to the victim, yes?"

"Yes. They didn't know where to look for the valuables."

"*Exactement*. Whereas a robbery scene where very little

is disturbed tells you the robber likely knew the victim and so knew where they kept the items worth stealing."

"Obviously, yes."

"Sigmund and I thought it could be of most use in murder cases, where things about the crime scene could indicate what type of person committed the murder." She smiled sadly. "The project rather fell away after he died, but maybe you could help me get it back on track."

In truth, it did sound interesting but the one lesson I'd learned from my time in the army was: *Never volunteer for anything. Ever.*

"Maybe," I said. "Though I don't work murders."

"I'll see that you work this one."

"Thank you, that'd be a good start." *Friends in high places, that never hurts.*

She nodded and looked at me in her direct way for a moment. Then she said, "You seem very calm for someone who just shot a man dead. Are you all right with it?"

"Very." I gave her a wry smile. "I've shot people who deserved it a lot less."

"That was war. This seems different, no?"

"Not in the moment."

"It's not the moment that interests me." She stared hard again, looking for cracks maybe. "When bad things happen to people, especially over a long period of time, they can resurface much later and give them mental or emotional issues."

"Bad things like a war, you mean."

"Precisely. Do you have any such issues?"

"If I say yes, are you going to ask a million questions and then present me with a huge bill?" She didn't laugh.

"We've all seen shell shock from the 1914 war, people's minds destroyed by the constant barrage of explosions around them. But that had a physical component, and I believe that damage can be done by stimuli that are purely psychological."

Despite myself, I started to pay attention. I'd gone through periods of anger and depression since shedding my uniform in 1918, at irrational and nonsensical moments, and particularly sounds, so I was inclined to believe her.

"Have you ever sat down and spoken with a psychoanalyst?" she asked.

"No." Nor would I. If I was going to pay good money to put my feet up on a couch, the person giving me their full attention needed to be a lot prettier and extremely undressed.

"Are you married?"

"No."

"And your sex life, may I ask how that is?"

"Madame, you may not." I was a little flustered at that question, for obvious reasons. I barely knew the woman, and she was old enough to be my mother. But as much as she made me feel uncomfortable, she perplexed me in a way I found fascinating. Lies and obfuscation were the currency in my daily life, yet she was so open, so direct. I found it both refreshing and curious.

Then again, here was a princess asking about my sex life after three servants were found murdered in her home, and she acted like *I* was unreasonably calm.

"I'm too busy. I'm trying to get promoted to the murder squad, so no time for women."

It was true. Getting close to someone wasn't writ large, or even small, on any of my career or life plans. I had my sights set on that murder division, and I'd found that while women liked the idea of being a policeman's girlfriend, they didn't usually like the reality. Late nights, last-minute calls to a crime scene, and so much talk of death and mayhem. Cops can be charming, but they're not usually romantic, so why start something I couldn't keep alive? I had other reasons, too, deeper ones, but she didn't need to know what they were.

"Fair enough," she said. "Do you think your blood pressure would go up if I reached for that pencil?"

"Depends on what you're planning to do with it."

"You are calm and unflappable when a man's life is in danger, your life even, but I think me merely picking up that pencil will cause you anxiety."

"Why would it?"

"Because you would begin to anticipate me tapping it. And you don't like that sound, not one bit."

"I don't know what you're getting at."

"Your colleague chewing gum is another one of them, *n'est-ce pas*?"

"I can't stand being around him, with or without gum," I said.

"Don't be flippant. Am I right or not, about the sound?"

"Sure, yes."

"What other sounds anger you?"

"'Anger' seems like a strong word."

"It's more than just annoyance, *non*?"

She asked me that several more times, but I couldn't figure out why and, in truth, she was right, but I dodged the question anyway. By that time, I wasn't interested in sharing anything other than a dinner table because by six o'clock my stomach was starting to rumble. Unfortunately, I suffered through two more hours of waiting around at the house, repeating my statement to more and more senior officers, and even getting my picture taken by some Boche propaganda flunky because Marie Bonaparte was more famous than I'd realized. The way they were playing this was inaccurate but impressive: humble Paris cop saves princess from murderous thieves, with German authorities rushing quickly to back him up and restore calm and order. A fine dollop of horseshit, of course, a man was dead, a cop no less, and one or more of those murderous thieves had gotten clean away. But they weren't going to let the truth get in the way of a good story.

The sun was going down when I stepped out of the Bonaparte house and started for home down rue de Rennes. I thought about the case, wondering what I could do to help catch the murderous thieves, and also how I could work harmoniously with GiGi. I wanted to solve this one, find the people who'd killed Marie Bonaparte's people, and it dawned on me I wanted to do that for two reasons. First, it'd help me in my quest to join the murder squad and second, because I wanted to impress the princess. I stopped to light a cigarette and leaned against a padded lamppost to take in a lungful of delicious Gauloise. The heavy smoke calmed me, but the lamppost didn't. The jacket that it wore was one of the many signs and reminders that my city wasn't as it should be—worried about air raids, part of the city's blackout regimen had included disabling some streetlights altogether and fitting others with dimmers. Two days later, the geniuses who came up with that policy realized that French people can't see in the dark, a realization prompted by a raft of complaints from pedestrians who'd walked into the metal posts, and even a few irate drivers who'd wrapped their vehicles around some.

I shook my head at the idiocy of it all and continued slowly toward boulevard Saint-Germain. As I turned the corner, I caught a whiff of cooked garlic and grilled meat, which made my mouth water and stomach grumble even more. I crossed the street and passed Les Deux Magots, hoping to catch a glimpse of one of the famous writers or poets who hung out there, but when I saw the place was shuttered and noticed that the entire boulevard was deserted, my heart sank as I remembered why. Those delicate aromas that had just tempted me, taunted me, were specters from earlier in the evening, lingering delights from before the restaurants and bistros had shuttered their windows and locked their doors to comply with German regulations. The boisterous smells of Paris were now themselves ghosts, haunting these dark and empty streets and reminding me, yet again, how my world had changed.

I was reminded, too, by a pair of Germans in uniform who were stumbling toward me, and didn't seem to like the look of me. When they got close, one of them tapped his wrist. *"Sperrstunde! Sperrstunde!"*

I knew perfectly well he was saying "curfew," but pretended I didn't. I started to reach for my warrant card but that terrified the drunk fool and he pulled out his gun. He pointed it at my chest while his colleague, as swarthy and un-Aryan as could be, came over to frisk me.

"I'm police. *Polizei,*" I said, knowing they'd find my gun and likely have kittens over it if there wasn't a good explanation. As it was, me being a policeman was seemingly hilarious.

Swarthy Fritz took my gun from its holster and they let me

show them my warrant card, in the sense that they snatched it out of my hand like schoolyard bullies. They had a good laugh over it, and then the proper Aryan pulled out a handkerchief and held it out to me.

"*Glanz mein Stiefel,*" he said.

"I have no idea what you're saying," I told him. I didn't speak much German and had no desire to learn. I also figured that whatever he was telling me to wipe with his damned hanky he was going have to ask a few more times before I complied.

"*Glanz mein Stiefel,*" he said again, this time with anger in his voice. He pointed to his boots and threw the handkerchief in my face. When I tried to hand it back, he stepped toward me and I could smell the sweetness of alcohol on his breath and see his watery eyes. He put a hand on my shoulder and pressed down, but I stood firm. The other man stepped forward and gave me an order that I still failed to understand, and also completely ignored. He spat on the ground and, while I was looking at that, he punched me hard in the stomach.

I went down on one knee and gasped for air, which for them was a good start. The Aryan Boche thrust his right boot in front of me and pointed to it and then the handkerchief. It dawned on me this wasn't a battle I could win, and they'd already made it plain they would use violence to get their way, so I started a half-hearted polishing job while they shared a chuckle at my expense.

In that moment I was glad for the curfew and the empty streets, so that my humiliation was more private than it might have been. I'd fought a war against these bastards once before, and won, yet here I was on my knees, the sidewalk hard under my kneecaps. But, more than sore knees, I felt what they wanted me to—the hot shame that burned inside my chest, the humiliation of being conquered and subservient, reduced in two heartbeats from proud policeman to meek boot-shiner. What they didn't know, or ignored, was that mixed in with that shame was a rising anger that burned my neck and colored my face bright red. I already figured the German pretense at decency was a sham—they were robbing Princess Marie of her home, and I knew firsthand of much, much worse right here in Paris, and I'd heard stories about what they were now doing to Jewish people in other countries. Which meant they'd do those things here, too, sooner or later.

And now here, in this moment, these drunken louts had ensured that whatever small chance the invaders had of living peacefully and respectfully alongside me in my city was wiped away with the dust of that bastard's boots, gone forever.

They eventually let me go with a kick in the arse, their parting shot as I picked up my gun and warrant card from the gutter where they'd been tossed. It was past eleven by the time I made it up the stairs to my apartment on rue Jacob, where I poured myself an oversize whiskey and went to bed, the hunger that had gnawed at me earlier now completely gone. That particular hole in my stomach had been filled by a vile broth made up of shame, humiliation, and the fist of a man I hoped very much I'd see again one day.

CHAPTER THREE

Tuesday, July 16, 1940

I took the usual walk to work the next morning, the warm sun rising to my left over the wide, slow-rolling River Seine, a sun oblivious to the changes my city endured and resisted each and every day. In truth, Parisians had been sick of the war and its privations even before the Germans' gentle stroll into Paris. In the weeks leading up to the occupation every man, woman, and child had been issued a gas mask in case of an air attack. These masks came in canisters, which everyone was supposed to carry with them wherever they went. But, in typical Paris fashion, I'd seen many women ditch the masks and use the canisters as purses to carry their lipsticks, compacts, and bus tickets. True to the old spirit of the city, those ladies may die in a gas attack, but they'd die pretty.

When I got to the office that morning, there were two notes on my desk from my secretary. One said that a journalist had come by to see me, and wanted me to go down to reception where he'd be waiting. The other, and the reason I had no intention of going down to reception, said that Section Chief Louis Proulx had been by already and wanted to see me *immediately*. What made that interesting was that Proulx was head of the murder division, not robbery.

I walked down the long hallway that connected our divisions—robbery occupied half of the third floor of the Préfecture, murder the other half. I passed through the large office where a half dozen detectives were stationed, as was my favorite police secretary, a peppy blonde named Nicola. She'd been at the Préfecture for some years longer than me, even though she was younger, and we'd worked together when she was assigned to robbery. She'd been promoted to this division about a year ago, and she'd joked that murder was a step up in life for everyone except the people we were there for. My kind of humor. That, plus the fact she was cleverer than most people in whichever room she happened to be in, made her my favorite sounding board (and occasional companion) while working cases. Now, I winked at her raised eyebrow but didn't say anything as I strolled past. I rapped on my superior's door and went right in.

Four men stared at me when I went in, and only one of them was Louis Proulx. Two of them were Germans, sadly, and the other was Roger Langeron, the chief of all police in Paris. Langeron was currently doing a two-step in his job, and had been since the Germans rolled into Paris on June 9. Every other government minister, bureaucrat, and flunky had long since stuffed their suitcases with papers and fled to Vichy where the new government was forming. The police, though, and in particular Chief Roger Langeron, had been left behind to make sure the carpet was red enough for the friendly invaders, and not stolen out from under their feet when they marched down the avenue des Champs-Élysées. Ever since their arrival, he'd been trying to figure out who was responsible for what, attempting to keep them happy (we'd all seen news reels of what they could do when unhappy), and still maintain control of the city of Paris.

But Chief Langeron was a good man and he had my respect. He'd worked his way up from the streets by being honest and thorough. He looked the part, too, with a tidy mustache and bald head, and bright eyes behind wire-rimmed glasses. The best thing about him, though, and not everyone agreed with me on this, was that he had recently put Louis Proulx as head of the murder division and, in turn, I knew Louis Proulx liked and trusted me.

Right now, Langeron was perched on the left side of Proulx's desk, which Proulx himself sat behind. The two Germans, to whom I now turned my attention, sat beside each other in chairs to my right. One of them I recognized from the previous evening, the little man in the black uniform of the SS. His hair was slicked back the way the SS liked it and I resisted an urge to stick my fingers into his too-close eyes. That smug face and his short legs told me he'd likely played the runt all his life and was loving his new power. The Wehrmacht officer beside him and in the gray-green was older, looked taller and rounder, and seemed more tired than malevolent.

As they stood to greet me, I stared at them, not trying to

hide the contempt I was fairly sure was written all over my face. I'd spent part of my life, and some of my soul, fighting these people twenty-five years ago, killing them and watching them kill my friends until we managed to drive them back into Germany. And here they were all over again, in my country, in my city, glaring at me like I was some kind of impertinent minion.

"Well then," Proulx said finally. "Inspector Lefort, I need to introduce you to majors Herman Jung and Ludwig Vogel. They both speak excellent French."

Both men snapped into a "heil Hitler" salute, Jung with noticeably less enthusiasm than his comrade, which I couldn't bring myself to mimic. They got a half wave instead.

"Sturmbannführer," Vogel said, looking back and forth between me and the chief.

"I'm sorry, what?" I asked.

"My title is Sturmbannführer, not major."

"Isn't it the same rank?" I looked to Chief Proulx for backup, but he just shrugged.

"It is," Jung said, failing to hide a smile. "Perhaps we can get down to business."

Proulx waved a hand and we all took a seat, the Fritzes where they'd been and me in the chair across from them, within kicking distance of Langeron's dangling foot. I wondered if he'd perched there for that very reason.

"So," I said as cheerily as possible. "Is this about the murders at Princess Marie's home yesterday, or has something else happened?"

"Something else," Proulx said. "Specifically, a dead German officer happened."

"And that's more important than three dead Frenchmen?"

"Infinitely," Vogel snapped. "Of course it is."

I looked at him. "Thing is, there's a war on and German officers are dying all over Europe. A great tragedy, of course," I said, with only the lightest dusting of sarcasm. "You're not expecting us to solve all of them, are you?"

"This one wasn't killed by the war," Vogel said, and his eyes glittered with anger. "Why do you think we're here?"

"That's what I'm trying to find out," I replied mildly.

"As I said, a German officer has been murdered." Proulx sauced the words with several layers of gravitas, and I said nothing else because it no doubt would have been the wrong thing. He continued. "The day before yesterday, he was stabbed to death in the Musée du Louvre."

"I thought the museum was closed?" I knew perfectly well *why* it was closed, too: the best pieces from the museum had been packaged up and shipped off to country homes and private cellars just before the Germans set foot in Paris. I also knew perfectly well that, while it was closed to the public, the Germans had been helping themselves to what was left under various guises of sequestration, confiscation, and repatriation.

"We are planning to reopen it in September," Vogel said, clearly enjoying the surprise on my face. "There is no reason we cannot all enjoy some art while we chase the English into the sea."

"Well, when you put it like that—" I began, but Chief Proulx interrupted, rightly worried about what I might say next.

"Anyway. This particular officer, Hauptmann Walter Fischer, was cataloging items in the gallery devoted to Near and Far Eastern antiquities when he was attacked and murdered."

"Oh. Who killed him?" I asked, with the most innocent expression I could muster.

Vogel muttered something in German and looked away, while Jung stared at me like he was trying to figure me out. Both Proulx and Langeron, as senior officers often did when I was in their presence, sighed heavily.

"You will have to excuse his sense of humor," Proulx said eventually.

"Or at least get used to it," I offered.

Proulx gave me a look that said, *Please, let me do the talking from now on.* "You are here because you are my best detective and it will be your job, your only job, to find out who did this."

"I'm in the robbery division," I said.

"Not anymore," Langeron spoke finally. "You have been promoted. You will take Marcel Rapace's desk."

"But not his partner, I hope." Me working with GiGi would guarantee nothing productive ever happened.

"I'll get to that in a moment," Proulx said, but I didn't much care for the look on his face when he said it.

"What about my robbery caseload?" I asked.

"It will be reassigned, even if it means the chief handles the cases himself," Vogel snapped.

"What about the Bonaparte murders? She specifically requested—"

"She is in no position to request anything," Vogel said. "That case will also be reassigned." A cruel smile appeared on his thin lips. "You will want to focus your entire attention on this matter, because you have one week to solve this."

"One week?"

"That's correct," Jung jumped in. "We are expecting a visit from the Führer this time next week. When he's here, he wishes to visit the Louvre and we do not need an ongoing investigation there."

"But he was just here," I said. Their beloved Führer had spent one whole day here, taking a whirlwind tour the same day he signed the armistice agreement with our cowardly leaders.

"And now he wishes to visit again," Jung said. "So this mess needs to be cleaned up before his plane lands."

"Well, I can't blame him for wanting to come back." True, but I was intensely irritated at the assignment and the way it was being assigned. "Look, if it's just a matter of moving the body out of the way before he gets here, I can get a couple of men to do that this afternoon."

"Don't be insolent!" Vogel snapped. "We have moved the body. You will find out who killed him."

I looked at Langeron and then Proulx. "So, why me?"

"That was our decision," Jung answered. "First, because we heard about last night and how you first realized the second intruder was still there, and second because we are hoping to continue good relations between our nations, good cooperation."

"Oh, so you'll all be leaving soon?"

Even the seemingly placid Jung bristled, which told me I was probably pushing my luck. He glared at me as he spoke. "We would like the Führer, should he find out about this incident, to then learn that a French policeman solved the crime. It will reassure him that things are as normal as possible here in Paris and that you are cooperating with us fully. That will please him."

"You should know, there are some crimes I am unable to solve. Not many, but some, so I assume he'll be reassured by a French policeman doing his level best, no matter the outcome."

"He will not." Vogel sounded emphatic on that point. "You will succeed or you will be viewed by the German High Command as having betrayed the trust we are bestowing on you. That is a very serious matter and will result in you facing some very pointed questions." He leaned toward me. "I will be asking them, and you will not enjoy how I do so."

I'd come across men like this before. Weak specimens who always use a weapon or some other tool to act out their twisted fantasies. In Vogel's case it was the power vested in his uniform and I needed to be very careful not to give him a chance to use it. In a normal world, the world of a year ago, Chief Proulx could and would have protected me from vindictive psychopaths like Vogel, but in this new world, he had no way to do that. Even Roger Langeron would be hard-pressed to keep me safe, if this bastard wanted otherwise.

And that meant, for all intents and purposes, I was on my own.

"Well, in that case," I said with my friendliest smile, "I'll get to work."

"Good." Jung nodded. "You can view the body, it's in the cellar."

"Which cellar?"

"Here." Jung pointed at the floor.

"You mean in a jail cell?"

"Your coldest one, I was assured. Anyway, it has not been touched."

"It got here by itself?"

"Except for transport," Jung growled, by now, and quite reasonably, fed up with my sense of humor. "No one has examined the body, is what I'm telling you."

"And no one probably should at this point." I grimaced. "Wait, there was no autopsy?"

"We know how he died," Vogel said patiently, as if explaining to a child. "An ice pick in the brain is always fatal."

"Yes, of course." I couldn't argue with that. "But I'll go pay him a visit anyway, I always like to see my clients in person."

"I'm sure that will be delightful for you," Vogel said.

"No, but at least I can make up for it later with a more pleasant visit to the Louvre. Quite the nicest crime scene imaginable."

Vogel and Jung stood, but it was the SS man who spoke. "No, you will not. The museum is off-limits to all French citizens at the moment. Including the police."

"I need to see the crime scene," I insisted. "You can't seriously expect me to—"

"I visited it myself, after the attending doctor had removed and disposed of the weapon, and I can assure you there was nothing there of evidentiary value." Vogel's smirk broadened and he put his cap back on with the stiffness of a pipe-cleaner figure. "So, there is no need for you to visit the museum, and even if there were, the Louvre is off-limits to you, Inspector."

CHAPTER FOUR

Roger Langeron escorted the two Germans out, as I slumped deeper in my chair and looked at Louis Proulx. "Tell me again why I got picked for this."

Proulx grimaced. "I'm sorry. That was my fault, partly anyway. They came in asking about you after last night, and wanted to know if you were really any good. I said you were one of the best. I promise, I had no idea what the assignment would be until after I gave them your name."

"Do me a favor next time. Tell everyone I'm your worst detective. Better still, unpromote me right now. I'm pretty sure there's traffic on the Champs that needs directing."

"The only traffic is German. When did you last see more than two French cars on the same road?"

"Not for a while," I conceded.

It was true. Most working cars had headed out of Paris weeks ago to the apparent safety of the countryside with their owners. The rest, as best I could tell, had been requisitioned by the Germans for use closer to the front lines.

"There you go then," Proulx said gruffly.

"Chief, maybe there are some draft dodgers to hunt down in Montmartre? Surely you can find something else for me to do. *Anything* else."

"I wish I could." To his credit, Proulx sounded like he meant it, for all the good that did me.

"Merde." Shit. I nodded to the envelope on his desk, the one with a swastika printed on the front. "That the file?"

"Such as it is."

I leaned forward and picked it up. "What's in here?"

"No idea, they didn't want me to look."

"Helpful pair, weren't they?"

Proulx fixed me with one of his loving but stern paternal gazes. "Look, this is serious. I don't know if he meant what he said, about what he'd do if you fail, but if he did then . . . well, you know those SS psychos don't play around. If they decide they want a scapegoat, you'll be it."

"Thank you, I'm very aware of what they're capable of." I tipped the contents of the envelope onto my lap. The top item was a glossy photo of a man in a German uniform. He was young, maybe midtwenties, with wavy light hair and a slight smile. He looked like a nice kid, if you ignored the black SS uniform he wore. One of those perfect Aryans that Hitler was always talking about. On the back someone had written *Walter Fischer.* "My victim, it seems. Handsome fellow."

Proulx looked at the picture when I held it up and grunted. "Huh. The envelope is pretty thin, what else do you have?"

There was no photo of the murder weapon, nor even a description or measurements to help me gauge its size. There was, however, a list of five names, typed onto a sheet of paper under a heading:

WITNESSES/SUSPECTS
Maurice Babin
Abraham Simon
Florence Petit
Nicolas Allard
Pascal Voclain

I passed the list to Proulx. "You know any of these people?"

He stared at it for a while. "No. But nice of them to provide your suspects for you."

"Maybe I'm supposed to pick one and pin it on him. Or her. Probably the Jewish-sounding fellow, Abraham Simon, wouldn't you think? They seem to be getting all the heat these days." *And everyone seems to be looking the other way.* "I mean, this is ridiculous, Chief, how am I supposed to investigate a murder with this kind of information?"

"I really don't know. I'm sorry."

"Jesus, this is a parlor game, not a murder investigation."

My irritation was growing and something else was, too, a darker fear that I was being drawn into a game too dangerous for any parlor. No, not a game. A trap. "Do they actually want it solved or is this all a farce? Should I just present myself to the firing squad tomorrow morning and get it over with?"

"Hang on a moment, show me that again." He took the list from my hand. "Maurice Babin. Where do I know that name?" He furrowed his brow in thought. "Yes, that's right, I'm sure it's the same person. His sister is friends with my wife, we've met a couple of times. He is, or was, a curator at the Louvre. Something about Chinese art, I think that was his specialty. That's right, it's coming back to me now."

"Well, good. And that fits with what they were saying about the gallery devoted to Eastern antiquities. What else can you tell me about him?"

"That's about it."

"That's all you know? You're as much use as those two clowns." I was only half joking.

"I'm sorry, I've met him twice, maybe three times, and I'm guessing he was the quiet type."

"Guessing?"

Proulx gave me a wry smile. "Well, if I don't remember him he can't have said much, can he? Can't have been very interesting."

"Unless you're into Chinese art, maybe. You can tell me where he lives?"

"Yes, of course, I can ask my wife for the sister's address." He reached for his phone and lifted the receiver. It took a full minute but then he was talking to his wife. "It doesn't matter why, I just need her address. No! It's her brother I want to talk to. Well, yes, I could've just said that but I wasn't expecting an interrogation. *Cherie*, please, I have someone in my office." He scribbled something on a piece of paper. "Thank you. Yes, *coq au vin* sounds delicious. See you later." He hung up and handed me the paper. "Apparently they lived together but she's down south. Given your time line, you might want to stop by tonight."

"At your place? For the *coq au vin*, you mean."

He shook his head. "I would recommend against. I married the one Frenchwoman who can't cook."

"My condolences."

"*Merci.* I compensate by drinking good wine with every meal. Lots of it. So, what else do you have to go on?"

The only other thing in the envelope was a typed summary of Walter Fischer's role, which was basically to sort the artistic wheat from the chaff. In other words, set aside the good stuff to be sent back to Germany, and leave the less-good stuff out to be put on display for the reopening of the museum. There was no mention of who he worked with, his schedule, or anything particularly useful to my investigation.

"They're really not going to let me into the museum to see the crime scene?"

"Doesn't sound like it. I can make a request, maybe go over his head."

"Thank you, I'd appreciate that. Well, there's nothing like a clean slate," I grumbled. "I suppose I better get started." I snapped my fingers. "Which reminds me: Who's my second on this? I'll take Achille, if it's all right with you."

Achille Boucher had been promoted from robbery to murder a couple months back, and he investigated cases the way you'd imagine he did when you met him. Slowly. But he was as thorough as any detective in Paris, and if you found yourself asking questions at midnight outside a rowdy bar in Pigalle, he's the guy you wanted by your side. Which is to say, his fists moved a lot quicker than his brain. And while time was of the essence here, I wanted someone with me who might spot the gaps I would likely leave in my haste.

"So, that's not going to be poss—"

"I know, he's on the double homicide in Vincennes. But that's open and shut, clearly the jealous lover. One of the other fellows can take it over."

"No, that's not the issue."

"Then what is? He hasn't complained about me, has he?" I was joking, mostly, as he wouldn't be the first detective to request a transfer away from me. I didn't play politics well, and some cops were more interested in climbing the ladder than catching criminals, which I didn't take to very well. He didn't seem that type, though.

"No, not at all. You two worked great together."

"That's my point."

"The thing is . . . I can't let you have anyone on this." I cocked my head to one side, not understanding because I knew that two detectives were *always* assigned to a murder case. "If that Vogel character was serious then I'm not willing to put another detective, another Frenchman, in his sights. It wouldn't be right. I'm sorry, Henri, but you're going to have to solve this one alone."

"You can't be seri—"

"On the plus side," he interrupted, "because of your anger issues, you'll have your own office, which never happens for the new men to the squad."

"It's a hearing issue, not anger," I said for the two hundredth time, and stalked out of his presence so he couldn't point to my face and prove me wrong.

CHAPTER FIVE

My new office was at the end of a row of four of them. There were eight detectives in my division—four of us had offices and the newest recruits, me excepted, sat at desks in an open area. We also had four secretaries, but I planned to use only Nicola. Her attitude could use a tweak, but then so could mine, and I think that's one of the reasons we tolerated each other so well. Marcel Rapace had been one of the more senior detectives and so had the largest corner office with a lovely view over the Seine. It *used* to be the largest office, that is, until they partitioned it to create another one, so now it was the smallest. I still had a view of the Seine, though, so I had one small mercy to be grateful for.

Except as I collected a notepad and pencil, and deposited my waifish file on my desk, I could see a column of German troops filling the quai de Gesvres, dozens of trucks and several hundred men on foot spoiling my view. It was hard not to welcome the rising tide of disgust that welled up inside me, to listen for the angry whispers in my head that came from the ghosts of the millions who'd died the last time these bastards had tried to take over the world.

It's something I need to make an effort to get used to, I told myself. *The dead are dead and these are different invaders. And they're here now, they're already here.*

But one little pep talk wasn't going to do it, of that I was certain. The ease with which they'd breezed into Paris was as shameful as the uncaring acceptance of it by those in the upper echelons of the government, those who were supposed to lead us, protect us. It had galled me when the suits and bigwigs sprinted out of the city to safety, and it galled me now to see the streets they'd left behind littered with the German invaders. I resented both groups, for different reasons but in equal measure, because I knew that although my life hadn't shifted too much, it would inevitably do so, and not in a good way.

I walked out of my office and stopped by to collect Nicola. Her blond hair was tied back and she was typing at the speed of lightning, completely ignoring the lump that sat on the corner of her desk trying to win her affections. Or at least some attention.

"Hey, Bruno." I pointed to the office door beside mine. "You live over there and no one's paying you to harass my secretary."

"No one's paying me not to, either," he said.

"True, but you'll earn my boot up your butt if you don't leave her alone and get back to work."

An empty threat, and we both knew it—if my boot went

anywhere near his ass the big oaf would snap my leg off and tickle my tonsils with it. But he slid off the desk anyway and wandered back to his office.

Nicola stopped typing and looked up. "You don't have to do that."

"I know, but I can if I want."

"Yeah, true. So what's going on? This have to do with your visit to Proulx?"

"Yep. I got that promotion to murder I've been hoping for." Her eyes lit up but I quickly squashed the excitement. "It's not good news, trust me."

"Why not?"

"A goose-stepper went and got himself killed with an ice pick. They want me to solve it and I have an entire week to do it."

"Just a week?"

"If I fail, I get to spend some time with a nasty little major by the name of Vogel."

"What does that mean, exactly?"

"I don't know, and I have no intention of finding out. I'm going to need your help."

"You are if you have to solve this in a week." She picked up a pencil. "Tell me what you need. Oh, and who else is assigned?"

"Just me."

"What? That's ridiculous, how can you be expected to do this on your own?"

"Thanks for the vote of confidence."

"I just meant—"

"In any case," I interrupted, "I'm not on my own, I have you."

She looked at me for a moment, to see how serious I was.

The honest answer to that was *very*. As smart and hardworking as she was, I'd choose her over any of the detectives in my unit, and a couple of them were damn good at their jobs. She was also more educated, though I knew she'd done that herself. She spent many weekends in the city's museums, a book of art under her arm. She'd tried her hand at painting a few times, but come to the conclusion she was better at studying art than making it. I'd learned a little from her, too, especially when it came to her favorite painters, most notably the American Mary Stevenson Cassatt who'd lived and worked in Paris and become one of the leading women Impressionist painters. But Nicola was also eminently practical, which is why I knew she could handle our next task.

"Let's start with the body," I said. "It's in a jail cell downstairs." I saw her look of confusion. "Come on, I'll explain as best I can."

She stood and took the pencil and notepad from me. "You talk, I'll write."

We set off along the hallway. "Their esteemed leader is visiting in a week."

She stopped in her tracks. "*Attends*, Hitler himself? But he was just here." She frowned, obviously unhappy at the idea of that little bastard polluting our city with his presence for the second time in two months.

"Maybe he likes Paris." I shrugged. "Anyway, they're handing off everything to us, even the body. If we solve it in seven days or less, they get credit and great propaganda for working with the locals, and if we don't, they have an easy scapegoat."

"You."

"Precisely. Either way they win."

"You'll look good if you catch the killer, though," she said, trying to be reassuring.

"Yeah, that's what I want. A reputation for working with the invaders."

"Ah, of course. On the plus side, you'll get some nice shiny German rations until a member of the Resistance kills you."

"Oh, you've read about them?"

"No, but I've heard about a few unhappy souls taking matters into their own hands." She was exaggerating for effect, and she knew it. Mostly, acts of rebellion were nonviolent but lately a couple of German cars had been burned and I knew of several cases where a Parisian's friendliness to one of our occupiers had landed him with a black eye or broken nose.

We started down the stairs, taking them all the way to the steel door that shut off the jail area underground. I banged on it and waited until the guard slid open the face-high hatch that let him vet visitors.

I recognized him, but couldn't remember his name. "I'm here to see a body. The German."

The guard nodded. "Just see it, or take the fucking thing away?"

"Do I look like a mortician? Open the door."

He did so with a loud clanking, and was about to say something else when he saw Nicola. "Oh, *merde*, sorry for swearing, mademoiselle. Didn't see you."

"I'll get over it," she said, and breezed past him.

The air was instantly cooler, and the light entirely artificial. There were twelve cells along each wall, most with steel bars so any guards sitting around the wooden table in the center of the room could see the prisoners, and the prisoners could see them. Usually they were filled with drunks sleeping it off, or petty thieves waiting to be processed, but today the place was empty. The lone guard had been sitting at the table reading a book, which was itself unusual in my experience. Behind him, the four cells along the back wall had solid doors and all were shut.

"The poor fellow has been lonely," the *flic* said. "He's our only customer right now."

"Why is that?" Nicola asked.

"When the Boche arrived, we didn't have anyone particularly bad down here, so someone on the top floor decided to release everyone." He gave a wry smile. "I think they wanted as many troublemakers out on the streets as possible for the bastards."

"Makes sense to me." I nodded toward the back wall. "So, which one is your guest staying in?"

"Last one on the left. And he's starting to smell, sir, so if there's any way you could have him moved soon, I'd surely appreciate it."

"I'll do what I can. Why are you down here guarding a dead body, anyway?"

"I've been asking the same question, sir. Ever since he started to smell, anyway. Before that I was quite happy to drink coffee and read my book, to be honest."

"A policeman who reads shouldn't be wasted, stuck down here in the bowels of the Préfecture. What's your name?"

"Daniel Moulin, sir."

"How long have you been on the force?"

"Coming up to three years, this December."

"Three years and you're down here? This is a rookie's job."

"I'm well aware, sir. I think I spoke my mind when it would've been wiser not to."

"The story of his life," Nicola said, jerking her thumb toward me.

"Open up that cell, Moulin, and when I'm done here, I'll see if I can't get either you or that body moved out of here."

"I'd appreciate that, Inspector. And no need for me to open that door for you, I left it unlocked. I was reasonably confident the man inside wouldn't try to escape."

Nicola and I moved toward the cell. "I knew you were too smart to be down here," I said over my shoulder.

When we got there, I pulled the door open and a thick layer of stench rolled out toward us. I put my forearm over my mouth and nose and Nicola stepped back, her face turned away and scrunched up in disgust. It wasn't that he was that far gone, it was more that whatever gases he was emitting had accumulated in that small space over the course of two days.

I gestured for her to wait for a moment, to let some of the more fetid air circulate out of the cell, and for my nose to adjust as much as it could. When we went in, though, Nicola kept her hand over her mouth as if that might help. I pulled out my pocket handkerchief and handed it to her. She took it and mumbled her thanks.

I was surprised to find the body dressed in an expensive gray wool suit and not the SS uniform in the photo. Aside from the nice duds, though, Walter Fischer had seen considerably better days. He lay on his back on the concrete bed, arms by his sides. Someone had put a small pillow under his head, and

I wondered if it'd been Moulin. I knelt beside Fischer to get a closer look, wishing I'd carried a second handkerchief for myself. The dead man's eyes were closed and his skin was an unsightly mix of yellow, gray, and white, as if a painter couldn't quite decide which was right and had mushed them together on his palette. His right ear was toward me, and looked to be the entry point for the ice pick. But the only sign of violence was a line of dried blood that came out of his ear and ran down to the hairline at the back of his head. I put my hands on his arm and rocked the body.

"Opinion?" Nicola asked.

"Dead. Definitely dead."

She kicked me with her toe. "Then we can go."

"Not yet." I went to the door. "Moulin, did anyone search him or leave a bag with his personal possessions. Anything like that?"

"*Non*, monsieur," he replied. "No bag of his possessions, but I have no idea where he was or what they did before they brought him here."

"When was that, by the way?"

"I don't know. It had to be during the night on Sunday, because I was sent here Monday morning."

"Did you put the pillow under his head?"

He looked sheepish. "Yes, sir. I'm sorry if that was improper, I just—"

"Never mind that. Was he stiff or floppy?"

"Stiff."

"Which means he was probably left at the crime scene for a few hours while they decided what to do, and then brought here." I ducked back into the cell and stood over the body. His tie had been loosened and the top button of his shirt was undone and I pointed out to Nicola that someone had removed his *plaques d'intentité*, what the Americans in the last war called dog tags.

With Nicola looking on, I started by checking the pockets of his jacket, but they were empty. Same for his pants pockets, which told me someone had kept hold of his wallet, keys, and whatever else he'd had on him. It looked more and more like that damned Vogel and his slightly less objectionable friend Jung planned for me to fail.

I wondered vaguely why they hadn't taken his clothes, or at least taken his jacket and shoes off, so I pulled his size forty-threes from his feet and looked inside. Nothing, but they were nice shoes, expensive ones from the leather. Nothing a French detective could afford, that's for sure, not even an inspector. *Too small for my feet, though. Shame.*

I wrestled with poor Fischer over his jacket, which he didn't want to give up without making the encounter much closer than I would've liked, partly because when I threw Nicola an inquiring look, of the *Help me, please,* sort, she just raised an eyebrow and stayed right where she was.

Eventually I prevailed, and didn't feel too bad about letting Fischer drop back on his bed with a *thud.* The suit jacket was expensive, too, nicely lined with a cream material that felt like silk, but may just have been fine cotton. It was Nicola who noticed that the lining had been cut horizontally in the back of the jacket. Someone had constructed a very clever pocket, although I had a hard time imagining what would fit in there without causing a hunchback-like bulge in the suit. I got my answer to that when I dipped my hand into the pocket and felt a piece of thick paper.

Nicola could see from my eyes that I'd found something. "What is it?"

It was a charcoal drawing, or maybe a thick pencil, of a woman in a somewhat suggestive pose with broad thighs and pendulous breasts. It looked unfinished because there was no context to it, no furniture or anything in the background.

"You're the expert, you tell me." I handed it to her.

She took it with one hand, the other still covering her breathing holes with my hankie. But that fell away as her eyes widened with surprise.

"*Mon Dieu*," she said finally. "Look at the signature."

"I did. I couldn't decipher it."

"*Oui*, it is scrawled quickly, but I think that's because it's one of his quick projects, almost a throwaway."

"You recognize it?" I was genuinely surprised. "It's not very good, you might want to tell the artist that. If he's even an artist, which I doubt."

She laughed. "Oh yes, he's an artist."

"From your disrespectful derision, I'm guessing it's someone I've heard of."

"Yes," she said. "Pretty much everyone has heard of Pablo Picasso. Even you."

CHAPTER SIX

Nicola and I stared at each other for a moment, then I said: "Picasso. You're serious?"

"I am."

"How can you be sure?"

She turned the drawing toward me. "The signature isn't clear, I'll give you that, but it does seem to start with a *P*, right?"

"Right, but—"

"Not done, hush." She gestured to the cell door. "But if we're finished in here, maybe we can talk outside? And I do mean outside."

I took a quick glance around and since I didn't fancy pulling Fischer's pants off, too, I let Nicola lead the way out into the slightly fresher air. We started for the exit door but Moulin stopped us, his eyes on the piece of paper in Nicola's hand.

"I'm sorry, sir, but you're not allowed to take anything out of here."

"Says who?"

"Those were my orders from Captain Fuller."

"Never heard of him."

"He's the one who assigned me here." There was a note of resentment in his voice, and we stood there looking at each other for a moment. "He was very clear that if I saw someone walking out with anything, I should prevent it." Slowly and deliberately, he turned his back on us. "I am certain that if I saw someone doing that, I would indeed stop them."

I smiled. "I have no doubt about it, you are a fine policeman after all."

With that, Nicola and I walked to the now unattended steel door and let ourselves out. We retraced our steps to my office and, once inside, I closed the door. Nicola put the picture on my desk and pointed at the signature.

"See how it's underlined? Picasso almost always underlines his signatures. He also writes them at a slight angle, which isn't necessarily something a forger would know."

"A good one would."

"True. But note the spacing of the letters, too. They're always the same distance apart, just like they are here."

"I see. Which means, if you're right, then our German friend might have been stealing art for himself," I said. "As opposed to stealing for the Fatherland, which was his job."

"Looks like it."

"But whether that has anything to do with his death, we don't know." I sat down and thought about it, but just came up with a handful of dead ends and several more don't knows.

"What else can I do to help?" Nicola asked.

"Plenty, I'm sure." I emptied the German envelope onto my desk, beside the picture. I pulled out the list of witnesses. "Can you look through our files and see if we have anything on these people?"

"Never heard of four of them." She studied the names. "But Maurice Babin is a curator at the Louvre. I've met him several times."

"I know. Eastern art."

"No, modern. Maybe he used to do Eastern but . . ." She shrugged.

"Wait." I sat up straight. "Like, Picasso modern?"

"I would say so." Nicola nodded. "Why don't you go ask him?"

"I will." I tapped the picture. "But I think I need to ask this fellow whether it's the genuine thing or not."

Her eyes widened. "You're going to interview Picasso?"

"He'd know better than anyone, wouldn't he?"

"Of course," she said. "But the newspapers said he moved to Royan."

"Where is that?"

"Not far from Bordeaux. You don't have time to go there, it's too far for just one interview."

"Damn it." My finger was still on the picture. "This is the only clue we have." But she was right. "Does he have a telephone? Can we find that out?"

"I can try, I'll do it now."

I looked over the meager information from the envelope, hoping I'd missed something somehow, but I hadn't. The file was so thin, there was simply nothing to miss. I turned my thoughts to the Louvre, and how I might get myself inside for a look around. I wondered if Maurice Babin might be able to help with that. While I was pondering my approach, Nicola came back in, brimming with excitement. I swung my feet off the desk.

"Let me guess, he has a phone and you have his number."

She shook her head. "Better than that. Much better."

"Spit it out, woman."

"He's here. In Paris. He kept his apartment on rue des Grands-Augustins." She lowered her voice. "But no one knows yet, he's trying to keep it a secret."

"How do you know?"

"I telephoned the university and spoke to my art history professor, and he—"

"Wait, you're taking classes at the university?"

She flapped a hand at me. "We can talk about that later, but yes. Anyway, he'd talked before about knowing Picasso and I told him it was very important, like life and death, so he let me in on that secret. It'll be public soon enough, just not right now."

"Rue des Grands-Augustins, you say? That just happens to be on my way home."

"Mine, too." She batted her huge blue eyes at me, not because she thought she could persuade me that way, but because she was trying to make me laugh. She was one of the few people able to. Especially a week before my likely torture and execution.

"Fine," I said. "Always good to have someone to take notes."

It was a little early to be heading to lunch, but in police work coming and going was a natural part of the day. Lunch was about the only time you could guarantee there'd be no one in the division offices, and even that took place in an ebbing-

and-flowing two-hour window. So no one said a word as Nicola and I made our way along the long corridor to the stairs and headed for the main doors of the Préfecture.

When we reached the street, we went our separate ways, just to be sure no one got any ideas, and just like we did every evening. We had to, so that no one would suspect or find out that Nicola and I lived together. And we didn't want people to know because, if they did, they'd make entirely the wrong assumption.

• • •

A light summer rain began as I crossed the Pont Saint-Michel, delicate drops dappling the river either side of me. The sudden shower had sent everyone scuttling for cover because I saw almost no one on the streets. Although that had been Paris for almost a month: empty. Our gray-green uniformed invaders had marched into a mostly vacant Paris three weeks ago. I didn't know exact numbers but had read that more than half of Paris's residents had packed up and fled south. I'd seen pictures of the roads, packed and at a standstill with cars, carts, horses, and people on foot carrying everything they could.

It had broken my heart to see a city normally full of life, now so devoid of it. Tourists from home and abroad came to Paris for the architecture and the art, but they fell in love with it for its vibrancy, its stylish, elegant, larger-than-life people. And those beautiful birds had flown south, leaving a gilded but mostly empty cage.

Pablo Picasso had gone, too, but he'd come back, and now lived and worked in a town house a stone's throw from the river, a place I'd walked past a thousand times without knowing what every Paris artist and socialite probably knew. I was familiar

with the man, of course, but only by reputation and while I
didn't dispute that his art was worth every franc he was paid,
I would never claim to appreciate it the way others did. *Others*
included Nicola, who was basically drooling by the time we met
up outside the entrance to the place.

"Did you put on some fresh lipstick?" I asked.

"What if I did?"

"He's married, you know."

"Oh, for heaven's sake." She rolled her eyes. "I'm meeting
one of the most famous painters of our time, I want to look nice,
not have his babies."

She led the way through the stone arch into the courtyard,
waiting for me to pull the bell ring. A young woman, maybe in
her late twenties, opened the door. She was pretty, with brown
hair and large brown eyes, but I was struck most by her frailty.
She stood in the doorway and leaned against the jamb, as if
the act of opening it required a rest. I introduced myself and
showed her my badge, hoping she wouldn't insist on seeing
Nicola's police credentials. She didn't, just directed us up to the
third floor.

"He's in his studio, working," she said. "Please don't stay
long, he doesn't like interruptions."

"We will be as swift as possible, madame, I promise."

Nicola followed me up the wooden staircase to the third
floor, where a pair of double doors stood open. Nicola and
I glanced at each other as we walked in, both in awe of the
space. To me, it looked like the inside of a ship. Thick wooden
beams jutted out from the walls and stretched up and across
the ceiling above us, and more beams, perpendicular to them,

striped the white to create the feeling that you were in the hull of a grand sailing vessel.

Nicola was focused more on the interior, a vast room that could have hosted medieval feasts. Paintings were stacked against every wall, and tables of varying heights and sizes spilled over with sculptures that, in all honesty, I couldn't tell whether they were finished or not. Hundreds of paintbrushes—thick, thin, tall, and short—poked their stems out of glass pots and coffee mugs, and the room was filled with the rich scent of oil.

Picasso himself stood with his back to us, but he knew we were there because he waved an arm for us to come over to him. As we did, I took a look at what he was working on: a three-foot-by-three-foot canvas that sat on a paint-spattered wooden easel. Either he'd just started or it was what they called Minimalist, a few bold strokes created a surprisingly (just to me, probably) lively and lifelike female form. Picasso turned finally and looked us both over, as we did him. He was dressed in a white smock that sported all the colors of the rainbow in one place or another, plus a generous daubing of black. He eyed me with interested suspicion and Nicola with just interest.

He put down his paintbrush carefully, as if it were made of glass. "Are you actually French police, or more Germans pretending to be?"

"We're French," I assured him, and gave him our names.

"I suppose I will believe you. They have women serving in the police now?"

"I am just his assistant," Nicola said. "And in truth I wanted the chance to meet you and tell you how much I admire your work."

"You are not *just* anything, my dear. You are kind to say that, thank you." He took her hand and kissed the back of it with a bow, then released her and shook my hand. "How may I be of assistance?"

"We are investigating the murder of a German soldier," I said.

"We've only managed to kill one?" he asked, with a wry smile. He had an animated, expressive face and there was a real charm about him. There was also an intensity in his eyes, such that when he looked at you, you knew you were getting his full attention.

"It's a start," I said, and he laughed. "Apparently this one was special. He was killed with an ice pick through his ear."

"Very dramatic," Picasso said.

"So was the location. One of the galleries at the Louvre." He raised an eyebrow but didn't say anything, waiting for me to continue. I pulled the drawing from my briefcase and handed it to him. "Is this one of yours, sir?"

"What makes you think it is?"

"My colleague here. She says she recognizes the slant and spacing of the signature."

Picasso resumed his visual interest in Nicola. "Clever woman."

"And the way you underline your name," Nicola threw out for good measure.

"Still could be a fake. If you know all that, any forger would." Picasso studied the picture for a moment. "But yes, this is mine. What does it have to do with your dead German?"

"I can't reveal that information right now, I'm sorry, sir."

Picasso smiled. "Sorry, are you? Let me guess, it was found on or near the body."

"How would you know that?"

"I see no earthly reason you'd bring it up otherwise. Unless, of course, it was found on the killer but then if you had him, you wouldn't be here."

"That's true enough," I conceded.

"Anything else I can help you with?" Picasso waved his arm at his studio. "They're not letting me show my work these days but that doesn't mean I am able to stop painting."

"Can I ask what you're working on?" Nicola looked past him to his easel and beyond. She moved toward a rectangular canvas, as if mesmerized by it. It was compelling, I had to admit, but in a confounding way. It seemed to hold two figures, one seated on a chair and the other lying on a bed. And I say *seemed* because the seated fellow had two triangles for a head and a body like a piece of origami. Likewise, the figure on the bed, naked I presumed, bulged and twisted in nonhuman ways and its head could've been sliced from a wheel of cheese.

"What do you think?" Picasso asked, looking back and forth between us.

"It's stunning," Nicola said, her voice a whisper. "What are you calling it?"

"It's not finished, and won't be for a while," Picasso said. "But I think it'll be called *L'Aubade* when I eventually show or sell it."

"*The Serenade?*" I supposed I could see it, the creature on the chair held what might've been a lute. The three eyes would've been a turnoff for me, but it takes all sorts.

"Prefer your art a little more conventional?" Picasso had that smile on his face again, the amused and indulgent one. "Renoir, Monet. Maybe van Gogh?"

"Love all those," I said, glad to be on firmer ground. I spotted a street scene that looked very familiar, even though it was painted in an odd style. Or maybe not finished yet. "This one, for example. You painted it?" I squinted at the signature, confirming with my own eyes and noting with some satisfaction that smarty-pants Nicola would've been wrong, since it wasn't underlined. I'd be sure to point that out later.

"Ah, yes, that one, I did. A street in Montmartre, you recognize it?"

"I do, yes. Different style than you do nowadays."

"Painters change, adapt, and evolve. I'd be a poor artist if I did the same thing over and over, wouldn't I?"

"True, I suppose." My eye fell on a pencil drawing that stuck out from under some papers on a long table. "I recognize that one."

Picasso plucked it out. "Sometimes I redraw older paintings for my own amusement. Nothing that will be sold or shown, of course. This one I finished in 1936, which I'm sure Mademoiselle Nicola will recall."

Even I was familiar with it, but I'd forgotten its details. It was a gruesome scene, men, women, and children in all sorts of torment, animals, too. Horrific in its simplicity, its contorted humanity, its bleakness.

"*Guernica*," Nicola said, moving over to my side. "That was the most amazing, moving piece I've ever seen."

"Thank you," Picasso said, with the slightest of bows.

"Right, yes, I remember now." I nodded slowly, my eyes

stuck to this crude yet compelling drawing. "*Guernica*, you did that."

"No." Picasso shook his head and his voice was solemn when he spoke. "The Germans did." He cocked his head and stared at me intently. "What is it you want to say?"

I needed this man's help, not his ire, so I did my best to keep my thoughts to myself, but he pressed me to speak up until I did.

"It's just that . . . I fought in the last war. Many of us did. We know what war is like firsthand."

"Ah, so you think instead of painting I should have been fighting." He laughed gently. "I'm a little old for that, now."

"As am I. But this isn't the first war in your lifetime."

"Very true." He nodded, then swept an arm to show me his studio. "What do you think this is?"

"Art," I said, confused. "Paintings. Sculpture . . . I'm not sure what you're getting at."

"No, you're not. Because you believe art is decoration. Adornment." He wagged a finger at me. "It is not. It is power. A weapon. Painting is an instrument of war for attack or defense."

"How so?" I declined to make a joke about hitting someone with a picture frame.

"How many men has Adolf Hitler killed with his own hands? How many has he shot?"

"I don't know. Not many, I suppose."

"Exactly! His power comes through his ability to persuade, to make people think a certain way. His way. Art has the same power. With a painting like *Guernica* I can have ten times the influence on those who wage war than any one soldier. A thousand times the influence. Pablo Picasso painting one picture is worth a hundred Picassos wielding a gun." He clapped a big hand on my shoulder. "Which is to say, I am fighting. I have been all my life. And as long as the murderous, conniving despots from the east are here in France, I will continue to do so." He took a deep breath and the anger melted from him. He pointed to the *Guernica* drawing. "You may keep that, if you like. I don't need to keep reliving it."

"That's very kind," I said. "But it would not be appropriate at this point, since I'm conducting this investigation." Nicola took the drawing from my hand and moved toward the table, eyes still on the picture. I continued. "And since you asked, there is one more thing."

"However I can help."

Picasso handed me back the picture found on my victim. I opened my briefcase, put back the drawing, and took out the photograph of Walter Fischer.

"Do you know this man?"

"I am very familiar with the uniform. But not the man wearing it, not this one."

"You're sure?"

Picasso gave me a hard look. "Some say I have an eye for pictures. So yes, I am sure."

"Right, of course." I tucked the photo away.

"Nasty business," he said.

"What do you mean, the murder?"

"Yes, I suppose." He took a breath and puffed his cheeks out, then exhaled. "The way we men treat each other. There always has to be violence, for some reason." He seemed to perk up, and pointed to an iron hook in one of the beams above our heads. "See that?"

"I do."

"You know the story of François Ravaillac, I presume."

"He killed Henry IV," Nicola said, saving my bacon.

"May of 1610. Stabbed him while he was in his carriage on rue Saint-Honoré, stuck him between the second and third rib."

"That sounds like a terrible idea, killing a king."

Picasso gave a sad laugh. "For Ravaillac it was." He pointed at the beam. "He was strung up, hung from that very hook while he was tortured."

My eyes widened with surprise and curiosity. "Are you serious?"

"As serious as the pincers that ripped off his flesh, as the molten lead poured on his body. And as the four horses that eventually tore him to pieces."

"That's quite a piece of history you have there," I said. Murder detectives, including me, are not squeamish, of course, but I silently gave thanks that the days of shredding people while they were still alive had passed. At least, I hoped they'd passed. . . .

"What else can I help you with?" Picasso asked.

I extended my hand. "I think that's a good note to end things on, so thank you for your time. We can show ourselves out."

He took my hand and shook it, then kissed the back of Nicola's again. Which, really, was the right order of things, even if we were there on police business.

Outside, the rain had stopped and the sidewalk and roads glistened in the late afternoon sun. Nicola, however, seemed preoccupied with her jacket.

"Just wait a moment," she said, contorting herself.

"What're you doing? I would recommend against undressing in the streets. In the old days you could get paid for it but I'm pretty sure the Germans are more law and order than licentious."

"Got it." With slow, delicate movements, Nicola pulled the *Guernica* drawing out of her clothing.

"Nicola! You took that?"

"Of course. He offered it as a gift."

"To me. And this is an investigation that involves him, we can't be taking gifts from witnesses. Heck, maybe he'll even be a suspect."

"Don't be ridiculous. If Pablo Picasso offers you one of his pictures, paintings, or drawings, you accept it. If he offers you a snotty tissue, you take it."

"Not likely." I shook my head, but I knew why she'd done it. "You keep that under wraps and out of sight until this investigation is over."

"I will, I promise." She smiled broadly. "And just imagine if he does turn out to be the killer, this'll be worth even more!"

"I suppose so. But if he doesn't, and I don't figure out who is, maybe you can sell it to pay for my funeral expenses."

"No, not that." She put a hand on my arm, a twinkle appearing in her eye. "I'm told the Gestapo and SS just throw their victims into the river. There'll be no need for a funeral."

CHAPTER SEVEN

I spent the rest of the afternoon alternately thinking about how I could proceed on the case and reading French history. The former was frustrating and filled me with worry, and the latter was a release from the former. I knew I shouldn't let myself be distracted, especially given my time constraints, but it was a habit I'd developed over the years—closing my door or hiding out in a café to read for at least two hours a day. It was, in my mind, essential to my survival as a human being and a functioning detective. I'd done a fine job convincing myself of that, and it applied whether I was in the middle of a big case or not.

I was interrupted briefly, by the familiar figure of Daniel Moulin. Nicola brought him to my office at his request.

"Since I have no one to guard and no more books to read, they're transferring me," he said.

"To where?"

"Some new unit that assists the Germans in keeping civil unrest to a minimum."

"You mean harassing people expressing their opinions and arresting those who don't immediately shut up?"

"That's my guess." He shook his head. "I don't suppose you have the ability to get me sent elsewhere? Anywhere else, in fact."

"I'm neck-deep in my own pile of shit," I said. "You sure as hell don't want to step in with me, even if they'd let you."

He pulled something from his pocket, and offered me some chewing gum. I shook my head. "Not for me, and not in my office, if you please."

"You don't want me to—"

"I do not."

He put the packet away. "Well, sir, if anything comes your way that can relieve me of my impending duties, I would greatly appreciate any help you can give me."

Likewise, I thought, but didn't say. "Will do."

We shook hands and I felt bad for the poor fellow. I, more than anyone, knew what it was like to be a stooge for the invaders. But I comforted myself with the thought that while he'd hate the work, at least his own neck wasn't on the line.

On the way home that evening, I stopped to get a bottle of wine for dinner. I was feeling down, and wanted something a little pricier than the usual cheap claret we sipped, and opted for a stronger, more robust Madiran. I knew the store owner and had bought wine from him for years, so he didn't ask too many questions when I asked to slip out of the back door once I'd paid.

"Is there something wrong, Monsieur Lefort?"

"It's probably nothing." I jerked a thumb toward the window. "But I thought I saw someone following me just now."

"Oh, *merde*," he said. He glanced nervously toward the store's large window. "That's not good. A German?"

"Like I said, probably just my imagination, but I'll enjoy this wine more if I'm sure."

"But of course, come with me, this way."

I followed him through to the back of the store and checked the alley when he opened the service door. The man I'd seen behind me, three separate times, on the way from the Préfecture had been small and thin but, for no particular reason, I didn't think it likely he was a Boche. No reason I could articulate, anyway. That said, the Nazis had already stacked the deck against me, it wouldn't be much of a surprise if they wanted to watch me spill my cards all over the floor. I shook the idea from my mind—if it was the Germans, I had no reason to care, and I couldn't imagine who else it would be. Paranoia was real for many people these past few months, for me, too, and I felt it best to tamp it down rather than entertain it.

The alley was deserted and, reassured I wasn't being tailed, I started walking and turned my mind to dinner, hoping Nicola wasn't cooking fish as it'd be overwhelmed by the hearty wine. Then again, treats like fresh fish were harder and harder to come by—already I'd noticed that eggs were more difficult to find and more expensive when you did.

But this was still France, so if it came to it, I'd starve to death with a belly full of red wine.

I trudged slowly up the stairs, the weight of the task in front of me heavy in my mind. I passed the front door of the apartment on the fourth floor and shook my head. The Leibowitz family had moved out the previous week after receiving letters from family in Germany about what the Germans had planned, and were actually doing, to Jews there. They'd told me and, while I was pretty sure they were exaggerating, I didn't try to stop them leaving. They had other family in America, a country I was growing more and more unhappy with. I mean, it's one thing to show up late to one major conflagration, but to drag your feet to two of them? This wasn't some petty squabble between neighbors, it seemed pretty obvious that the small man with the even smaller mustache wanted to conquer the entire world. And, whether America liked it or not, they were part of that same world, which meant that sooner or later that nasty little Nazi would focus his beady eyes (and his armies) on their shores.

As I unlocked my apartment door, I heard voices inside the apartment, two women talking. One was Nicola and the other . . . I couldn't place immediately. There was laughter, though, so I wasn't worried and focused on not dropping the wine as I went inside. To my surprise, I saw Nicola in her leather armchair (I had my own, across from it) and Princess Marie Bonaparte on the sofa beside her.

Nicola bounced to her feet. "Henri, look who's here!"

"I see that. Welcome, Princess Marie."

She waved a hand. "Please, call me Mimi. These days it's good not to draw attention to yourself if you have a title."

"I shall try to do so." I walked to the kitchen and put the wine down. A recipe book caught my eye, shiny and new, and sticking out from between older and familiar recipe books and a large, dusty English-French dictionary that hadn't been pulled out, let alone cracked open, in a few years.

"You're buying new books?" I called to Nicola.

"A gift," Mimi Bonaparte called back. "From my kitchen to yours."

"Very kind." I slid it back into place and wandered into the living room. "To what do we owe the pleasure?"

The two women exchanged conspiratorial glances, and Mimi answered. "Yesterday you offered your assistance with my theory on aspect association. I would like to take you up on that."

"I see." I poured myself a glass of water and sank into my own chair. "The thing is, this is going to be a busy week. I'm not sure I'll have much time for psychological theories."

"Nicola told me. And I don't plan to take up any of your time, just be available if you need an ear."

"Ears are always good," I said, noncommittal. And then they exchanged looks again. "What are you two not telling me?"

"Well," Nicola began, "I just thought that . . . I'm not sure how to put it, but—"

"Maybe I can try," Mimi said. "I think there are numerous ways in which I can help you and, like I've said, one way you can help me. I'm here to trade."

"Trade?"

"There are aspects of your life that are going to hold you back," Mimi said. "Slow you down. And this week of all weeks, you don't need that."

"Amen," I said. "But I have no idea what you're talking about."

"Yes, you do. We talked about it at my house."

"Remind me."

"Nicola told me that if she wants to eat an apple or a stick of celery, she has to do so in her own room with the door shut."

"Not true," I protested. "Sometimes I'll go to my room, or for a walk."

"I think you know what point I'm making."

"That I have good hearing. Too good hearing."

"No. I told you that Sigmund Freud and I were working on several psychological studies. One related to people just like you, normal people who become outraged at certain sounds."

"I don't think I'm unusual in that regard. Everyone has noises they hate."

"True," Mimi said. "And everyone has food they hate. But that's not the same thing as having an allergy to food."

"You think I have an allergy to noises?" I laughed, but no one laughed with me. "Seriously?"

"Yes," Mimi said. "I am certain of it. My interest is whether it is a psychological issue or purely a matter of biology."

I had no idea what to say to that. I could hardly argue that my reactions to certain sounds were *normal*, I knew they weren't. But to rise to the level of some kind of . . . what? Medical condition? Sign that I was mentally unstable?

"I'd assumed that I just have good hearing. Combine that with my general distaste for the people around me and voilà."

"That fails to explain your annoyance at Nicola's eating apples."

"And celery," I reminded her.

"You also smoke too much," Nicola said quietly, filling a brief silence.

"Anyone who smokes, smokes too much," Mimi said, nodding. "And that has both physical and psychological components, too."

"So I'm a lab rat now?" I said. "Ladies, many thanks for the attention but I have one overriding concern this coming week, and that's to catch whoever killed a German officer at the Louvre. If I don't do that, well, I suspect I'll never have to worry about chewing gum, celery, or cigarettes ever again. Neither will you."

"Understood," Mimi said. "But that also means if you fail then I will lose the best subject I've ever had, for two studies. That does me no good."

"Respectfully, not a huge weight on my mind." My stomach was starting to rumble and I didn't smell anything cooking. "What are we all eating tonight?"

"Mimi said that if you agree to her plan, she'll provide us with fine wine and food." Nicola was a good cook but didn't enjoy it, so the idea of someone else providing would be a huge incentive for her.

"Oh, there's a plan already?"

"One hour every evening," Mimi said. "You sit down with me and answer my questions. In exchange, let's say after two or three sessions, you get free wine and free food for the foreseeable future. So, to present my full offer, you will be getting free food and wine, maybe I can help you stop smoking, and possibly even stop you from exploding every time someone eats a carrot near you."

"Look." I sighed. "Normally, I would love to assist, I would. But right now I don't have the time or energy to be spilling my guts figuratively the same week I may be spilling them literally."

I patted my stomach. "And doing without all that rich food and wine might be good for me. Counteract the many cigarettes I plan on sucking down to steady my nerves."

"Henri, please think about it before you say no." Nicola stood, her big blue eyes wide with pleading. "I have to run next door to get supper. Is fish all right? I saw Robert earlier and he said a fresh catch came in today."

"That sounds delicious," I said, not mentioning the Madiran.

"Good." Nicola wagged a finger. "Please, just think about what she's offering."

"I did." I turned to Marie Bonaparte. "But I am curious about something. With all the trouble filling our city, with all the lost and lonely and miserable, why pick on me?"

"We're a perfect match," she said. "I'm interested in crime, have been ever since it was suggested to me that my father and grandmother engineered my mother's demise when I was born."

"Sounds like an interesting childhood," I said. Behind me, Nicola let herself out of the front door. "You should find a good psychoanalyst to talk to."

"I did. Sigmund Freud."

"Ah, yes, you mentioned him. Was it helpful?"

"Unimaginably so, as it would be to you."

"Then, when you resurrect him, I'll sit down with him. Lie down," I said, giving her my friendliest smile. "Or whatever the current seating trends are in psychoanalysis."

"You don't take the science seriously?" Bonaparte said.

"Not true. I know from my own life that a good ear and sensible advice can turn a man around. Or at least let him know in which direction he should be headed. What you do seems to be a professional embodiment of that."

"It is," Bonaparte agreed. "Though I would suggest that's a very superficial abridgment of what I practice. But this means that if it's not psychoanalysis itself you're dismissing, it's me."

"Incorrect again." Truthfully, I was starting to enjoy this verbal sparring, but I absolutely did *not* want to spend an hour a day, in what was bound to be the most trying week of my life, talking to this insightful woman. Guarding my secrets on top of guarding my life seemed like too great of an ordeal, even for good food and wine.

"Then explain," she pressed.

"It's me. You see, another way of stating things might be to say it relies on the client shelling out their life savings for the privilege of exposing their greatest faults and weaknesses. Given that I am light in the former category and plentiful in the second, that doesn't seem like something I should pursue."

"I told you, I'm not charging. I'm paying, and quite well, I think."

"And for that very reason my continued refusal should be a bright and obvious sign that the other side of the equation is so loaded with rotting compost that I don't want anyone digging through it, even for a case of Château Pétrus."

We sat in silence for a moment or two, then she tried again. "Maybe I can help you solve your case?" she offered. "On top of all the other benefits."

"In my business, we call those *alleged* benefits. As opposed to actual harm to the hours in my day, depletion of my mental energy, and the embarrassment of revealing all those secrets you're wanting to pry from me."

"Well, let me assure you," she began, as prim and outraged as I'd yet seen her. "I guarantee total confidentiality. That's absolutely the most important tenet of what I do. Anything that you tell me, stays with me."

"You'd keep things from Nicola?"

"You would be my client, not her, so absolutely. Of course."

"What if I've committed a crime? Aren't you required to reveal that to the authorities?"

"No, I am not. Anyway, you're a police officer so I highly doubt that anything you confess to me would be much of a crime."

The front door opened again, and Nicola came in carrying something wrapped in newspaper.

"I'll help in the kitchen." I stood and offered my hand. "Lovely to see you again, Princess Marie."

"Please, Mimi." Marie Bonaparte made no move to get up or shake my hand. "And let me offer you something more for your time."

"I don't plan to swap my inner thoughts for pastries and meat."

"And wine," she said with a laugh. "But I already offered those, so that's not what I meant."

"Money?"

"No, no. That would set a very bad precedent, me paying my own clients."

"Shame," I said. "I could spill my guts for a few hundred francs an hour."

"That's not the offer."

"Then what is?" I said, trying to keep the impatience out of my voice. "I feel like I'm about to get tricked here, since you want my honesty."

"Not at all. The offer is that I spill my secrets to you."

I wasn't expecting that. "You spill . . . ?"

"I tell you my secrets. It's a show of trust, and it'll give you a measure of how open I want you to be with me."

I thought about it for a full second. "No."

"Why not?"

"Two reasons. First, you're a princess, which means you have precisely zero secrets that would be either interesting or relatable. Second, how would I know you're telling the truth?"

"Ah, the trick you're so afraid of." She laughed again. "You're wrong about me not having secrets, let me assure you of that. And when I tell you what they are, you'll know I didn't make them up. I promise. Just give me thirty minutes of your time right now. Then you'll have all night to think it over and if you decide you're not impressed with my honesty and openness, and my secrets, then I won't ask you again."

Nicola's voice floated in from the kitchen. "Sit back down and do it."

I looked at this odd woman sitting before me, a gentle smile on her lips as she held my eye, her hands clasped on her lap. Truth be told, I'd found her interesting from the moment I'd met her, and who wouldn't want to know a few secrets about a princess? Especially one related to Emperor Napoléon Bonaparte? And listening to her wasn't a commitment to anything, she'd said so herself.

I sat back down.

• • •

When I was comfortable, she cleared her throat and began. "My father and grandmother engineered my mother's death and kept me a virtual prisoner to ensure I survived long enough to inherit

my fortune. If I died before I became an adult, they lost everything."

"Sounds terrible."

"It's not even the start of it." She spoke softly, calmly. "My
father also withheld any affection from me, even though I
craved it. He didn't recognize or encourage my intellect, which
I also craved. In November 1907 I married a man who was in
love with his own uncle."

"His uncle?"

"Yes, which was less than ideal because we are still married
and he is Prince George of Greece. He was thirteen years older
than me and, I believe, that age difference and his position allowed me to transfer my affections from my father to him. How
am I doing?"

"That seems like his secret, not yours."

She smiled. "Then I shall continue with some of my own. I
have had multiple affairs, one with Aristide Briand that lasted
almost ten years."

"The prime minister?" Now that was a surprise. Not just the
existence of the affair but her frank admission to it.

"Yes, the prime minister."

"All right. That's better. Keep going."

"I found that marriage is security but it is also a sacrifice.
In one of my writings I called it an entombment of oneself."

"Maybe that's why I've avoided it."

"Perhaps. In addition, I am frigid and have been ob-
sessed with that aspect of my life for . . . well, all of my life.
I even had three operations to lower my clitoris in the hope
that would allow me to achieve . . ." She laughed when my

mouth opened involuntarily. "Am I making you uncomfortable, Henri?"

"I . . . no . . . not at all," I lied. "I just wasn't expecting . . . that."

"Well, then I shall just say that the operations were medically successful, sexually less so. Any questions so far?"

"Not about that." I shifted uncomfortably. "What are your other interests, I mean apart from picking through people's minds?"

"Crime." She smiled broadly. "Remember, a mass-murdering predecessor is in my blood, so how can I not be fascinated with crime? I have been my whole life."

"Have you ever committed a crime?"

"Yes, but only in response to one."

"Intriguing," I said. "Do tell."

"A man, a junior politician, found out about my affair with Aristide and he tried to blackmail me." She frowned. "I had been blackmailed once before, when I was young and naive, so I have a particular distaste for such people. They are, in my opinion, the lowest of the low, greedy little cowards."

"You killed him?"

"Oh, no. I should have liked to, but I'm not sure I have that in me. No, I gave him a taste of his own medicine."

I leaned forward, fascinated. "How so?"

"On the pretense of paying him, I invited him to my home and served him a glass of wine while we settled on final terms. It turns out that a young Beaujolais masks the bitter taste of certain sedatives."

"You drugged him."

"I did." She smiled primly, then went on. "Once he was sound asleep, I let two friends of mine into the room. Horace and Giles. They are . . . entertainers, of a type that princesses are not supposed to know of, let alone associate with."

"Do you mean . . . prostitutes?"

"I do. Did I mention that I am quite a good amateur photographer?"

"No, is that relevant to this story?"

"Most certainly. While Horace and Giles disrobed each other, and then my unwelcome guest, I set up my camera. The result was a series of photographs that would have ensured this low-level politician's career was over the very next day, had they found their way into the world."

"Good heavens," I said, stifling my laughter. "You really did that?"

"Absolutely. I still have the pictures, if you'd like to—"

"No, no, I most certainly would *not* like to." I looked at her for a moment. "That is quite something, and I have to confess that I've never met anyone as direct as you. Has it never gotten you in trouble?"

"With whom?" She leaned forward and patted my knee. "Henri, my wealth and privilege have insulated me all my life. By now, well, people are used to me, to how I am. At my age and my place in society, what can anyone do to me?"

"Take your house, to begin with."

"Ah, yes. But I can always buy another one."

"You miss my point. These people, these Germans, they don't care about your money and status. If they can take your wealth, they will. If they want to take your life, they will do that, too." I fixed her with a stern look. "I'm just saying, your outspoken and straightforward ways may not be as consequence-free as they used to be."

"Warning noted. Now, unless you have more questions, I should take my leave and let you eat."

"Sadly, I have no more questions."

"Then I shall leave you to enjoy your meal, and think about continuing our association. I know that my own forthrightness will remain between the two of us, and I hope it will lead you some way toward trusting me."

I nodded slowly. I was certainly closer to that than I'd expected to be.

"I shall think about it and let you know."

"Excellent. In any case, I'm sure we'll be seeing a lot of each other."

"How so?" I asked, surprised.

"Well, as you know, the Germans are taking over my home."

"Yes, and you're leaving for Africa."

"In a few weeks, yes. But until then I need somewhere to live." She gave me her friendliest smile. "And Nicola was kind enough to let me know that the apartment right below yours is most likely for rent. Furniture and all."

CHAPTER EIGHT

Wednesday, July 17, 1940

Every murder inquiry will throw up a surprise. Sometimes two, or even more. This investigation didn't have time for many so I suppose I was lucky to find out straightaway that my victim, Walter Fischer, cohabited with the man at the top of my list. I made that discovery early the next morning, when I stopped at the address that Jung and Vogel had given me.

Maurice Babin wasn't someone you'd automatically associate with art. Rugby, yes. Bar fights, absolutely. He was at least six feet five inches tall, and his circumference was about the same. His facial hair, on his chin and on his head, was well-kempt but with the suggestion that a strong breeze would set everything off. His eyes darted this way and that, like he was afraid to miss something that was happening, either action or conversation.

He mumbled something unintelligible when he saw my police badge but let me in anyway. We stood inside his ground-floor apartment and I could smell the coffee he'd been making when I knocked, and he offered me a cup. I accepted, and when it was made we sat at a small table between the small living area and even smaller kitchen.

I asked him about the dead man.

"I barely knew him" was his leading line, which caused me some suspicion considering the apartment they lived in had, from what I could see, just one bedroom.

"Right." I looked around to confirm my suspicions. "So, who had the couch?" He turned his doleful eyes on me and I felt like a bastard. "Look, I don't care about any of that, I just need to find out who killed him."

We each stared into our coffee, then I sat back and surveyed the small living space. I pretended not to notice the tissues cast about like there'd been a snowball fight but he wasn't fooled and, in turn, he stood and pretended cleaning them up was just a little tidying for an unexpected guest.

I didn't like that he was fraternizing with the enemy, and I realized that was what made me have a dig at him. But I wanted to tell him I meant what I said, that I didn't care he was homosexual, that I'd seen so many variations of hate that almost any type of love was acceptable to me, but I didn't have those words and I knew he'd not believe them even if, magically, they came to me. The thing about living through a war, surviving months of trench life and being sent on idiotic missions (including jumping out of airplanes), was that it all tended to focus the mind on what mattered. Surviving, first and foremost, and then the frills: family, friends, good food and wine. Plus, all the relationships I'd seen in my life had been counter to the books I'd read, and I didn't know or care what made other people happy. I just knew it when I saw it, and that was enough.

"Yes, please," he was saying. "Find out, and catch who killed him."

"When did you last see him?"

"Before he went to the museum on Sunday. He left around noon."

"Did he usually work on Sundays?" It hadn't crossed my mind until then that maybe Nazis took weekends off, too.

"I only knew him three weeks, but he worked every day of them." His giant hands smothered his coffee mug like he was strangling it.

"And what exactly did he do at the museum? What was his job?"

"He was supposed to catalog the art, for a couple of reasons. His first responsibility was to put aside items that were German for return to his Fatherland."

"Ah yes, Germany, famous for its many artistic masterpieces."

A small smile crept onto his face. "I said something similar. He didn't like that, he is—was, very patriotic."

"I'm sure. That doesn't improve the quality of German art, though. You said he was sorting it for several reasons."

"*Oui.* He was the one to decide which art would be put back on display. They are reopening the museum in September. Did you know that?"

"Someone mentioned it, yes." I took a sip of coffee. "Why was he chosen for that job?"

"He was a lecturer before the war, a professor. Art history at Heidelberg University."

"Makes sense. How do you get from that to signing on with the Waffen SS, I wonder."

"You know . . ." He paused and slurped at his coffee. "I had wanted to have that conversation with him. Tried a few times but I think . . . I got the impression he didn't even know himself. Maybe it was to avoid being drafted into the Wehrmacht infantry, maybe there was an allure, all that power. I sometimes think he didn't really know what he was getting himself into. Naive patriotism, so to speak."

"So he wasn't your traditional sadistic, bullying SS officer?"

"Not at all. He looked the part, I know. Handsome, elegant, the poster boy for the Nazis. But he wasn't like that, he was kind and gentle. Which is why you have to find out who did this to him."

"There are several reasons why I have to do that," I assured him. "Do you have any idea who might have wanted him dead? Any reason?"

"No. Not at all."

"Did he work closely with anyone at the museum?"

"Two people. Florence Petit and Nicolas Allard."

Two of the names on my list. "And what do they do?"

"Mademoiselle Petit is another art expert. She's been at the museum for ten years."

"And Allard?"

"Oh, he's the muscle."

"As in protection? Security?"

"That fool?" Babin laughed softly. "I'm sorry, that's unkind. But he is quite literally a fool. He's harmless enough, though. And no, not security, his job was to do the carrying, the fetching, the moving, and I think the shipping. He is strong and obedient, two very valuable qualities these days."

"More so in an army than a museum."

He got up and moved to the window. "Except we don't have much of an army anymore, do we?"

"True enough." I recalled the other two names on my list and ran them by him.

"Abraham Simon, yes. He's a frame-maker."

"He works at the museum?"

"No. I mean, sometimes he comes there to do work, but he's not an employee."

"Any reason to suspect him of committing this crime?"

"Not that I can think of." Babin shook his head slowly. "He makes and refurbishes frames for high-end artwork. If a painting needs extracting, he can do it, or if we need a brand-new frame for a freshly painted piece, he'll sometimes advise and create it."

"You only know him professionally?"

"That's correct, and not very well in that regard. Plus, he's at least sixty."

"But he works with tools and builds frames all day. There are plenty of strong sixty-year-olds, you know."

Babin shook his head. "Wait until you meet him."

"I will, thank you." I paused, because there was another

question burning a hole in my tongue. "How is it that you and Herr Fischer . . . ?"

"We met at the museum, I work in a different part usually." His eyes watched me, wary, and I could see he didn't trust me with the truth. "We connected . . . socially, and he didn't like where he was billeted. That's all there is to it."

"Right, thank you." I stood. "Well, I should be getting on. Do you happen to know how I can contact Mademoiselle Petit and Monsieur Allard?"

"At the museum. I suppose they are still working there."

"Yes, of course." I went to shake his enormous hand and looked past him, through the window, into the small, walled yard. The only object of interest, to me anyway, was a shed in the back corner. A shed that had a door that was a slightly different shade of brown than the rest of it, and a door that had been secured with a large, very shiny padlock.

● ● ●

The Germans had forbidden me to enter the museum, so if I was going to locate the two people my victim had worked with, I would need to linger outside and catch them coming in or going out. By the time I left Babin's place, he'd told me which entrance to the Louvre they all used, but I had to assume they'd be at work already, so I turned my focus to another name the giant had given me, even though Babin didn't think much of him as a suspect—Abraham Simon.

Simon had a shop on rue de Seine, and a bell on the back of the door jingled when I went in. The place smelled of wood and varnish, and looked more like a storage space than a store. Something, maybe sawdust, irritated my nose and I sneezed loudly.

A small man appeared in the archway that, I assumed, led into the back of the store, maybe his work space. Small, yes, but quite distinctive with a full, dropping walrus mustache that was as gray as the frizzy hair that grew in clumps on his head. He gave the impression of age, but his eyes were ice blue, the kind of captivating blue that a movie star would die for.

"No need for that racket," he said genially. "I heard the bell."

"Excuse me." I dabbed at my nose with a handkerchief.

"It's the sawdust. It'll settle down in a while." He cocked his head. "You're not a customer, how can I help you?"

"How do you know that?"

"You didn't come in holding a painting. I suppose one could be in your briefcase but then again . . . it's a very battered brief-case."

"Meaning?"

"I don't mean to be rude," he said, always the precursor to rudeness. "But most of my clients have tweed suits, new leather shoes, and . . . not battered, old briefcases."

"It was my father's."

"I see." Those fierce eyes held mine, and his walrus mus-tache twitched like it had a life of its own. "So, how can I help you?" I showed him my badge and saw the wheels turning in his head. "This is about the dead German."

"It is. Did you know him?"

"Of course." He perched on the edge of a heavy pine table and I noticed his hands: great, outsize hands that looked like they'd belong to a lumberjack, not a frame-maker. "Some of the more expensive pieces down there required my atten-tion. My expertise."

"Why?"

"It's not always a good idea to ship paintings in their frames. At least, to do so requires a lot more traveling space, larger packing crates. As I'm sure you're aware, transportation space and wood for crates are beginning to be in short supply."

"Yes, of course. So you would go to the museum and take paintings out of the frames."

"Correct." His smile was kind, but he didn't offer any more explanation.

"How many times have you done this?"

"Twenty, maybe thirty."

"All for Walter Fischer?"

"And Mademoiselle Petit. One or the other will send for me when I'm needed. I usually spend an entire day there, rather than making individual trips."

"I see. What happens to the frames when you remove them?"

"That all depends. Sometimes they are put into storage at the museum, or somewhere else. Sometimes they are destroyed, the cheaper ones that is."

"How well did you know Fischer?"

"Not very well at all." He shrugged. "He was always there when I was, but I don't speak German and I also don't speak to Germans who speak French."

A touch of resentment then, but not enough to turn down whatever the invaders were paying. "Why did you work with him, if you're so opposed to exchanging niceties?"

He laughed. "Do you think in the last month, in the coming months, there will be a lot of people coming in here to buy frames for the new art being created? Do you even think there will be any art created while these people are here?"

"I have no idea." But I thought of Picasso and his involuntary moratorium.

"Well, I do. And the answer is no. Therefore I have to make my living while I can, the only way I can. After all, I am too old to rob banks."

I gave him a sympathetic smile, I wanted him to know I was asking not judging. "Actually, I don't think there's an age limit. You just have to be able to run away quickly."

"Then I am definitely disqualified." He laughed again. "Anyway, the Germans pay well and they pay promptly. For now, at least."

"I'm glad to hear that." I asked him about Petit and Allard, both of whom he only knew from his work at the Louvre, recent acquaintances. He knew Babin rather better, from the Parisian art scene, but I didn't press him on what he knew of the relationship between Babin and Fischer. If it became relevant, maybe, but I had no clue what Simon already knew. No need to embarrass a grieving man, if I didn't have to.

The one man on the list he didn't know, and no one seemed to, was Pascal Voclain. I had Nicola working on looking all these people up, and I figured I'd have time to stop at the Préfecture and check on her progress before walking over to the Louvre to try and catch Petit and Allard. I had descriptions of the two from Babin but to be sure, I had Simon describe them, too. Both men agreed that Petit had a penchant for white silk scarves, and that the beefy Allard was so slow of mind, he could've seen the murder being committed, and had no clue what happened.

"The poor man has the intelligence of one of my picture frames, sadly," Simon said, actually looking sad. "I think from the 1914 war, at least that's what someone told me."

I'd seen hundreds of men permanently damaged by that war. Not all had lost an arm, a leg, or an eye. Just as many had lost their minds and yet those were the ones who got the least sympathy. Mocked for being idiots, if they were lucky. Locked up for being lunatics if not. I'd come out relatively unscathed and had been handed a medal and a small pension on the way out. Most got nothing, except for a lifetime of sick memories and nightmares repeating like a scratched record. I knew how lucky I was, and I felt for Allard, wanted to meet him all the more.

I thanked Simon for his time and trudged back to the Préfecture to find Nicola at her desk, absorbed by the file that was open in front of her. She noticed me come in and looked over, tapping the file with one finger.

"You're going to want to see this."

"What is it?"

"Our file on Pascal Voclain."

"Looks thick." I leaned over her shoulder and looked at a photo clipped to the front of some pages. Voclain was short and stocky, with an impressively large mustache and small, beady eyes. "What's it say?"

"He's well known to us. History of petty stuff when he was young, then grew up into more adult crimes. Burglary, assault, a touch of pretty much anything you can think of, except honest hard work."

"See any possible connection to Fischer or this case?"

"Two weeks ago, Paris police arrested him outside the Louvre because he was threatening violence against some Germans. Against one in particular, and he even took a swing at him." She looked up at me. "Go on, you're a detective. Guess who."

CHAPTER NINE

I took the file on Pascal Voclain from Nicola and retreated to my office. It got any detective's juices flowing to discover someone with a motive to harm a victim, and especially when that someone has a history of violence. It's rare that a person goes from zero to murder, there's almost always something in between, so it seemed likely to me that my killer had hurt someone before. And that's true even if the violence is behind closed doors where no one can see, as I well knew from my own past.

I'd just flipped open the file when the telephone on my desk rang. I was surprised, mostly because working telephones were a rarity, but also because this office was so new to me I didn't expect the Préfecture's operators to know I was in here. I hoped it wasn't for Marcel Rapace—a distraught lover, maybe, wondering why he'd not been in contact. . . .

It wasn't.

"*Bonjour*, Henri Lefort."

"Henri, *bonjour*." I immediately recognized the slightly deeper voice of our visitor from last night.

"Princess Marie, what a surprise."

"I told you, call me Mimi."

"Very well, Mimi."

"Thank you. Anyway, I wanted you to know that I will be moving some things into the apartment beneath yours tonight."

"Oh," I said. "That's wonderful news."

She laughed. "You're a terrible liar."

"Well, at least I tried."

"You did, thank you for that. I think. I was wondering if you'd reached a conclusion. I need to know whether to schedule you or another client for this evening."

I'd thought about it on and off all morning, and each time I reached a different conclusion. On one hand, I was fascinated by her and wanted to spend more time talking. I also knew that I had some things buried deep inside me, specters and memories screaming at me from the darkest corners of my mind, and those would only go away when subjected to the bright light of day. Plus, if she could really help with my aversion to certain sounds, well, then I could start going to the cinema and theater again, which would make Nicola very happy. As would allowing her to eat carrots and celery in the same room as me.

Then again, I had very good reasons to keep some things secret, and I wasn't sure I could trust myself to sieve selectively through them under the questioning of such a brilliant woman. Everyone had done bad things in the war, but not everyone had done what I did. And as open and forthright as Mimi had been with me, her world was so far removed from that life in the trenches I doubted she'd really understand. And, as I thought more about it, I realized that this mattered, her understanding, not just because it might lead to her doing me some good but because I liked the woman, and I liked that she liked me. Not in a sexual way, but precisely the opposite—she was interested in Henri the person, just as I was in Mimi the person. And it was a budding friendship I didn't want to drown under a ton of historical shit that, so far, I'd been able to keep anyone else from stepping in.

"Henri?"

"I was thinking, sorry."

"There will be wine. Good wine."

"Is that ethical, getting your clients drunk?"

She laughed. "If one glass of Château Pétrus gets you drunk, you definitely have issues we should discuss."

"Well, that's for damned certain. Wait, did you say Pétrus?"

"I most certainly did. A glass every session, if you want it."

"Well, you should've mentioned that up front." If I saved up every centime I'd ever made, I wouldn't be able to afford a case of that stuff.

"Then it's agreed, I will see you when you get home. Just knock on the door and I'll take no more than an hour of your time." She said it like I'd agreed, but I caught the note of hope, of anticipation in her voice.

"I'll be there," I said. "I can't promise I'll want to answer all of your questions, and I might just drink your wine and leave, but I'll be there."

"That's all I ask right now," she said. "Thank you, Henri, you won't regret it."

I wasn't so sure about that. From what I knew, these people liked to talk about family, and I wasn't ready to go there. And I knew she'd want to talk about the war, what I did in it, which was inextricably intertwined with family. I shook my head as I hung up the phone, wondering what I'd gotten myself into. By agreeing to analysis, I had possibly handed her a key—not to my psyche, which was just fine and dandy, but to my past.

Which, by any measure, was decidedly not.

•   •   •

The custody sheet was at the back of the Voclain file, and it showed that two weeks previously the man had been taken to a cell downstairs, and thrown in the drunk tank to cool off. That, of course, meant he was probably one of the many who'd been released without charges being filed. What an irony it would be if Voclain turned out to be our man: released because the Germans were here, only to kill one of them. Or maybe not irony, maybe wish fulfillment on the part of whoever held the keys downstairs.

The question was, why did Voclain have a problem with Fischer in the first place? Merely because he was German and in Paris? It struck me as strange, the likelihood that a man prepared to steal from anyone with a coin in their pocket, or assault an elderly man (which he had, according to his file) would have a patriotic streak. Men like Voclain, in my experience, had allegiance to just one cause: themselves.

Of course, the best way to find out would be to ask him. I spent half an hour on the office phone, calling the regular list of jails around the city in case he'd used his freedom to violate some other poor soul, and struck lucky with the second to last.

The humorless jailer I spoke to said he was being held for assaulting a tree.

"I'm sorry, can you say that again? I thought you said *tree*."

"I did."

"Ah. Thing is, I'm not sure that's a crime. Is it a protected species?"

Silence for a moment. "The report doesn't mention the type of tree."

"Right. Oversight on the part of the arresting officer. Can you hang on to him until I get there?"

"Well, if you're telling me that's not a crime then I should really release him."

"True, but remember we don't know the type of tree, do we?"

He sounded doubtful. "You really think that could make a difference?"

No! "Yes."

"Oh." He was still unconvinced.

"Where did this happen?" I asked.

"Luxembourg Gardens. Yesterday afternoon. Why?"

"I was going to check out the crime scene, but there are a lot of trees there. How about I come down and interview him, see if he'll tell us?"

Another pause. "I suppose."

"Great, thank you. I'll be there midafternoon, so don't let him go before then."

"I thought you were going to come now!" he protested.

"Important police business to take care of first."

"But this means I'll have to feed him lunch."

"Of course you will." I became stern with him to get my

point across. "There may be a war on, but we're not savages." I hung up before he could protest further.

Lunch was on my mind, too, so I checked my pocket watch and guessed that Mademoiselle Petit might be heading out for hers in the near future. I tucked the Voclain file into my brief-case.

"Where are you going?" Nicola asked as I closed my office door.

"Interview two suspects. Witnesses. Whatever they are."

"Names on a list."

"Right. But that list is all I have, and there's no time to waste."

"Any luck so far?"

She looked at me, almost pleadingly, and I wanted to take the time to tell her, to reassure her, but I couldn't. What I could do, though, was remain positive.

"A few bits and pieces, yes. I'll fill you in later."

I made good time to the Louvre, thanks once again to the absence of the usual tourists and wandering locals getting in my way. Mostly I saw groups of Germans, either in their civvies and leaning casually over the bridges, or in uniform marching smartly from hither to thither for no apparent reason. They stayed out of my way and I theirs, all of us keen not to offend. For now, anyway.

I'd noticed a new feature to the occupation in the past week, and I saw several of them on my walk. Parisians had started to call them "little gray mice," and they scuttled about the city always on a mission, but usually uncomfortable, watching their surroundings. They were young German women in gray uniforms and little hats, sent to do the secretarial and administrative work that the Boche so loved. I rather assumed they were there to provide the soldiers some comfort of an evening, too, but that was purely supposition on my part. And while I resented their presence, as I did for all Germans, I actually felt a little sorry for them. They looked harried and lost. They didn't have the arrogance of their uniformed countrymen, nor their brethren's power or strength such that they could inspire fear, respect, or even cooperation. And without those shields, these little women scampered through the streets, smart enough to know they were despised, and low enough on the totem pole to know they might be targets for those Parisians desperate to lash out at the city's invaders.

The door at the back of the Louvre that Babin had mentioned was, like Picasso's home and studio, one I'd strolled past a thousand times and not noticed. Fortunately, someone had kindly placed a bench in the sheltered Place du Louvre so I could sit and watch it. My stomach rumbled and as my eyes maintained watch, my mind wondered what they'd be seeing on a plate in an hour or so. Lamb was supposedly in short supply, so might be wise to traipse on over to a place in the Marais I knew that braised it so very well. While I still could.

The door opened and closed several times before disgorging the delightfully pretty, white scarf–wearing Florence Petit and I almost immediately discounted her as a suspect. A terrible thing for a detective to do, I know, but it wasn't just because she was so pretty. She was, in keeping with her name, extraordinarily petite. Not small, I bet no one ever called her that, because she carried herself with a great confidence and dressed like a movie star. But strong? Probably not. Additionally, I doubted she'd have been able to reach Walter Fischer's earhole, let alone have the power to skewer his brain with an ice pick.

I walked up to her, and when she saw my official credentials she looked a little startled, but quickly regained her composure, and I led her back to the bench so we could talk.

"When was the last time you saw him?" I asked, after giving her my condolences.

She looked confused for a moment. "Well, I mean, I suppose technically the last time I saw him was when I found him dead."

"Ah, good to know."

"You're the case detective." Her eyes narrowed in suspicion. "How can you not know that already?"

"Because I was assigned this case by the Germans, who saw fit to move the body before calling me in, and then banned me from the Louvre."

"You're not even allowed in there?"

"That's why I was waiting out here."

"That makes no sense!"

It does if you don't much care for the detective to solve the case. "I agree. But that's where we are, so I'd appreciate any help you can give me."

"Of course, I'll do what I can."

"Can you describe exactly how you found him? How he was lying, where, that sort of thing. Every detail you can remember."

"Yes, of course." She looked down at the pavement and I knew she was conjuring up the scene. "I don't usually work on Sundays; I wasn't meant to be there. But I'd left my purse behind after popping in on Saturday to check on Nicolas."

"Monsieur Allard."

"Yes. He likes to work on weekends when it's quieter, he's not much of a people person, you might say. Anyway, I'd come in Saturday and left my purse behind so went back on Sunday to get it."

"You didn't need it Saturday night or Sunday morning?"

"Oh, I did. It just took me a while to realize where I'd left it."

"Right, makes sense. Go on, please."

"I let myself in through this door." She pointed to the one she'd just exited. "It opens into a short corridor, which leads to a large gallery area. It's not used for displaying, but for storage and sometimes repairs. Anyway, off the main gallery area are two other large rooms, almost the size of the gallery space but not quite. In one we put items that will be displayed in September, when the Louvre reopens, and in the other we put items that are to be shipped off. On one side German art, and on the other everything else."

"I knew items were being shipped to Germany, repatriated someone said, but where else are you sending things?"

"Everywhere. Some to the new government buildings, some to Italy. Quite a lot there, actually."

"Why?"

"The same as the German art."

"Repatriation." I nodded, as it made sense that the fat, stupid version of Hitler called Benito Mussolini would want to get his hands on as much valuable art as possible. And the Italians had produced way more of that than the Germans, to the best of my knowledge. "And your job, what is that exactly?" I asked.

She smiled and her lipstick seemed to glitter in the sun, deep red and very kissable. "That would depend on who you ask."

"Explain that."

"My boss is Aldrik Graf. He used to be some sort of attaché to the German embassy here, arts and culture or something like that. When the Germans took over, he was put in charge of the Louvre, which sounds like a big job but because it was closed at the time, it really wasn't. His main job was to hire a few people to catalog, sort, and ship out the artwork. Or leave it behind."

"Was it his idea to reopen the museum?"

"No, it was mine."

"Impressive."

"No, this is what I'm trying to tell you. That's my job, or part of it. The Germans see me as some sort of liaison, having me involved was a matter of establishing some goodwill. Can you imagine how it would look if the Germans started emptying the Louvre themselves?"

"That's what's happening, best I can tell."

"Maybe. But people aren't protesting because they see people like me and Nicolas in there, supposedly protecting French interests. They are clever, they have more French people in there than Germans. Way more."

"Wait, *supposedly* protecting French interests?"

"We do what we can but I serve at the pleasure of my boss, right? I make too much fuss and he can get rid of me." She snapped a delicate finger and thumb together. "Just like that."

"So if someone identifies a piece they want to ship away, to Germany or Italy for example, you're supposed to point out that it's French."

"How hard I point that out depends on its value."

"I don't understand."

"I have limited power. I save my loudest protestations for the pieces I think are worth the most, would be valued by the French people the most."

A beggar had spotted us and was drifting our way, a woman dressed in rags and carrying a dozen or more bags. She looked like a slow-moving, grubbily disgusting Christmas tree. When she was ten feet away I was able to confirm that she did not, however, smell like one. She extended her hand, her eyes on the woman beside me like Mademoiselle Petit was a priceless doll waiting to be picked up. And traded for booze, most likely.

"Back off, madame," I said firmly. I held up my badge to make sure the message got across. "Police business, keep moving."

The woman licked her lips, which, given the grime that covered the rest of her visible body parts, probably qualified as a full meal. But she drifted away muttering to herself, or maybe us. I turned my attention back to my witness.

"So tell me about Walter Fischer."

"Herr Fischer would have called me a pain in the arse."

"Why?"

"He was a stickler. Everything remotely German had to be shipped off, even if it was worthless, or maybe the artist wasn't really German. For example, we had a sketch, it was never even a painting, by Raymond Wintz. It was called *The Blue Door*, quite famous."

"I'll have to take your word for that."

"Right, well, my point is," she said patiently, "that Fischer had heard of it and assumed the artist was German because of his name. He insisted the painting should be sent back to

Germany." She straightened her spine and a smile appeared on her face. "I won that particular battle."

"Well done."

"But you see, to win it I had to provide evidence, do research that showed Wintz was born right here in Paris. I simply don't have the time to fight every battle that way. Some I have to let go."

"And that pains you."

"Of course." The stiffness, the pride, disappeared. "We have lost a lot of art. Most of it unknown but all of it valuable in one way or another."

"Did you get on well with Fischer otherwise?"

"There was no otherwise. He was quiet, very professional. He never . . . you know."

Well, he wouldn't, would he? "That's good. Do you know anything about his private life? Family?"

"*Mon Dieu, non.* We never talked about anything like that. He could have had millions of friends, three wives, sixty kids, and a dog, and I wouldn't know."

"So you never had lunch with him. A drink."

She shook her head. "I barely had a conversation with him."

"I assume you have no idea who would want to hurt him."

"None at all."

"What about Nicolas?"

Her head snapped around and her eyes burned with intensity. "Now you listen to me. Nicolas is a good man. He lost everything fighting for France, including his mind. He may hate the Germans, Walter Fischer included, but his life was destroyed by violence. There is no possible way he would commit an act like that. He came here to keep away from people, he wanted nothing to do with any war or any kind of conflict. The last war finished him. I don't know what he saw or did, and I don't want to. What I do know is that he's suffered enough for a thousand lifetimes and so I'm begging you, *begging* you, to leave him alone."

"Mademoiselle, I would dearly love to do that. Believe me, I fought in that war, too, and I've seen what it can do to a man. If you can provide an alibi for him for Sunday, I will not need to trouble him. Maybe he was at church all day?"

She threw her head back and laughed. "That is one place I can promise you he was not. He spits every time he passes Notre Dame, or any other church."

"The war did that to him, too, eh?"

"Most certainly it did." She put a hand on my arm. "Let me do this, please. Let me talk to him and see where he was on Sunday. Please, if I can't find out then . . . well, we'll see. But let me talk to him first."

I sat back against the hard bench and thought. Eventually I turned to her and said: "I'll let you do that. But make no mistake, if I'm not completely satisfied with whatever he tells you then I'll be speaking to him myself. You need to know that my neck is on the line with this investigation and so, as war ravaged as he may be, I'm not about to stand in front of a brick wall wearing a blindfold just to spare his feelings."

"I understand," she said. "Thank you for letting me do this for him. I'll talk to him about it this afternoon. I'll come to the Préfecture when I have his answer." She stood and extended a hand. "I am late for a lunch appointment. I will see you at six."

I stood and took her tiny hand in mine. *"Merci,* mademoiselle. In the meantime, I need to figure out how an ice pick made its way into the Musée du Louvre."

A look of confusion passed over her face. "An ice pick?"

"Yes. The murder weapon."

"Oh, *non,* monsieur, you are mistaken. It wasn't an ice pick at all."

CHAPTER TEN

I managed not to explode in front of Florence Petit, saving a string of swear words for the fresh outdoors. I needed answers to this case, not more questions, and I sure as hell didn't need the psychotic bastards overseeing me to be feeding me lies and false information. I calmed myself, thinking maybe they were mistaken and not misdirecting, but if that were the case it meant I was being overseen by imbeciles, which was of cold comfort.

I needed some time and fresh air, so didn't mind at all that it took me almost an hour to walk to the *commissariat de police* on rue du Bouquet-de-Longchamp, due west of the Préfecture in the Sixteenth Arrondissement. Two German soldiers in steel-gray uniforms stood sentry outside the white building, and in front of them a half dozen cigarette butts littered the cobblestone street, which irritated me.

"Make sure you pick those up. If you have to be here, at least keep the place tidy." One of the soldiers started to bristle so I tacked on, "I can have a word with my friend and colleague Sturmbannführer Ludwig Vogel, if that would help." The sentry probably had no idea who that was but, if he did, he knew not to risk the man's wrath, and if he didn't he at least recognized the SS rank.

They both gave me hard stares but I breezed past them like I didn't care. Mostly because I didn't. Behind the counter, a bored policeman looked up from his newspaper, but stayed put in his creaky wooden chair.

"Can I help you?"

"You most certainly can." I showed him my badge and he must have recognized my name because he scrambled to his feet.

"Yes, sir, we spoke on the phone earlier. Your man is still here."

"I meant to ask this before. Why is he in your jail if he committed a crime in the Luxembourg Gardens?"

"I have no idea, sir. Something to do with the current situation, I expect. Maybe you could ask those two jokers outside, they might know."

"I don't think they like me very much."

"Oh?"

"I scolded them for dropping cigarette ends on the ground."

"Good for you, sir." A new respect shone in his eyes, and I guessed he was too timid to challenge the newcomers directly. A lot of people were, but then again I probably would have been, too, if I'd really thought that pair of slobs might do something to me. With a jolt, I remembered the drunk Germans who'd not cared a jot about my status as a detective and, resolving to be slightly more judicious with my insolence to the invaders, I gestured past my junior colleague.

"Shall we?"

"Oh, right, the prisoner. Follow me, sir."

He held up a hatch in the counter and I tucked in behind him as he led me through a locked door, down a long corridor, and through another locked door into the small station's jail area.

"Here we are." He looked over his shoulder at me. "Got nine cells, all are full. But I put your fellow in one by himself so you could talk to him in private."

"Very thoughtful."

It was hot in there, and loud with the babble of muffled male voices. The smell wasn't great, either, a mix of stale sweat and piss.

"You'll be all right talking to him alone? It's shift change so I'm the only one here right now, I should get back out there in case someone comes in."

"This fellow punches trees, not people, right?"

"Yes, sir," he said, perfectly serious.

"Well, then, I should be fine."

"Tell you what, I'll let you have the key." He handed it to me and pointed to the steel door I needed. "He's all yours."

"Thanks." I watched him leave and then wandered over to the cell. Someone had drawn the number four on the wall in chalk beside the door. I put the key in the lock and turned it with some effort, which was actually quite reassuring. It swung outward and, probably out of habit, Pascal Voclain stood at the back of his cell, hands on his head facing the wall. *Jailers have you well trained*, I thought.

"Monsieur Voclain, please, sit down." I pulled the door shut behind me, unable to lock it because there was no keyhole on the inside. I gestured for Voclain to sit on his concrete block of a bed, and I sat on the one opposite it, but closer to the door. After about three seconds, I enviously eyed the thin mattress on his bed. Voclain himself was a healthy specimen, short but broad, and I remembered the large mustache and close eyes from his picture.

"What do you want?" he asked.

"Some information."

"Why should I help you with anything?"

I jerked my thumb toward the door. "The *flic* who has the keys to this place. He told me you were arrested for fighting with a tree."

"I was drunk."

"Was the tree?"

His eyes narrowed. "What?"

"Look, if you want out of here, I can arrange that."

"Sure you can."

"Seriously. I outrank that guy and anyway, the tree doesn't want to press charges."

"Why do you keep saying that shit?"

"Basically because it's true. You're here on a ridiculous charge and I can either talk to the jailer and get you out or I can walk out now and forget to mention your name to him."

He sat back and eyed me for a moment. "What information do you want?"

"I want to know why you tried to punch that German."

"Which one?"

"You've tried to punch more than one?"

"Tried and succeeded, you could say."

"Well, good for you. Keep up the good work. The one I'm talking about was named Walter Fischer and you took a swing at him outside the Louvre a couple of weeks ago."

His face darkened and I knew he remembered. "Why do you want to know?"

"Because he's dead, and I'd like to know if you went back to finish something you'd started."

"He started it, not me."

"How so?"

"The day before I'd seen him coming out of the Louvre." He sat forward and gestured for me to do the same. "I don't want anyone else hearing this."

I shifted forward, all ears. I should've been all eyes, too, but I wasn't and so didn't see his fist coming my way. I reacted pretty much as that tree had: not at all, not until the punch connected with my jaw, anyway. Pain exploded across my face and my brain rattled in my head, then the concrete floor raced up to meet me and everything went dark.

For what may have been a long time, or not.

Hands tugged at me, pulling me upward, and I groaned at the pain in my face. The jailer plopped me on the concrete bed I'd fallen from, and I slowly worked my jaw to see if it was broken. The pain was bad but not broken bad, which was a relief. I wasn't likely to solve this case as it was, taking away my ability to speak would have been a definite nail in my coffin.

"Are you all right?" the jailer was asking.

"Yes, I think so. That bastard coldcocked me. Damn it."

"It stinks in here, let's get you into some fresh air."

"Yeah, thanks." I looked up and saw blood on the front of his uniform, and a piece of cotton bandaging sticking out of each nostril. I wanted to laugh at how ridiculous he looked, but considering it was my fault I decided just to let him help me outside. I slung my arm over his shoulders and leaned on him. "He got you, too, huh?"

"Yep. Never saw him coming." We moved out of the cell and past the others, which had multiple pairs of eyes staring out through the food hatches, and anonymous voices shouted at us, asking what was going on. Cool air drifted over me the second he swung open the main door letting us out of the cell area.

"Sorry about this," I said. "I guess we were wrong about what and who he likes punching."

"Oh, please don't worry, there's no harm done," the jailer said. He half carried me through the reception area and out the main doors.

"Apart from him escaping," I said.

"Escaping? Not really." He pointed down the street, to where the German soldiers stood over the form of someone lying in the middle of the cobbles.

"*Merde*, they shot him?"

"Both of them did. Making sure, I suppose."

"He's definitely dead?"

"Oh, most definitely."

"*Merde*," I said again. "The only thing worse than an escaped murder suspect is a dead one."

"Murder suspect, eh?" He blew out his cheeks. "I didn't know that."

"It hardly matters now."

"Well, on the positive side you can just blame him and close your case now. Nice and easy."

"Right," I said. "Because that's how police work should go." Although in this instance, for an idiot, that wasn't a half-bad idea.

CHAPTER ELEVEN

I waited at the Préfecture for Florence Petit, waited a full hour, and she never showed up, which put me in a bad mood. Worse mood. That's why it took me until I was halfway back home before I again noticed someone was following me. The same someone as before, and that bad mood wasn't about to put up with whatever bullshit game this *mec* was playing.

I took a meandering route, not to shake him but to make sure I was right. Once I'd decided I was, I slowed until he was close by and then dipped into a *tabac* and waited for him. He'd have to pass by, the store was little more than an alcove. It took me a moment to realize I was sharing the doorway with a sack of bones held together by baggy clothing and some string. The wretch looked up hopefully at me, and I looked down at where he sat, his one leg extended out. So many of these men littered the streets of Paris, my comrades in arms two decades ago, heroes when they came back from the trenches, but most days invisible to those of us in full working condition. Even to me, truth be told, not because I was insensitive to their plight but more because I didn't need reminding of the past.

I pointed at the missing limb and stated the obvious. "The last war?"

"Bien sûr." Of course. He nodded and gave me a grimy-toothed grin. "I ain't fighting much in this one."

"You, me, and the rest of the French army," I said.

"Cowards. All of them."

"Just the ones at the top." I dug into my pocket for some change and showed it to him. "This in exchange for not looking at or talking to me for the next couple of minutes."

He eyed the money, then me. "You hiding?"

"Lurking."

"Don't make a difference to me." He held up a dirty hand and I filled it with coins. He busied himself counting and recounting them, but kept his side of the bargain. A moment later, my tail reached the *tabac*. He glanced inside and hesitated but kept going, the look and the hesitation telling me he was following me for sure. I stepped out behind him, wanting to get a better look but part of me, the sadistic part, also wanted to make him uncomfortable. He crossed the street, so I followed him, getting a good look at his face in the window of a hat shop on rue de l'Université.

It was the same *mec* as before, short with slicked-back hair and narrow, nervous eyes. And none of the arrogance of a Gestapo or SS bastard. And that meant he was French, a civilian,

and for the life of me I could think of no reason why I'd be followed by one of my own.

One way to find out, I thought. A few long strides later, I
had my hand on his shoulder, and I spun him around and shoved
him against the same window that had revealed his face to me.

"Who are you and why are you following me?" I growled. I
had him by the lapels, and, as I was six inches taller, his terrified eyes looked up at mine.

"I wasn't, I was in front of you. How could I be—?"

"Don't." I lifted him onto his tiptoes. "Lie to me."

"I'm not," he said, but his white face and terrified eyes told
a different tale.

"I saw you yesterday and today you were behind me. So you
have one chance to tell me the truth, otherwise you'll be swal-
lowing your teeth for dinner."

He stared at me for a moment, then his body sagged. "All
right, all right. I'll tell you."

I relaxed my grip a little. "I'm listening."

"I'm a journalist. A reporter."

"There are no newspapers anymore."

"I know. Fine, I *was* a journalist. Now . . ." He waved his
arms in despair. "I get by how I can."

"Following policemen?"

"Not usually. I was hired to follow you. To find out more
about you, like where you live."

"By who? Why?"

"I don't know." I pushed him against the glass and he cried
out. "It's true."

"I told you not to lie to me."

"Someone from a news agency in England. He sent a wire

and some money, it didn't give details but I needed the dough so I did it."

"There was a name. Of a person, or a newspaper." I could see by the slide of his eyes he was withholding information so I gave him a slap on his cheek.

"Stop! It was Reuters, the news agency."

"*Connerie*," I snapped. *Bullshit*.

"It's true. I don't know why, just that they saw the propaganda the Nazis put out after you saved Princess Marie Bonaparte two nights ago."

"How do you know?"

"When I got the telegram, I thought it was a joke. A trick. I went to the Reuters office here and they didn't know anything but let me call London. I spoke to someone there, he said that's all I needed to know."

"Who did you speak to?"

"I don't know, I was passed around until this *mec* knew what I was talking about."

"What was his name?"

"I don't know, I'm telling you!"

"Then what did he tell you to do?"

"Just find out about you. Where you live, who with. And get a picture if I can."

"Did you take one?" I snarled.

"No! And you lost me yesterday, so I don't even know where you live."

"Why does he want this information?"

"I don't know," he whined. "I promise, I was just doing what I was asked, what I was getting paid for."

"Show me your identification papers."

"What?"

"You heard me. Now." I released my grip on him.

"Yes, fine." He dug in his jacket pocket and showed me his papers. Enzo Riva was his name.

"You're Italian?"

"People always say that. My family is from Nice."

"Never been there." I shoved his papers into my jacket pocket.

"Hey, I need those, what if I get stopped?"

"Then you're in trouble, so don't."

"Monsieur, please . . ."

"Come to the Préfecture. Tomorrow, at nine in the morning. Have a name for me, the person who hired you to follow me."

"I can't, I don't know how to get his—"

"At five minutes past nine either I will have this man's name and you will have your papers, or . . . well, I strongly suggest we stick with that option."

Enzo Riva wilted in my grip so I just let go of him and walked away, not looking back. Either he'd do as he was told or he wouldn't, there was only so much I could control.

I set a course for home, and let my mind wander a little, away from a mystery I couldn't yet solve, and toward an enigma I could at least examine a little more closely. I couldn't help but be a little intrigued about Princess Marie Bonaparte, both as a person and as a potential balm for my psyche. There was also something enticing about the notion of sharing a secret I'd kept locked up for twenty years, something exciting about maybe, perhaps, being able to trust someone with it. (Nicola didn't count, not really, because it was almost as much her secret as mine at this point.) All the more exciting because these days trust was becoming the rarest of commodities. And, for a reason I couldn't articulate, I really did feel like I could trust Mimi.

One way to find out, I thought. *And that glass of Pétrus sounds particularly alluring after today.*

·   ·   ·

"So do I lie down, or how does this work?"

I hadn't been in my downstairs neighbor's apartment for over a year, but it looked a lot like mine, just with nicer furniture. Marie Bonaparte led me through the main room into one of the two bedrooms, which she'd set up as her office or study. The room held a desk, a bookcase, and two leather armchairs that had been placed opposite each other but then swiveled so that if two people sat in them their right knees almost touched. We settled into them and she took out a notebook and pencil.

"I was promised wine," I reminded her.

"Ah, yes, my sincere apologies." She pushed herself up and walked quickly out of the room. She returned less than a minute later with a large glass of red wine. "Decanted, don't worry."

"Not one for you? I don't like to drink alone."

"I'm working." She flipped open the notebook. "Tell me about your parents and childhood."

"I'm not ready to talk about that. Try something else." I took a sip of the wine and let it roll across my tongue, filling my mouth with the softest and most delicious flavor I'd ever encountered. I closed my eyes to savor it more intensely.

"Don't make me take that away from you."

I opened my eyes and swallowed. "I'm carrying a gun, just try."

"Well, then," she said, smiling, "let's talk about that."

"Me carrying a gun?"

"You in the 1914 war."

"What if I don't want to talk about that, either?"

"Then I'll take my wine back."

"Fine. What do you want to know?"

She thought for a moment. "Did you lose anyone important in the fighting?"

"Everyone did."

"Don't be flippant. Who was the most important person you lost?"

That was easy. "Myself."

"Explain."

"Can we start with something easier?"

"We can." She settled back in her chair. "Tell me which regiment you were with."

"Fifth Army, Second Army Corps. Designated to defend the Ardennes but I got moved around a fair amount."

"You saw a lot of fighting?"

"Saw it and took part in it. Even got a medal for it."

"For something specific?"

"Yes. A mission I went on. Actually, it was my avenue out of the war."

"Do you feel like telling me about it?"

I fell silent, my mind working overtime. I could tell her, of course. I didn't have to tell her *everything*, but I could tell her most of it. I took another gulp of wine.

"It was around this time of year, 1918, and there were six of us. A special mission to bring back a spy who had some important information."

"He had information but no way to give it to you except personally?"

"He was a German. He saw the way the war was going and he wanted to switch sides. He would only tell us in person, once he was safe."

"Why did you get sent?"

I laughed gently. "Mimi. Your wealth and privilege, and your gender, have spared you from knowing the vagaries of war and the command structure."

"Meaning?"

"Meaning my life was governed by men I'd never seen, making rules I knew nothing about, and giving me orders without telling me why. From my perspective, it seemed like a good way to get out of the trenches, out of the firing line for a few days."

"And did it?"

"Out of the frying pan and into the fire." I suddenly brightened. "Come to think of it, I suppose you could say that on this mission, I solved my first case."

"Is that so?" Her eyebrows arched in surprise. "Now I'm very curious."

"We'll get there," I assured her. "But I don't want to get ahead of myself."

"Fair enough. So, these men with you. Who were they?"

I conjured their faces and was surprised how easy it was for me to picture them.

"The *mec* in charge was a Brit. Captain Hangerland. Some kind of special operations soldier, I liked him. Then there was Claude Boudin, who was there for his muscles not his charm, he was built like a brick shithouse, all angles and solidity. Even his eyes looked like black ball bearings hammered into two slits in a concrete face, and he didn't so much speak as rumble."

"You liked him, too?"

"At first I just avoided him. I wasn't much more than a small, scared kid and he seemed like the kind of monster who lived under your bed."

"Who else was on the mission?"

"There were three Americans. Two of them had been friends before the war, joined up together: Mario Guerra and . . . I can't remember his real name. Hangerland called Guerra 'Mex' and I only knew his friend as 'Tex.' One's family was from Mexico, obviously, and the other Texas."

"And the other American?"

"Mike. Mike Ashton, he was from New York City."

"You liked him?"

I'd not expected to feel any emotion, but when Mimi asked that question a wave of sadness welled up inside me.

"*Oui*," I said. "He was young, like me. Too young to be there. Of all of them, I liked him the most. He was also a corporal, smart guy, and so technically second-in-command." My heart had tripped over itself as I pictured seeing him there for the first time.

She nodded and let me have those seconds to myself. Then she asked, "You said three Frenchmen, I only know of you and the brute, Claude Boudin."

"You're good with names," I said.

"No, I'm terrible." She tapped her notepad. "I wrote it down."

"Ah, of course. The other Frenchman was . . . Jean. Grenier, I think. Yes, that sounds right." I shook my head at the memory. "He didn't make the mission."

"Why not?"

I sighed, and told her how, after we were first pulled to-gether, we'd all piled into a truck to go get kitted out and fed.

We'd barely gone fifty yards when the familiar whistle of an incoming shell made us grip the wooden slats of our seats and look around for a place to hide. But there was nowhere to go so for a moment we froze in place like statues, following the shell's growing scream as it hurtled closer and closer.

Captain Hangerland yelled something and we hit the floorboards as one. Seconds later the shell screamed over us and exploded in front of the truck, all but shattering my eardrums. The front of the vehicle had reared up like a bucking bronco, hanging in the air for a second, then slamming back into the ground at the same time the canvas canopy shredded in that deafening blast of heat and sound that rattled us like dice in a cup. Sitting there with Mimi Bonaparte, holding that glass of fine wine, I remembered those seconds when metal, mud, and rock rained down on us and, as I'd done too many times before, I opened my eyes to see a man with half his head missing and his brains leaking onto the floor in front of me.

Again we sat in silence for a moment, and I appreciated that. Eventually she spoke. "Not a great start to the mission."

"No." I grimaced. "Poor Jean Grenier. And it didn't get much better from there."

"Tell me, but first I'm curious about something."

"What?"

"The makeup of the mission. Why three Frenchmen and three Americans, all led by an Englishman?"

"They didn't tell us, but we assumed it was for two reasons. First, no side wanted to sacrifice just their men for the mission. Second, we figured they didn't trust each other, didn't want an all-Brit team to get their hands on this spy and keep him for themselves."

"Did you all speak French?"

"No, the operational language was English. I had an actual Englishman teaching me as a kid in Castet, and had an affinity for languages."

"Is that why you were chosen for the mission?"

"Not a question I can answer," I said, keeping it vague.

"No, I suppose not." She scribbled something into her note-pad. "Please, continue."

"I suppose the most remarkable thing about the operation at the time was that it required us to jump out of a plane. None of us had been near one, let alone jumped out of one—in fact, we didn't even know it was possible." I smiled at the memory, at the shock and fear that had gripped every single one of us. Only the threat of a bullet in the head from Hangerland had got us to don what he called "aviatory life buoys." Now known as parachutes, and much safer than they used to be.

"I can't imagine how that would have been," Mimi said. "How terrifying."

"Yeah. And one of us didn't make it."

"Oh, no. I'm sorry. Who?"

"The one Hangerland called Mex."

I'd jumped first. Not by choice, but by dint of Hangerland's boot. Behind me, in order, it had been Claude Boudin, then Mex, then Tex, then Mike, and finally Hangerland. One second that foot was in my back, and the next the door was open and I was flying.

Floating.

No . . . falling.

Pull the cord. Pull the fucking cord.

Except, one thing about falling is that gravity doesn't work the way that guy under the apple tree, Newton, said it would. Not everything goes downward.

I scrabbled at my shoulder where the short rope had been, and slapped at my chest as the wind blinded me and my stomach spun inside me. I felt dizzy, sick, elated, but most of all desperate. I heard a scream above me, a scream of fear, and when I tilted my head backward I saw it, a flicker of white against the black sky. *The cord.*

I reached up and grabbed at it, fingers grasping at the air as my legs scissored below me, as if I could somehow get purchase, regain balance. But there was nothing beneath me except the wind, buffeting and bullying me, and in a full, round second, I realized what I'd done. I'd jumped out of a fucking plane.

Two fingers felt the thin rope, caught it, and my fist closed around it the way I'd held the grip of my pistol the first time I'd needed it. Really needed it, in my first engagement in a German trench with one of those Kraut sons of bitches charging at me with a bayonet.

And the magic was the same, in a way.

The bullet I fired in that first battle halted time, slowed a charging man in mid-stride and then stopped him cold. Saved me.

Same there, high in the sky. When I pulled that cord my whole body jerked like that German had but this time it was me who slowed, then stopped. Even the wind stopped whistling, and I felt like I was hanging there, with the black, star-dotted sky above and the invisible earth somewhere below. The moon had withdrawn from this affair, hiding her face from us as if too terrified to watch human beings leap into nothingness. I didn't blame her.

Once I'd caught my breath, the cold closed in on me. So did a new set of fears, too, the ones I'd ignored until now: the insane height, the dark night, and the overall fright of what I was doing settled into my bones and squeezed my heart, chilly tendrils of fear snaking through my guts and up my spine.

I kicked my feet in the air beneath me just to move a little and I looked around, hoping to see one of my comrades, a friendly face or maybe just someone as scared shitless as I was. But the space around me was empty. Utterly empty. I tried telling myself this was a dream, but I knew that it couldn't be, because it was the exact opposite. In dreams, the craziest things imaginable come to life, they taunt and torment you. They tease and tantalize, but, above all, in those moments they seem real.

This did not seem real.

I felt like I was floating, but I knew I must be hurtling toward the ground. And, even if this was a gentle descent, when would I hit it? I tried to control my breathing and looked down toward my feet but I couldn't see them, let alone the earth below. It could be a field, a forest, a barbed-wire fence where I would land. From here it was all one black hole, a chilling, giant black hole sucking me in, sucking me down.

And then Mario Guerra whistled past me, a flash of his white face, eyes wide with shock and fear, his hands up like he was surrendering, and above his head a thin stream of white that was his aviatory life buoy, and my mind contorted this image into an empty bubble coming from a cartoon character's mouth.

Then he was gone.

In a flash of surprise, both his and mine, he was past me

and sucked down into that blackness, hurtling to the ground in the way I wasn't.

And so I floated.

"My god," Mimi Bonaparte said. "How awful. How absolutely terrifyingly awful."

"It was. Except the largest part of me was glad that my parachute had worked. I felt relief as much as terror, to be perfectly truthful."

"Understandably. What happened next?"

"The rest of us landed in a field behind enemy lines. Only Hangerland had our orders, the details, and we eventually found each other as dawn was breaking. We holed up in a barn for a few minutes, just to collect ourselves and figure out the way. We also picked up a replacement for Mario."

"How so?"

"It was weird. He was an American, a prisoner of war who'd escaped and was trying to find his way home. He had a dog with him. Some of the team didn't want to have anything to do with him, but Hangerland figured we'd lost one American but gained another. I think mostly he knew the poor fellow wouldn't make it to safety without our help, and it wasn't like he was an extra mouth to feed."

"The dog was."

"Everyone fell in love with that dog. We told Ben—Ben Hardy was his name—even if we cut him loose, we'd probably keep the dog." I smiled at the memory. "He was a mutt, some German shepherd with maybe some Labrador in there. He was brown and very proud, so Ben had called him Leo."

"You like dogs," she said. "I saw the photo upstairs with you and a dog. I always think it says a lot about a person, whether they like or own pets. Anyway, what happened then?"

"We made our way from the barn toward a wooded area about three miles southwest. Just following Hangerland, it was like any other march a soldier does. More nerve-racking, of course, but we fell into a rhythm and just kept going."

"I don't mean to upset the rhythm we have here," she said gently. "But you mentioned solving your first case and I'm not really seeing . . ." Her voice trailed off.

"And I told you we'd get there." I remembered my wine and drank some. "But let me ask you something first. Do you remember Gustav Pohl?"

"The anarchist? I remember reading about him, yes. What does he have to do with all this?"

I thought about how best to explain it. "Let me put it this way. As a young soldier you do a lot of waiting, and a lot of traveling. Most of it pointless. I was on a train once, a group of us, when a couple of my comrades found a *mec* with some literature on him. Anarchist literature. I saw the pamphlet myself, it talked about living without a real government, no taxes, no wars. Gustav Pohl was going to lead Europe into a new age. Point was, that didn't go over well on a train crammed with angry French patriots. The poor, idealistic sap, probably harmless and just misguided, was dragged to the rear car, shot, and thrown onto the rails."

"Murdered?"

"I suppose so, yes, though I'm sure they'd say they were executing a traitor. Anyway, I watched the whole thing and what surprised me as much as the anger directed at him was how he'd been defiant to the very end. Almost crazed with the passion that he was right and the hundreds of angry soldiers around him were deluded and so, so wrong. Even in those last seconds he was unrepentant." I shook my head at the memory. "He was devoted to his cause beyond any other, beyond even living."

"What a subject he would have made," Mimi said.

"I imagine so. But back to the story. We found our way to the wood and planned to stay there for the rest of the day and overnight, just to make sure we knew the lay of the land and were well rested. That's where it happened."

"The crime?"

"The crime and the unmasking of the criminal."

"How intriguing," Mimi said. "Please, go on."

"I would." I looked at my watch. "But I think our hour is up."

She looked over at the clock on the mantel. "So it is. But you can't leave me in suspense like this. What was the crime, and who was the criminal?"

"The crime was murder." I stood and slowly drained the last of my glass to keep Mimi in suspense. "And the criminal wasn't just a murderer. He was a traitor."

CHAPTER TWELVE

Thursday, July 18, 1940

The next morning on the way to my office I took a moment to linger on Pont Neuf. The air was still cool and the river chugged along beneath me, gray and fast, letting me wonder about the people at either end of this body of water. How was their war going? Were they hopeful or desperate, living as normal or trapped like us, in a livable but alternate world?

I leaned over, elbows on the parapet, and followed a tree limb with my eyes, watched it twist and bob in the swirling water. This was my place to think, the place where I would switch off the active part of my mind and let some of the background thoughts twist and bob themselves into place. This was a place to come to when I was starting to get stuck.

The tree limb swept under me and out of view, so I turned

my gaze on the water itself. The River Seine was like a cinema screen, gray and waiting for projections onto it, and those came when I stared down for long enough. I saw shapes in the water that shifted and disappeared, then re-formed and vanished once more.

I'd fallen in once. A police party on a boat with a few too many bottles of wine, and even though I'd been fished out within seconds the river had shocked me. She was cold, so cold, and her eddies and currents had grabbed and held me down the moment I went in, long and hungry fingers pulling me in to drown. In those few cold, wet seconds the river had seemed alive to me and once I was back on board the boat, safe but shaken, I looked down at her slow-rolling, glistening surface and called her a two-faced liar.

She tried to make it up to me after that with inspiration, and I let her in moments like this. But today wasn't one of our good days. After ten minutes of quiet staring, I straightened up feeling none the wiser, and noticed two men in civilian clothes approach. They were in their twenties, fit and well-groomed, and they were looking around like tourists. German ones, I guessed, since we didn't seem to get any other types anymore.

"Excuse me," the taller of the two said in French. *Yep, German.* "We are looking for rue de l'Odéon. We forgot our map. Is this the right way?"

His accent was good, and my initial concerns about being approached by an off-duty German soldier were assuaged by his politeness and deference.

I gave him a friendly smile. "Ah, you are looking for Shakespeare and Company, am I right?"

"*Oui, monsieur,* that is correct."

Shakespeare and Company was an icon, a bookstore that championed literary greats before they were great, and hosted them like celebrities after they became so. It was also the sort of place you could buy books that were banned elsewhere. I knew that *Lady Chatterley's Lover* was one such example, and I presumed these two gentlemen were en route to a similar shopping trip. *Good for them for expanding their horizons and providing business to a Paris store*, I thought.

"Ah, you are headed in the wrong direction," I said. "You must have memorized the other rue de l'Odéon, there are two and it's easy to mix them up." I pointed back the way they'd come. "You need to head back across the bridge toward the Louvre, and keep going along rue Pont Neuf until you hit rue Saint-Honoré. Turn left there, got it?"

"Left onto Saint-Honoré?"

"*Exactement*. And then the correct rue de l'Odéon will be the . . . one, two, third street on the right."

"Got it! *Merci*, monsieur, *merci beaucoup*!" They both gave me a small wave, as if unsure whether to shake my hand or not, and turned and walked back the way they'd come.

I almost felt bad, sending them a good mile in the wrong direction. But they were in my city and had no right to be here, to be visiting our churches, strolling through our parks, or even browsing in our bookstores. And for me, personally, pinned into this dog of a murder case by the Germans, it was a small act of resistance, a tiny cut I could inflict on the morale of the monster who had devoured so many of my countrymen and looked set, unless things perked up quickly and considerably, to devour me at the end of the week. I trudged back to my office at the Préfecture with my back a little straighter than before, but with one eye out for a couple of Boche who might realize they'd been sent in completely the wrong direction and come looking for their impostor of a tour guide.

When I got to the Préfecture the journalist Enzo Riva was waiting in the large reception area. Several *flics* were standing there smoking, their bicycles leaning against the paint-peeling wall. Riva was twisting the brim of his hat in his hands, which told me he was nice and nervous.

"Monsieur, please, I cannot tell you his name," he began, before I even opened my mouth. "Journalists cannot reveal their sources."

"I don't want your source; I want the name of the journalist asking about me. It's different."

"He said not to tell you."

"Who did?"

He gave me a look. "I'm not stupid."

"That has yet to be determined. His name, please."

"I can't."

"You're sure?"

"*Absolument.*"

"Well then." I turned to the uniformed officers. "You there."

"*Oui?*" It wasn't the most enthusiastic *oui* I'd ever received, but at least they were paying attention. And, more importantly, they were my subordinates.

"This *mec* just exposed himself to me. Put some bracelets on him and find a nice uncomfortable cell, will you?"

"Wait, what?" Riva protested. "I did no such thing. He told me to meet him here, I didn't do anything at all."

The two *flics* dropped their cigarettes and shuffled toward us.

"Name?" I asked Riva, in my politest tone.

"I . . . I can't."

"Be gentle taking him down those hard, concrete steps," I told the uniforms. "They can be slippery."

That amused the *flics* and I could see they were now looking forward to this little task. Enzo Riva, less so. His eyes were wide with fright, I could see he had no desire to wear scrapes and bruises for a week on another man's account.

"Wait, stop. I'll tell you," he said, his hands up in surrender.

"You have three seconds," I said.

"Lawrence Clayton," Riva said. "He's an American stationed in London. That's all I know, I promise."

"Stand down, gentlemen," I said, sending the beat cops back to their corner and two fresh cigarettes. I turned back to Riva, my mind working overtime. "Why is he so interested in me?"

"I don't know, he wouldn't tell me." He must have seen the disbelief in my eyes. "I mean it, and that's normal. If he thinks he has a story he wouldn't want me to scoop him." He looked at me for a second. "That name mean anything to you?"

"No."

"You don't know him?"

"Never heard of him. What kind of journalist is he?"

"American is all I know."

"What did you tell him about me?"

"What I already told you. Nothing."

"Does he know you're giving me his name?" I wagged a finger. "And don't you dare lie."

Riva looked sheepish. "I was going to tell him. I called him this morning but he wasn't there. On assignment out of the office; they wouldn't say where."

I nodded. "All right. You can go." I escalated from wagging to jabbing him with a finger. "But if I catch you tailing me again, I won't file that complaint I just made about you because you won't have anything to expose, do you understand?"

I watched him leave and stood there a moment, thinking about why an American journalist working out of England might be so interested in me. But I didn't have much time for side adventures, so I made my way upstairs to the murder division where Nicola was waiting for me, which was always a comfort. Trouble was, Sturmbannführer Ludwig Vogel was also waiting, which was not. The former looked apprehensive, the latter just plain angry.

"Where have you been?" he demanded.

"Doing my job."

"Eating and drinking in the cafés no doubt."

"Well, that *is* what they're there for." He turned a darker shade of crimson, so I backed off a bit. "I have been out interviewing witnesses, the people on the list you gave me."

"And what have you found?"

The truth was that I'd found a pretty lady, a homosexual relationship, a drawing by a famous artist hidden on the victim's body, and discovered that he, Vogel, was wrong about the murder weapon. None of which it seemed sensible to share right then and there, so I prevaricated.

"Nothing concrete yet. I'm still trying to figure out everyone's role, the relationships between people. Once I've spoken to everyone, I expect things will fall into place more quickly."

"Do you think it's someone on that list?"

Not necessarily, no. It was your fucking list, not mine. "It's possible."

He straightened up suddenly, like someone had rammed a cannon rod up his derriere. "I know who did it. And I am very disappointed that a detective of the Paris police does not."

That surprised me, and I half hoped for a confession so I could slap some handcuffs on this fool and maybe slap him around a little.

"Who do you think did it?" I asked.

"It was Maurice Babin."

"What makes you say that?"

"I received information that he and my . . . the victim were engaged in improper and immoral acts." *There goes one cat out of a very full bag.* "Additionally, Babin has a part-time job in a restaurant, which means he had access to the murder weapon, an ice pick." *That cat remained put, thankfully.* "He is also a large man, and could easily have overpowered Walter Fischer and stabbed him like that."

"I'm still not seeing a motive. Nor evidence that Babin was at the museum that afternoon."

"He was, he must have been. I am suggesting that he followed Fischer in, slipped in behind him. Simple." He puffed himself up again, and I figured a righteous speech was coming. I wasn't disappointed. "As for motive, I think it's plain. Walter Fischer was a loyal and respected member of the Waffen SS. Somehow, Maurice Babin lured him into an unseemly and improper situation, possibly by physical force."

"Wait, now you're saying that Babin raped your comrade?"

"Silence!" Vogel was beet red, and he lifted a quivering finger toward Nicola who'd been watching us like our conversation was a tennis match to the death. I noticed that the rest of the squad ringed the room, also watching us silently. "How dare you say such things in front of a lady. How dare you imply that a soldier of the conquering German Fatherland would have . . . succumbed to such depraved acts!"

"Hang on, you're the one who said—"

"There can be no question. Babin is a pervert and had means, motive, and opportunity to kill Hauptmann Walter Fischer." Vogel pointed a finger at me. "I expect this investigation to focus on him and I will expect to see your report, and all supporting evidence, on my desk by the end of the week. Friday at six o'clock, not one second later."

I fought the urge to let him know I usually knocked off around four on a Friday because, again, this didn't seem like the right time or place.

"Understood," I said, and accompanied it with a polite nod. I just hoped that I'd managed to hide the disgust that filled me to the brim.

When he'd left, I retreated to my office and everyone else did the same except Nicola, who followed me into mine. "What was that about?"

"Our friend Vogel doesn't like his comrade's choice of lover." I plopped down in my chair. "On one hand, I have an easy suspect to arrest, which would pull me out of the stew come the weekend."

"But on the other hand . . ." she began for me.

"Yes. On the other hand, I'm not sure how I feel about getting an innocent man hung by his neck, just to save mine. Maybe I should blame the dead guy, Pascal Voclain, after all."

I could. I knew I could. But the thought was of no comfort, oddly. I'd done a lot to survive over the years, a lot no man would be proud of, but since becoming a police officer I'd done things the right way. No cut corners, no evidence tampering, no easy outs. Much about this case irritated me, from the limited access to the ridiculous time line. But one thing that annoyed me the most was the fact that the Germans were forcing me, potentially anyway, to pollute the one thing that had been good and pure in my life: my job. Yes, I could blame a dead guy and walk away with my own neck unstretched, but I'd never done anything close to that before and I hated that these jackbooted bastards were making me consider it now.

•   •   •

Nicola sat on my desk, about a yard away from my feet, which were elevated to help me think, a pencil and paper on her lap. Always ready to help, that one.

"So what's your plan?" she asked.

"I don't know."

"Well, let's look at the options. You can continue to investigate everyone and maybe solve the crime, or sit back and blame Voclain. Or let Babin take the fall because maybe he *did* do it, we don't know."

"Maybe he did," I said. "But I'm not seeing a lot of evidence to support that idea."

I could see in Nicola's face she had more confidence in me than I did, that she knew I'd not just let Babin take the fall and walk away. Ironic, really, because I was taking a risk that maybe didn't need taking and I wasn't big on that kind of thing. I'd seen too much in life to think very highly of noble self-sacrifice, mostly because it always involved a darn sight more sacrifice than nobility. But we both knew she was dangling the options in front of me to poke me into doing the right thing. I was about to let her know that one thing I *had* figured out was that the murder weapon wasn't an ice pick but a chisel, but she was already on to the next helpful step.

"Let's go through the people on the list," she said. "Tell me what we know so far, because talking it out always helps."

"Talking it out always helps *you*," I corrected gently, and with an added smile so that I didn't get the Walter Fischer treatment with that pencil.

"Keep joking, *mon ami*, see what happens."

"Right, fine. Let's start with Maurice Babin. Housemate and lover of the victim. Also in the art business, so had access to the museum or may have just followed his lover in and killed him, like Fritz said."

"Motive?"

"Hey, in a relationship there's always a motive to be found. Jealousy, anger, revenge, money. But none that apply, as far as I know now. But he has no alibi, I'll add that to the mix."

Nicola had scribbled the names on her paper, from memory. "Next is Abraham Simon."

"The frame-maker. Old fellow but with large and presumably strong hands. No known motive, didn't know the victim hardly at all, although also in the art business. And access to the museum."

"Alibi?"

"Depends on the exact time of death, which we don't know. He was at our friend Pablo Picasso's place for lunch and stayed in the afternoon to work, talk about framing some paintings. He wasn't sure what time he left because they were drinking wine as much as working."

Nicola gave me a small smile. "Ooh, a reason to go back and talk to Monsieur Picasso again. I can do that for you."

"You can come *with* me," I said disapprovingly. "Let's finish the list and then we can go on the way home. Again."

"Florence Petit."

"Ah, a pretty thing. Smart, too, if I'm not mistaken. Says she didn't know Fischer well because he kept to himself and was all about the work."

"Of stealing art to send to Germany."

"When you put it like that, everyone on the list has that for a motive."

"Isn't that exactly what he was doing, though?" she pressed.

"It's not being pitched that way. 'Repatriation' is the word they're using."

"Well, I'd imagine Petit and the others are pretty unhappy about Germans looting the Louvre, no matter what they call it."

I thought about that for a moment. "I have to think Fischer was on the up-and-up, though, because I honestly didn't get a lot of outrage from them."

"From who?"

"From any of them."

"Except he'd stolen that Picasso drawing."

"Small potatoes, given all of the art they handle each and every day."

She shrugged. "Maybe they know something we don't. Or maybe all the German art he was sending back was terrible. Anyway, more about Petit, please."

"Very pretty, did I mention that?"

Nicola rolled her eyes. "Definitely innocent then, in your mind."

"Of course!" I grinned, but then did my best to get back to being serious. "I really don't think she'd have the strength to kill him. Or even the reach. And she has no more motive than anyone else there, if it's art related."

"Isn't she the one closest to him, in terms of working with him and seeing what he's repatriating?"

"Yes, I think that's true."

"Then maybe she saw him put in something non-German, or even put something aside for himself, confronted him about it."

"Right," I agreed. "I mean, like you said, he took that Picasso drawing, and there's no reason to think that was either the first or last time he purloined something for himself. Imagine it, Fischer gets defensive, she's angry, he attacks her to stop her telling anyone and she defends herself."

"Why wouldn't she just say, if that's what happened?"

"No." I gave her a look. "Because he's a Nazi, and those people have no mercy. If one of them is killed, they will hang someone from the highest tree. You've seen the stories, you know they don't care about women and children any more than they do their male enemies."

"Nice of them not to discriminate."

"Look, I'll tell you this much. If I killed an SS officer in self-defense or even by accident, no way I'd admit it. No way. And remember, she was there. She found the body."

"But if that was her thinking," Nicola insisted, "if she wanted to distance herself from it, she could've just turned around and walked away. Let someone else find the body and not even be involved."

"What if someone saw her leave? If she's seen leaving without reporting it, she's an easy suspect."

"True." Nicola gave me that disapproving look. "Apart from being too pretty to do it, of course."

"Much too pretty."

"She also missed a meeting with you, about the big guy. Isn't that a little suspicious?"

"Not really. Just protecting him, most likely." And if he was as damaged by war as I suspected, I couldn't blame her. "Let's move on, because we're just playing guessing games right now. Who's next?"

"Pascal Voclain," she said. "If it comes to it, maybe you can find a few reasons it was him and leave it at that."

"If I can't catch the real killer, you mean."

"Without meaning to pay you a compliment, I would suggest that if you don't nab one of the others for this, it probably *was* him."

I was grateful for the moral support and her belief in me, but I'd never labeled someone a killer purely by the process of elimination. In my book, doing so in this case would be excusable in one sense, but I wasn't sure I would see myself the same way after. And if I was going to live through this I was going to have to live with myself afterward.

CHAPTER THIRTEEN

As soon as I stepped out of the Préfecture, a small man in a worn and dark blue corduroy jacket strode up to me. At first, I thought he was going to ask for some spare change, but a split second later I knew exactly who he was, mostly from the notepad and pencil he pulled from his pocket. But he also had a look to him I'd seen before, and it was the kind of look a vulture gives a dying sheep as it circles slowly overhead, eyes narrowed and hungry, greedy even.

"Henri Lefort?" To my surprise, that look had suddenly changed and he was staring at me like I was a work of art, his eyes running all over my face.

"*Oui, je suis* Henri Lefort." My guard was up immediately, and he could tell.

"You speak English?" he said, in English. I'd noticed English people doing this and it never failed to annoy me. It was an assumption on their part more than a question, that was what got me. Imagine me going to China, approaching a complete stranger, and asking if (in other words *assuming*) he spoke French.

"*Non*," I lied, in French.

He puffed out his cheeks. "*Alors, je peux essayer,*" he said. *Then I can try.* He started slowly, introducing himself, and his French was actually quite good. "*Je suis* Lawrence Clayton, I am a journalist."

On fucking assignment indeed. "Congratulations. No comment."

"But you don't even know—" He moved to block my way. "Please, I just want to talk to you about saving the life of Marie Bonaparte, but also about the last war."

"Someone already wrote the Bonaparte story and I'm too busy."

"Please, it's important." He shook his head as if in wonder and all but whispered, "You look so like him."

"Important enough to have someone follow me, I gather. Not interested." I started to walk away but stopped. "Wait, Enzo Riva said you were in London yesterday. How did you get here so quickly? And why? And who do I look like?"

"More slowly, please."

I repeated my questions, enunciating as best I could.

"Ah, I got here with difficulty," he said. "And because Enzo said you were not cooperative, I thought it best I come myself. Give me a few minutes to explain. Please."

"You have two."

"I saw the story the Germans put out, the propaganda. It

had your picture and . . . it was amazing. Incredible even. I was in London and I spent all night on the phone with people in the States, getting them to dig up records and photographs and files."

"Did any of those records and files tell you I'm in the middle of a murder investigation?"

"You said two minutes."

"And you're wasting them."

"I saw your photograph. I fought in the war, too, and I couldn't be sure but you looked very much like someone I knew there. I mean, older, obviously, he was just a kid but I still couldn't believe my eyes, I thought you *must* be him."

"They say everyone has a double somewhere," I said with a shrug.

"Yeah, they do. But I had to be sure because I never knew what happened to this guy. So, like I said, I got people at the New York office to do all my digging, and I think I have some surprising news for you."

"Thirty seconds."

"This guy I knew. He was your brother."

I raised an eyebrow as high as I could, and followed that up with a patronizing smile. "My brother."

"Yes. Interested now?"

"Not particularly."

"Why not?"

"Because I don't have a brother. Especially an American brother. Because, as you know, I'm French."

"Yes, I know you are. But let me tell you what I found."

"Your two minutes is up."

"Please, wait." He was almost begging me now. "I have

people working on it still, to find out more. But yes, I'm convinced you have, or had, a brother."

"You're insane." I threw up my hands. "And even if you weren't, which you are, why do you care if I had a brother?"

"Because of what I found out about him." His eyes were wide, imploring me to ask what he'd found. When I didn't, he told me anyway. "You're the hero, former military now a respected detective, and you saved the life of Princess Marie Bonaparte."

"I mean, not really. All I did was—"

"Look, in the eyes of the public you most certainly are, and that's what matters. Henri Lefort, hero of the Republic of France." He looked me in the eye for maximum effect, and spoke slowly but clearly. "Contrast that with your brother who, if I'm right, was a cold-blooded murderer."

•   •   •

Finding a place to eat or drink coffee in Paris had become a game of checkers. The Sixth Arrondissement, where I lived and lurked, had many cafés, bistros, brasseries, and restaurants close to each other, a plethora of eating and watering holes. But if there was a group of German soldiers in the one you stopped at, you'd hop past it to the next and hope it wasn't being patronized by more of the cabbage-crunchers. It wasn't that they did anything particularly offensive, it's just that they were there. Laughing, joking, telling tall tales of their war exploits.

Like conquering us.

I'd walked away from Clayton without saying a word. He struck me as one of those journalists who'd write a story first and check out the facts later. Maybe. And I didn't want to give him a single word he could twist and use against me. So I just walked away, left him standing there with a pencil in one hand, a notepad in the other, and his pleas for me to stay and talk falling to the cobbled ground around him.

I was also late for my rendezvous with Nicola, and she gave me her *Well, that's typical* look when we finally met up. I didn't bother her with Clayton's tall tale, though. I wanted us both fully focused on the job ahead of us. Namely, saving my neck. We'd arranged to meet at a favorite café, our sights set on a little lubrication before stopping by the artist Pablo Picasso's home. But six or seven uniformed men were destroying plates of food, their table littered with empty wine and beer bottles.

"Straight to work?" Nicola asked, turning her back on the place.

"I suppose so."

We walked in silence through quiet streets to Picasso's home, where he met us at the doorway with the same expression of distaste Nicola had worn five minutes earlier at the café, suggesting he was less than thrilled to see us again. Me, anyway; his eyes sparkled a little when he caught sight of Nicola behind me but even so, he didn't invite us in. A whiff of perfume escaped through the door, a light mix of lavender and some other flower I couldn't name, and Nicola and I exchanged knowing looks.

"I am busy," he said. "Come back tomorrow."

"Just one question for now, monsieur. Was Abraham Simon at your house on Sunday?"

"Yes. He was here for lunch."

"Just lunch?"

He was quiet for a moment. "It was a long lunch that began late. And he did stay and look at some paintings afterward. He took some measurements to make frames."

"What time did he leave?"

"I don't recall. Is he a suspect or something?"

"If you could just try to remember the time that he left."

He pursed his lips. "Maybe six."

"That's a very long lunch."

"As I said, it began late. And we drank wine while we worked, which makes the exact time hard to remember."

"But you think around six."

"Yes. I think. Now, if you'll excuse me."

And with that, he was gone and we were left facing a closed door. We wandered away, apparently thinking the same thing because soon Nicola said, "He's covering for him."

"It certainly sounded like it."

"I mean, it's possible they were drinking and lost track of time, but there's a big difference between lunch and six, especially when you're overly defensive about it." She glanced over at me. "And obviously you smelled the perfume, too."

"I did. Recognize it?"

"No." Her eyes twinkled with mischief. "Did you?"

"Very funny. Hey, look where we are. Buy you a drink?"

Café Hugo sat at the end of rue des Grands-Augustins where it met the quai of the same name. Fortunately it was being patronized by locals, or maybe quiet Germans in unusually ragged civvies, so we took a table in the shade of the awning. A young waitress who looked Italian or Spanish came out to take our order. We decided to split a bottle of Bordeaux.

"I've been meaning to ask," Nicola began when the waitress had gone back inside. "Why would the Germans hand you a list with names of suspects?"

"You notice it didn't have any German names on it?"

"Ah, yes. To make sure you pin it on a Frenchman. Guilty or not."

"Right. I myself have been wondering how they managed to come up with that list so fast."

"German efficiency," Nicola said. She frowned but sat silently while the waitress brought out the wine and two glasses.

"*Merci*. You can leave it," I said. "I'll open it myself."

She gave me a lingering smile and drifted back into the restaurant, slowly enough so I'd notice the look she threw me over her shoulder.

"Maybe my luck has changed," I said, reaching for the corkscrew she'd left behind.

"She's too young for you. Barely even twenty."

"Nonsense. Twenty-five at least." I started work on the cork. "Anyway, you looked like you had something bothering you."

"Yes, actually. What you said about the promptness of that list reminded me. Have you noticed how the Germans seem to know everything?"

"Like what?"

"They just . . . know where everything is. I don't mean the individual soldiers, I mean the entity. Like, they wasted no time figuring out where to set up their various headquarters. The high-ranking officers seemed to know which houses to move into, and who to move out."

"You mean, they knew where the rich Jews all live."

"Right. It's like they spent no time figuring out where anything was because they already knew."

I popped the cork and poured us each a glass. "Maybe they had spies here. I don't know."

"It's been bothering me, is all." She sighed and took a sip, then smiled at me. "Maybe she's not too young after all. Maybe we just need to have as much fun as we can, while we can."

"Fun. I've almost forgotten what that is."

"And they've only been here three weeks." She sighed. "You want to eat here? I can cook if not."

I looked at my pocket watch. "We can stay here. We have enough time to eat and drink the place dry before the damn curfew."

Her face darkened. "Prisoners in our own city. In our own homes."

"Careful," I joked, "the walls have ears."

"I wish they did, I'd put an ice pick through one of them."

"Oh, that reminds me. It wasn't actually an ice pick that was used."

Her wineglass halted midway to her mouth. "No? What was it?"

"A chisel. Frame-makers have sets of them, all different sizes."

"A frame-maker, you say." She looked past my shoulder to the street. "You mean like the one strolling toward us right now."

• • •

Abraham Simon nodded a *bonsoir*, and those ice-blue eyes held mine for a split second, but he didn't slow down as he passed us on his way to the open doors of the café.

When he'd disappeared inside, I said: "Interesting."

"What is?" Nicola asked, sounding not very interested.

"One might think he'd stop and ask for an update on the case."

"Perhaps he's late for a meeting," she suggested. "I think I shall go use the powder room, if you'll excuse me." A good idea, since the powder room was inside and downstairs, letting her see who Simon was meeting with, if anyone.

"I'll order another bottle while you're gone. Same again?"

"Yes. And get some ham to go with that bread. While it still lasts. I hear rationing is weeks away."

"Which means it's probably days away."

"Then you'd better top up on snails, too. God forbid you have to go out and catch your own in the countryside."

Nicola passed the waitress on her way inside, and when our pretty server got to the table I asked her name.

"Véra Clouzot," she said. "And you?"

I stood to introduce myself and she blushed, then her eyes slid toward the café entrance Nicola had just used. "It's all right," I reassured her. "We're not together in that way."

"Oh, good. Some men, they don't mind making a pass as soon as their wife or girlfriend is out of sight."

"How exhausting. For them and you."

She laughed. "I know, what are they thinking?"

"They aren't." Something clicked in my memory. "Say, isn't this the café that several people got sick in, from the food." That came out more bluntly than it was supposed to. "Sorry, I just meant—"

"Please, don't worry." She leaned in and lowered her voice. "Several *Germans* got sick here from the food."

"Ahhh, I'm with you." I gave her an approving wink. "In that case, I will have another bottle of wine, a plate of ham, and as many snails as you can catch and plate in the next ten minutes."

She covered her mouth as she laughed again. "Of course, monsieur, I will run as fast as I can and catch them myself."

"You are so beautiful, you could just call and they'd come running to you." My turn to blush, I hadn't done this in a while.

"You are very kind, monsieur."

"Oh, no need to be so formal. Just Henri is fine."

"Henri then. *Enchanté*," Véra said, and then she turned her body to go but her eyes lingered on mine for an extra second or two. When she walked back into the restaurant there was an extra swing to her hips, if I wasn't mistaken.

A few minutes later, Nicola reappeared.

"That was odd," she said. "He disappeared."

"What do you mean, *disappeared*?"

"There are two rooms downstairs. I looked in both and he's not there."

"Maybe the restroom?"

"Yeah, well, I'm not looking in the men's restroom. I'm not that curious."

I stood. "Well, I am." I made my way into the restaurant and to the iron staircase that wound its way to the lower floor, where the bathrooms were. The doors to the men's and women's stood open, both obviously empty. I looked around but the few tables down here were empty, the frame-maker nowhere in sight. I made my way back upstairs and outside.

"Any luck?" Nicola asked.

"No, maybe he's in the kitchen?"

"Oh, because he's a chef now, too?"

"No, but I don't like my suspects disappearing on me or otherwise behaving oddly." Simon's disappearing act worried me, and I was grateful for the distraction of Véra carrying full plates. "Ah, the food."

We sat back as she unloaded the wine and nourishments onto our small table, and from the speed and the fact that she made it all fit I could see she'd either been doing this awhile or was spatially gifted. She left us with that pretty smile and my eyes lingered on her form as Nicola started talking.

"Have you seen those yellow stars they're putting on businesses now?" she asked.

"Not yet, but I will. Just like they've done everywhere else they've conquered. And you mean Jewish businesses."

"What do they have against the Jews anyway?"

I poured the wine and looked around. A table of four men in nice new suits had taken a table three away from us. "I have no idea. But keep your voice down."

"Right, of course. I'll keep my voice down, my head down, and anything else those bastards want."

I winked. "Not everything, I hope."

"Oh, hush." She raised her glass, but lowered her voice like I'd asked. "*Santé*. To Paris, as it once was and will be again."

"I'll drink to that."

We sat there as the light grew dim around us and I was once again aware of the noise. Or, specifically, the lack of it. There should have been cars and motor coaches trundling past on the quai but there were practically none. A lot more bicycles, I noted, but the eerie silence that the city had fallen into under German occupation continued to unnerve me. That they would requisition cars and limit fuel wasn't strange, of course, but this unnatural quiet was the result of them doing so. On nights like this, on that very night, I missed the swirl of traffic and people, the swell and eddy of men, women, and machines that I liked to sit and watch at the end of the day, with a glass of wine in my hand and a plate of food before me. But now the women were afraid to venture out, their men were still heading home from a war too easily lost, and the machines that once prowled the city's streets were either bringing them home or on their way out of Paris, headed south. All these things had sucked the vitality out of Paris herself, left behind like an abandoned woman—still beautiful, but sullen without that which fleshed out her spirit: her people.

An almost silent Paris was something I'd never seen before, and I didn't much care for it.

"It'll be dark soon," Nicola said, pouring the last of the bottle into her glass.

"Hey, I'm paying, so I get the last drop."

"Too late."

Véra appeared with the bill without asking. "I don't want my customers getting in trouble over the curfew. That's when we see them. They always come around sundown, patrols looking for trouble. And I've heard people aren't just getting arrested, they are getting shot."

"On the spot?"

"On sight, yes."

Sundown had been a dangerous time twenty-something years ago, when tiredness and sleep crept over us in our trenches and made us vulnerable to stray bullets, to random assaults, and a desire to end it all there and then. A lot of men died around sundown when they might otherwise have lived. And here it was, happening again.

"Well, thank you for looking out for us, and your other

customers." I left cash on the dish and we stood. "And you stay out of trouble, too."

She raised one very sexy eyebrow. "Some trouble's worth getting into. Hope to see you again soon, Monsieur Henri."

My eyes were on stalks as Nicola dragged me away from there, but as we passed by the side of the café I saw Véra again. She stood in front of a small window facing us, her hands on the heavy curtains about to pull them shut. She paused though, and despite my attraction to her I could hardly fail to notice that our friend Abraham Simon sat at a table right behind her, one that bore what looked like a sumptuous and leisurely dinner, lit by candles. My eyes drifted back to Véra and that little smile playing on her lips, but not before I'd seen who else was seated at the table with Simon. As she drew the curtains together, Nicola let out a little gasp and I knew she, too, had seen them, had taken in the view of that dimly lit room and a meal being shared by Florence Petit, Nicolas Allard, and the short and sturdy figure of Pablo Picasso.

CHAPTER FOURTEEN

Nicola and I walked quickly and in silence, heading south away from the river where we'd be more likely to attract attention, and both of us wanting to mull over what we'd seen before suggesting explanations for it. The first hurdle for me was that there was no reason that group of people *shouldn't* be having dinner together. They were all in the art business, one way or another. I would certainly expect them to know *of* each other, if not actually be friends.

Except for two things.

"Did you see another entrance to the café?" I asked Nicola.

"No. I'm pretty sure there isn't one."

"Apart from the delivery entrance in back, you mean."

"Right. For the kitchen." Nicola was obviously thinking

along the same lines as I was. "And why are they being so cavalier about curfew?"

"Maybe Picasso thinks he can ignore it because he's famous."

"Maybe," she said. "But the others aren't, and I don't think the Boche give enough of a damn about his fame to extend it to a frame-maker and a dullard. Maybe the pretty girl, but not them."

"The windows are blacked out with curtains, maybe they think they're safe." I thought that through a little more. "But even if they are safe inside, they still have to walk home."

"Maybe they'll go to Picasso's," she said. "That's close enough."

"Yes." I looked over at her, a thought taking shape in my mind. "It is quite close, isn't it?"

We turned into the narrow rue Christine and about ten yards into it, I saw a movement to my left, a shifting shadow in a doorway that made me turn and reach for my gun. I whipped it up and pointed it at the figure, ready for the attack and just as ready to kill him. I'd seen the reports firsthand—since the lights had been turned off in Paris there had been a surge in muggings around the time of the curfew. Not only was it easy for thieves to sneak up on their victims, if someone was out past nine o'clock they couldn't very well report being attacked.

"Please, don't shoot," a voice said. "I am not a criminal."

His voice was husky, low, and French was not his first language.

"Step out," I said, as Nicola moved behind me. "Slowly and with your hands up."

He did, and Nicola and I instinctively took a step back. He looked like a giant, well over six feet tall and built like a one-man tank destroyer. His dark skin and dark clothes explained why we'd not seen him at first.

"Please, don't shoot," he said again, and I recognized his accent.

"Who are you?" I asked.

"My name is Grégoire Burton."

I smiled and switched to English. "You mean your name is Greg Burton."

His eyes widened. "You speak English. You're—"

"I do," I said. "And I was. Who are you and why are you out here?"

His eyes shifted to my gun. "Promise not to shoot me?"

"Not yet," I said mildly. "Speak."

He glanced left and right, as if legging it might be his best option, but the street was narrow and we were too close for it to be the right decision.

"Greg Burton, that used to be my name. I came to Paris after the war."

"The war has just started," I pointed out.

"No, the last one. I came here in 1918."

"From America?"

He smiled. "Kind of. I was with the 369th Infantry."

"And you stayed after the war."

"A simple choice for me."

Nicola cocked her head. "Wait, why an easy choice?"

Burton took a deep breath. "Stateside we were trained as soldiers. How to march, salute, fight. Then they shipped us over here and turned us into laborers. We volunteered to fight for a country that treated us like slaves, and our reward was to be treated like slaves in a foreign country."

"And it is better here?" she asked.

"In April 1918 my unit was assigned to the French army, mostly because white American soldiers wouldn't fight alongside us Negroes. We wore US uniforms but the French gave us weapons, helmets, and everything else. They also gave us respect. We were treated by the soldiers and the commanders like any other unit." His voice softened. "That broke my heart."

"But it's why you stayed, why it was an easy decision," Nicola finished.

"Right. Very easy."

"That's all well and good," I interrupted. "But what are you doing out here on the cusp of curfew? You know how the Germans are, they hate people with dark skin even more than they hate the Jews."

"My girlfriend is Jewish," Burton said. "We lived in a small apartment in the Fourth. She got me a job in a restaurant, I helped the chef. He was Jewish, too."

I heard something in his voice. "Was?"

"He was taken away a week ago, and I tried to fill in, keep things working while keeping my head down. And then this evening, I came home to find my street blocked off." His voice thickened. "There were soldiers coming out of our building with people. One of them was my girlfriend."

A moment of silence hung between us, but eventually I managed to speak. "That's starting to happen too much. I'm sorry."

"Wait a minute." He raised his head, looking at us with suspicion. "Why are you out here? And you have a gun. . . ."

"I am a policeman, but please don't worry. I'm not one of

those policemen. I don't care who's Jewish or what color your skin is." It struck me that until all this racial purity nonsense, most Parisians hadn't cared much about these things. I supposed I knew people who were Jewish, but it never seemed like much of a factor in my life, knowing that. Same with Black people, who had a harder time prewar, but I'd not cared one way or the other. Now, it seemed, everyone in Paris, in France, was being made to pick a side.

"Look, you're not safe out here, come with us." He hesitated, so I asked, "Do you have any other options, people you know and trust?"

"Maybe. Maybe not."

I knew what that meant. "You don't want to impose on them, get them in trouble."

It was a dilemma I'd heard about before but with Jewish families, mostly. They knew they had to hide but they couldn't do it alone, they needed help. Trouble was, I knew of several French citizens who'd been arrested for hiding people that the Germans were looking for, so it was a huge risk and not something to ask of a casual friend. But this man and I had something in common, something he didn't know about, and that meant I couldn't leave him out here at the mercy of . . . god knew who, or what.

"I'm not your pet mouse. I mean, would *you* want to adopt me?" He smiled and shook his head. "I'm not exactly easy to hide."

• • •

Nicola went into the apartment first to distract the concierge. He was a good man and I knew he could keep a secret, but hiding someone from the Nazis was one secret no one should have to keep for someone else. Especially when the Germans would happily torture it right out of him should they be so inclined.

Burton and I waited in the street for a full minute and then I led him into the foyer and we headed for the stairs. I was used to climbing them, of course, but not this fast and we were both panting when we reached the top. I fumbled with my key and we moved quickly inside.

Burton looked around. "Nice apartment. You one of those crooked cops who take bribes?"

I laughed. "If I was, I'd have handed you over straightaway."

"True enough."

He waited in the dark until I'd lit two gas lamps, which were more reliable than the electricity lately, then he went to the window and looked out over rue Jacob, but peering through the heavy curtains from one side like he was used to being careful about being seen.

"You eat anything today?" I asked in English.

"At the restaurant right before I went home. Tried to go home."

His head dropped because, now safe, he was starting to feel the full import of what had happened.

"Do you know where they took her?" I asked.

"I assume Drancy, where they take all of them."

Drancy was a detention and distribution camp that the Germans had set up in the northeastern suburbs of Paris. From there people were shipped out to camps, or to Germany to work. The bus was a one-way, and probably permanent, trip out of Paris, and we both knew it.

"What will you do?" I asked.

"I don't know."

"Could you go back to America?"

He snorted. "Yeah, maybe I should go sign up again. They'll get into this war eventually, they'll have to, and we can do it all over again. I'll volunteer and they'll treat me like I'm nothing. But at least maybe we'll win again and I could come back." I gestured for him to sit, just as Nicola rejoined us. "We should speak in French so your wife can understand."

This wasn't the time to be explaining *that* situation so I just said, "French, sure."

"Isn't it something?" He shook his big head. "I come here, live here, to get away from the racial discrimination of my homeland. Then they invade and it's worse than before. At least the people over there don't execute you for being Black." He sighed. "Well, I suppose sometimes they do. Just not quite so systematically."

"Well, whether you go back to America or stay put in Paris, that's a decision for another day."

"You're sure you don't mind me staying?"

"Do you chew gum?" Nicola asked, a small smile on her lips.

"Or have a penchant for carrots or celery?" I added.

"No, I don't much like chewing gum." Burton spoke slowly, clearly confounded by her questions. "I like carrots, but cooked ones. Not celery in any form. Why?"

Nicola jerked a thumb toward me. "Rules of the house. But you seem to abide by them already, so as long as you don't slurp your soup, you can stay," she said. "Since Henri is a policeman, they won't search here, and if they do, we'll get a warning from one of your colleagues, right?"

"That's the idea. But she's right, you're safer here than any-where else. Just until you figure out what you want to do."

He raised his head and looked back and forth between us. "Thank you. Thank you for your kindness."

"You'll have to sleep on the floor in my room," I said, "but we have plenty of blankets, it won't be too bad."

"I expect it'll be warmer and more comfortable than that doorway."

"Safer, too."

We fell silent as the sound of marching boots drifted up from the street and I went quickly to the window and looked down. Patrols were rare this side of the river, the Latin Quarter was one of the safer places to be, for now, so the sound of such determined boots spiked my blood pressure, and Burton's too from the look on his face.

"What are they doing?" he asked.

"It can't be for you, for us. The concierge didn't see us come in, and I'm sure no one else followed us."

A moment's pause. "Are you?" he asked.

He was right. In the darkness that was now Paris at night it was impossible to be completely sure. I just grunted in reply, which was no doubt very reassuring.

We stayed like that until the twelve-man unit passed under my window and turned the corner into rue Bonaparte. Only then did we relax. Nicola got up from her armchair and went to the kitchen, from where she called out.

"I need a drink. You boys?"

"Good idea. Red wine for you, Monsieur Burton?"

A grin spread over his face. "Perfect, thank you."

Nicola popped the cork and I fetched three glasses. She poured generous servings, and the gentle *glug-glug* of the wine flowing from bottle to glass was itself a comfort, a promise of relief to come but also a reminder that some of the small things in life were still available to us.

I took a sip of mine and then remembered. "*Merde*, I have to go see Mimi."

"I'll keep a plate warm for you," Nicola said.

"Go see who?" Burton asked.

"An hour of therapy."

"Therapy?" he said. "I don't understand."

"Psychoanalysis, they call it," I said with a cheery smile. "Basically, I'm trying to figure out if it's this war that's crazy, or me."

CHAPTER FIFTEEN

"You're late, and is that wine on your breath?" Mimi Bonaparte said as I collapsed into my leather armchair across from her. She stood with her arms crossed looking down at me with disapproval. For a moment the only sound was the heavy *tick-tock* of the clock on the mantel.

"Not as much as there should be." To my left, on a side table, another glass of Pétrus sat waiting for me. I checked to make sure there were no flies taking a bath in it, and helped myself to a slow, sweet sip.

"Well, in any case we should get started." She was annoyed with me for being so late, but I'd told her I had a job to do that week, so figured that was her problem. She sat down opposite me. "Or should I say, continue. I believe you were about to solve a murder and identify a traitor."

"Ah, yes." I settled back in my chair and stared into the ruby-red wine, letting my mind wander back two decades, to that small wood that had held our campsite. I half closed my eyes. "I don't recall exactly what I told you, but here are the important points. First, we buried Mario Guerra where we found him. Wrapped him in that treacherous parachute and buried him in some foreign field. I can still see the clean gash in the silk that had made him fall thousands of feet."

"Just so awful," Mimi said, quietly.

"Tex said a prayer over him." I tried to recall the incantation. "Ah, yes. 'For thine is the kingdom, the power and the glory, now and forever. Amen.' And then Tex crossed himself like the good little Catholic he said he was, and we walked away. Well, limped away, he'd hurt his ankle landing, but you get the idea."

"Yes, and you went to the woods."

"We gathered in a burnt-out barn, first. Ate a little something, talked. Worried about Tex as he seemed to have cracked a little. Right up until the minute we moved out of that barn he just sat there, digging in the dirt floor with a stick like a child." I shook my head at the memory. "And then someone shot Claude Boudin in the head."

Mimi sat bolt upright. "What?"

"I didn't mention that before?"

"You most certainly did not."

"Ah, my mistake. It happened soon after we left the barn, we'd made it about a quarter mile, Hangerland in the lead and Tex limping along in the rear. Out of nowhere, a shot rang out and Boudin dropped dead in the dirt."

"My goodness, the poor man. Who shot him?"

"We never saw him. We just took off running, didn't stop

until we hit the trees. Even Tex with his injured ankle kept up with us, ran like the wind."

"You just left Boudin there?"

"We certainly did." I smiled grimly. "War can be like that. Unceremonious."

"Yes, of course, I'm sorry. I wasn't judging your decision. Of course, you had to protect yourselves."

"Yes. We did."

•   •   •

We set up camp twenty yards inside the tree line, staying close enough to the edge of the woods to have a good view of the fields to our south. Smart-ass that I was, I questioned Captain Hangerland about that decision.

"Shouldn't we camp on the north side, so we can scout where we're going?"

He was kind, or tired, enough not to bite my head off. "No, Corporal. Someone out there shot Boudin and that means there might be him or more than one person out there looking for us. If they come, they'll come the way we did. From the south."

He was right, and I decided there and then not to second-guess his orders anymore. We settled down on the leafy ground, our backs against the base of oak and elm trees, and each of us dug through our packs for a bite to eat. It felt almost cozy in there, and I was more than happy to be off my feet in the shade, waiting for the sun to set, for nighttime to wrap that dark cloak of security around us for a few hours.

As if he could read my mind, Hangerland said, "I know it's still light but get as much sleep as you can, chaps. We'll move out after dark, and tonight and tomorrow are going to be more dangerous and more exhausting than today."

I almost laughed. The day had begun with all of us jumping out of an airplane and ended with two of our party dead. I didn't say anything, having decided to give Hangerland and the others some respite from my wit, so I just watched as he took out a portion of his parachute that he'd stuffed into his pack.

"What's that for, Captain?" Ben Hardy asked. His voice was quiet, as his dog Leo was snoring gently by his side.

"Little trick I learned from my colonel." He tried to rip the cloth but it held fast, so he took his knife and made a cut, slicing a square off. "When you're sleeping outside, lay a piece of cloth under your head. It'll keep the bugs off, and your mind will translate it into a pillow. Well, sort of. Better than twigs and leaves getting in your ears, that's for sure. Here, help yourself."

I watched as Hardy struggled with trying to tear his own pillow and he, too, resorted to using Hangerland's knife, patiently cutting a tidy square for himself before offering the material to Tex. He cut a piece and held the cloth out to me.

I shook my head. "No, thanks, I'll be fine without. I'll use my pack." I lay back, and eventually drifted off to sleep.

At ten that night Hangerland roused me.

"Your turn for watch duty," he said, his voice a whisper so as not to wake the others. "We'll bug out in another couple of hours."

I pulled myself into a seated position, leaning against a tree until I got my bearings. I looked around and saw the huddled bodies of my colleagues. Someone was snoring gently, Tex maybe, and when I looked up the sky was clear and lit with stars. I stared for a moment, looking at the heavens and listening to the American Mike Ashton shifting in his leafy berth at the foot of a tree. Once he was quiet, I stood and picked up my rifle.

We were supposed to walk back and forth across the south end of the woods, staying two or three trees deep within it so that we'd see intruders before they saw us. For once I did as I'd been told, but every time I passed through the middle section, near where we were camped, I looked over toward my sleeping colleagues and wondered about them. Wondered about all of them.

After my third pass, my bladder let me know it needed to be emptied so I propped my rifle against a tree, stepped up to another one, and unbuttoned my pants. I tried not to let out a loud moan of relief, and aimed for the broad base of the tree so my stream would be quiet.

"You're not very good at this, are you?" said a voice behind me, and the stream dried up in an instant. As did my throat.

I turned my head and saw that my rifle had disappeared. Mike Ashton stood over my right shoulder, my rifle and his swinging loosely in his hands.

"What the fuck?" My heart was thumping like a jackhammer.

"You're supposed to be on watch." He smiled and his eyes sparkled. "Yet here you are, with your dick literally in your hand."

"You've never taken a piss?" I laughed. "I'm impressed."

He shrugged. "Sure, but when I'm on guard duty I face the way I'm supposed to face. As long as I spot them before they spot me, it doesn't matter if my dick is out, does it?"

He had me there.

"Why aren't you sleeping?" I asked.

"I did. For about five minutes. Then I decided to check to see if you were doing your job." His tone was mild, not accusatory. "I'm used to doing these missions with people I know and trust."

We talked for a long time, almost two hours, the length of my shift, whispering in the dark while facing south, talking about the mission, about other things, and hoping Boudin's death wasn't a harbinger of our own.

•   •   •

"Two hours?" Mimi said. "Shouldn't he have been sleeping?"

"We had a lot to talk about." I drank some wine and smacked my lips. "And please, stop interrupting, I need to tell this story my way."

She held up an apologetic hand. "I'm sorry. Do go on."

•   •   •

Eventually, Ashton stood. "I want to check out where we're going, the far side of the wood. It's only about a hundred yards."

"You don't need more sleep?"

"I'll sleep later. If I get three hours, maybe four a night, then I'm fine. And anyway, I have a strange feeling about this mission. A feeling I don't like."

We have that in common, I thought, but I just nodded and we stood in silence.

He seemed different at that very moment, not the quiet, easygoing American I'd chatted with before. Maybe it was just because he had a bad feeling, but it also occurred to me that maybe he'd done this sort of thing before. Which meant that he knew how dangerous things would be getting, where as I, a mere trench grunt, had no clue what we were in for the next day.

At the end of my two hours on watch a figure approached

from where my comrades were sleeping. As he got close, I could see it was Captain Hangerland.

"Captain, everything all right?" I whispered when he reached me.

"Not sure. You seen Ashton?"

"Yes, sir. He couldn't sleep, or didn't want to, so he went to check out the north side of the wood."

"Damn it," he muttered. "We need to stick together." He squinted his eyes as he looked at me as if something were wrong.

"You want me to go find him, sir?"

"No, I'll do it. You stay here and keep an eye out. He may be an American but this is my mission and he needs to do as he's told."

"He said he had a bad feeling, sir."

"A bad feeling? What the devil does that mean? Pure nonsense. Damned fool can relieve you when I bring him back; till then you sit tight and keep your eyes peeled."

"Will do. Sir."

Hangerland patted me on the shoulder, which surprised me. "We'll make a soldier of you yet, boyo."

I watched him walk away into the night, and heard his footsteps cracking through the woods for a full minute after the dark swallowed him up. I presumed he wouldn't tear into Ashton when he found him, too loud and too risky, but I did wonder how it'd go if he tried. The American had given me a glimpse of the soldier in him and I wasn't sure the captain knew what he might be up against.

It was another long hour until I saw Ashton again. He appeared from the interior of the woods and stepped into the small clearing where I'd made a comfortable nest to stand guard. Sit guard in this case. I scrambled to my feet, eyeing my rifle to make sure he hadn't nabbed it again while I was looking the other way. He smiled, and said, "You're safe, don't worry."

From his light fingers or from the Germans, I wasn't sure which, but I didn't say so.

"Hangerland find you?" I asked instead.

"Yes. Thanks for telling him where I was. He was not happy."

I shrugged. "He's the captain and he asked. You wanted me to lie?"

"It doesn't matter now."

"OK. Well, I'll leave you to it." I unscrewed my canteen and took a swig. "See you later. And shout if you see any Krauts, I'm going to lie down."

"I will. And I think we leave in an hour, so enjoy it while you can."

I walked back to the campsite, where Tex and Hardy lay thirty yards apart, the former cuddling his backpack, the latter curled into his dog, a beast so tired his only reaction to my cracking twigs ten feet away was to let rip with a gigantic fart that he accompanied with an even louder snore. I stumbled a good few yards away to avoid the gas attack and sank to the forest floor, too tired to bother making myself comfortable. Too tired, also, to notice that Captain Hangerland was nowhere to be seen, and all my worldly cares disappeared as sleep hit me two seconds after my head hit my pack.

Ben Hardy woke me at dawn by shaking my shoulder and hissing in my ear.

"Henri. Hey, Henri."

For a blissful moment my eyes opened to the gentle glow of a morning that hadn't quite broken, and to the fresh and clean smell that only nature can bring. Then I felt the dew that had settled into the crotch of my pants, smelled Hardy's fetid breath in my face, and remembered where I was and what I was doing. My mood soured.

"Hardy, go away." I closed my eyes.

"We're supposed to get going in the night but it's morning. I've been awake for an hour and the captain's not here."

"He's probably using the bathroom facilities."

"His rifle is gone but his pack is here still."

"So what? Maybe he went hunting for breakfast." My head hurt and Hardy's general aroma on top of his breath wasn't helping. Leo was sitting nearby watching us, looking as rough as I felt.

"Something's wrong," he said. "We should've been on the move hours ago. We need to find him."

"Send your dog. He should be good at finding people, right?"

"I'm serious."

"Look, I'm about the lowest-ranking man here, go run it by Ashton or Tex."

At the sound of his name, Tex pushed himself up onto one elbow, his eyes blinking away sleep. "What's going on?"

"It's morning and Hangerland is missing," Hardy told him.

"For the love of god," I protested. "He's not missing. He's just not here."

"Taking a piss, I expect," Tex mumbled.

"Thank you!" I said.

"For an hour?" Hardy insisted. "We should pack up and go find him."

Tex pushed himself upright and ran a hand through his hair. "We do need to get moving."

I looked around. "Where's Ashton?"

"On watch," Tex said. "I tried to relieve him but he doesn't sleep much apparently."

"I'm here," said a voice, and Ashton stepped into our little gathering. "Did someone say the captain is missing?"

"Pissing," I said. "He's *pissing*."

•   •   •

I smiled as the tinkle of wine Mimi was pouring into my glass gave a soundtrack to my story.

"Sorry, I'm trying not to interrupt, I didn't mean to distract you."

"Anytime you want to refill my glass with that quality of wine, don't hesitate," I reassured her. "Now, where was I?"

"Hangerland is missing. Let me ask, had no one seen him all night?" Mimi asked.

"Best we could figure out, the last time anyone had seen him was when he'd gone to find Ashton."

"Were you suspicious?"

"I'm getting to that." I took a sip, set the glass back down, and continued.

•   •   •

"We should go where he last was, where I was," Ashton said. He picked up his and the captain's packs and we all scrambled to follow. Leo was the slowest to get going, and he didn't even have a rifle or pack to carry.

We walked in two mini columns, Ashton on the left in front of Hardy and Leo, and Tex on the right with me behind him. I was sure we'd find Hangerland squatting behind a tree with a handful of leaves ready to go, and was more than happy to let those guys take the lead on that discovery. But Tex did have one question.

"Hey, Ashton, how come you didn't wake us up? You knew we were supposed to leave around midnight."

"I'm just a foot soldier, I do as I'm told."

"Meaning?"

"Meaning when I spoke to the captain last night, he made it very clear that I was to wait for him to give me orders before I did anything, and not to make any decisions for myself. At all."

That did sound like Hangerland, but the farther we walked the more the hair on the back of my neck started to tingle. There were no other visible paths than the ones we were taking, winding animal trails through the oak, elm, and birch trees. As I ducked and occasionally walked into the branches around me, I realized that this part of France had somehow survived being blasted into smithereens. I mean, an intact wood with healthy, standing trees was a rarity wherever I'd been stationed, so as I walked I took the time to appreciate not just the cover from German eyes, but the softness of the ground under my feet, the greenness of the leaves that brushed me, and the gently peeling and gnarled bark of the trees.

Ahead, Tex had spotted something a lot less bucolic, and considerably more unpleasant.

"Fuck," he hissed, and hurried forward, dropping his rifle and pack to the ground.

He'd gotten a little ahead of me so I trotted up behind him to see Captain Hangerland lying facedown on the ground, and not in a way that would suggest he was sleeping. Tex squatted and grabbed Hangerland's shoulders, grunting as he turned him over. Despite the horror of it, I knelt beside him, unsure what my leader was doing there, confused as to how this had happened.

It was crystal clear, however, that he was dead.

• • •

"Dead? But how? You're dragging this out too much," Mimi said.

"This is psychoanalysis, not story time," I reminded her. "I'm supposed to be able to go at my own pace, am I not?"

"Yes, yes, of course."

"Wasn't that our agreement?"

"Yes, but . . ." She took a breath. "Fine. But please, tell me what had happened to the poor captain."

"I will." I took another long, slow draft of Pétrus. "Ah, that's delicious. So very delicious."

• • •

To me, it looked like some marauding Fritz had run a bayonet upward through Captain Hangerland's jaw and into his skull. And left it there. Two feet of steel buried in his brain, the rest of the bayonet streaked with blood, and fallen leaves glued to the handle that protruded a foot or more from under his chin.

I looked down at Hangerland's waist, and swore quietly.

"What?" Tex asked. Just then, Ashton and Hardy crashed through a bush to our left and stopped short at the gruesome sight on the ground. Leo trotted in right behind them and stood there looking at us, his head cocked to one side and a confused look on his face. I knew how he felt.

"It's his own bayonet," I said. "Someone killed him with his own . . ." My voice trailed off.

"How is this possible?" Hardy said, his voice quavering.

"It doesn't matter how," Ashton said. "He's dead. What matters is what we do next."

"If this means there's a murderous German around here somewhere," Tex said, "then I think that's something we need to know. It matters."

Ashton knelt beside Hangerland, laid a hand on his chest, and closed his eyes for no more than three seconds. When he opened them, he looked toward the north edge of the woods. "We have our orders, our mission. And if there is a German around here, all the more reason to get on with what we're supposed to be doing."

"We can't just leave . . ." But Tex must have remembered that we'd left his best friend behind, and Boudin, which meant that we had to leave Hangerland behind, too.

Ashton searched the captain's pockets, eventually finding and brandishing the written orders for the mission.

"We need to see those," Tex said. "Everything's changed now."

"No, it hasn't." Ashton tucked the papers into his pocket. "You have a new commander, is all. Me. Look, whether you like it or not, I'm a corporal."

"And how old, exactly?"

Ashton stiffened. "Rank doesn't take account of age. I'm a corporal, you're not."

Tex chewed on this for a moment, but Ashton was right—despite his age, he outranked us all. He was in charge.

I didn't much care, not in that moment. I just looked down at Hangerland, frozen in death, skewered like a piece of meat with his own weapon, and wondered, *How can this be?*

"Let's go." Ashton shoved the papers into his inside jacket

pocket, and we followed him along the narrow trail toward the northern tree line. I got there last and found my comrades kneeling and looking out over a pasture toward a road about a quarter mile away.

"Shit," Ashton said.

My eyes followed where everyone else was looking: the road. The extremely busy road, to be precise, the road filled with the gray and green of German vehicles, and with a long line of horses carrying packs and people. As I watched this procession the sound of engines rolled over the lush green grass, the low growl of trucks rumbling alongside the higher, angrier roar of German motorcycle riders zipping along. I'd never had a chance to get close to a motorcycle, but from a distance they looked fun and frightening at the same time. Although crouched in the woods with a hundred, maybe a thousand, Germans zooming by, right there and then it was more on the frightening side.

"What's the plan now?" Hardy asked.

"The plan just died," our new leader said.

"That's a lot of reinforcements headed to the front," Tex said as he sat down. Leo looked over at him and did the same thing. "I guess we're fucked."

"Until nightfall we are," Ashton said. "Or until that convoy passes by."

I dropped my pack and sat on it. As tired as I was, the proximity of our mortal enemy had my adrenaline surging and I noticed I was shaking, from fright as much as exhaustion. One eagle-eyed German and we'd be surrounded and likely executed on the spot.

But there was another reason I was scared. It was a thought

that had nagged at me since late the previous evening, not one I could prove with any real surety but one that, if I was right, meant that our mission was doomed. Not just because it required us to jump out of an airplane, or scuttle across enemy territory, or babysit and return a spy, or even cross a major German transport artery.

No, the terror rising in me came from a source much closer, the growing belief that there was a reason we'd been dying off one by one. There was no marauding German hunting us, there was no one-shot sniper picking us off as we crossed muddy fields. There hadn't even been a parachute accident.

As I sat there on my pack, feeling the cool morning breeze on my cheek and watching the lightening of the day, I ran over the supporting evidence in my mind, looking for a wrong step, hoping I'd see a blatant misunderstanding in what I now thought had happened. But the more I thought about it, the surer I became: one of the men sitting with me in that tree line was a traitor. And because I knew it wasn't me, I also knew I had to find out who it was before I, too, wound up with a bayonet in my head or a bullet in my back.

I sat with my rifle on my lap, partly for comfort and partly for deterrence, and after thirty minutes of eyeballing my comrades I realized there was no way I was going to find out if I was right by staring at them all day. I needed to figure this out another way because the more I put it together, the more I was sure there *was* a traitor among us and, even though I had my suspicions as to who it was, I had no real proof.

And that meant, unfortunately, getting off my ass in order to save it.

I stood slowly and stretched.

Ashton looked over his shoulder at me. "Make a good target that way."

"Not for long." I jerked my thumb toward the interior of the woods. "I need to take a dump."

Hardy turned. "Maybe someone should go with you, in case that Kraut is out there still."

"I don't plan to be long," I said. "I also don't want one of you people standing over me while I fertilize a tree, thank you very much."

"You sure?" Tex said. "Ben's right, we don't know whether that guy is still out there. Maybe even watching us right now."

"If that's the case, if he's really that good, it won't make much difference if you all make a ring around me and wipe my ass while I'm fully armed."

No one said anything for a moment, then Hardy leaned back against his tree. "If you're sure, have at it." Leo just watched me with his head cocked.

"I am." I gave them a wave and started into the trees. Only when I was sure that they couldn't hear me did I break into a run.

I kept up a steady, loping pace and kept my eyes busier than my legs. My target was the barn half a mile behind us but my head was on a swivel in case a random patrol, lone German, or even an angry farmer made an appearance. I was also very aware of a bundle of muddied clothing directly in my pathway. Maybe it was good that Claude Boudin was still there, unmoved and unmolested, but the closer I got to him the more my eyes stayed on his body. A cloud of flies buzzed over his corpse, and his presence there seemed like a warning, a threat dropped in front of me, because if the mean-eyed Boudin could be felled so could any of us. That aura of threat seemed to expand as I moved toward him and doubt ran through me like cold steel. Could the man I suspected have really done this? What if I was wrong, so wrong?

But I kept running so I could find out, so I could know.

Maybe so I could keep living, too, and keep a couple of my fellow soldiers alive alongside me.

●   ●   ●

"But where were you running *to*?" Mimi asked, and I could hear the exasperation in her voice.

I took a deep breath. "In a few minutes I'm going to tell you something I've not told another person in more than twenty years. I'm sorry if you're impatient but this is the story of my life, one of the most important things that's ever happened to me. I have to tell it the way that's right for me to tell it."

"I understand," Mimi said. "It all seems so crazy."

I gave her a wry smile. "Oh, you have no idea."

●   ●   ●

Forty minutes after I'd set out, I stumbled breathless back into the group. Mike Ashton leaped up when he saw me and grabbed me by the lapels. His face was red and eyes bored into me. "Where have you been? What were you doing?"

"I got lost."

Tex and Hardy got to their feet and closed in on me.

"Jesus, Henri, we went to look for you," Hardy said. "Where were you?"

I was torn. I wanted to drag Ashton away from the others and tell him what I'd found, what I knew, but he didn't seem to be in any mood for rational discussion, and neither did the others. Even Leo was on his feet, head forward and tail quivering.

"All of you, back off." I glanced past them, through the trees, at the rolling lines of Germans, their horses, vehicles, and guns. I worried for a moment we were being too loud, but the steady rumble told me I could probably scream and still not be heard. So I raised my voice. "I said, back off."

Ashton didn't, instead he pushed me against a tree and stuck his face inches from mine. "We have a mission. We are a team. If we don't do this together we will die. All of us will die out here. Where did you go?"

I held his eye for a long moment. "Fine. You want to know where I went? I'll tell you." He still had me by the lapels but I wagged a finger in his face. "But you listen to every word I have to say before you speak." I looked past him to the others. "You, too. Stay the fuck put and listen. Just listen."

Something shifted in Ashton's eyes and his grip loosened. "What's going on?" he asked.

"There's no Kraut in these woods," I said. "Boudin was killed by one of us. So was Hangerland." I looked past Ashton. "So was Mario Guerra."

Ashton pushed me hard into the tree again and his eyes narrowed. "No! It's not possible." Behind him, Tex and Hardy looked at each other, confused.

"It's true." I put my hands on Ashton's wrists and held his look with one of my own.

"You're saying . . . there's a traitor here?" he said, and looked over his shoulder, then back at me.

"Yes."

"Who?" he demanded.

I shifted and then looked at my suspect.

And named him.

"Tex."

In a second, Mike Ashton had his pistol in his hand, pointed at the Texan without even looking at him. "Justify that statement," he said, without taking his eyes off me.

"It didn't make sense. Two snipers shooting at us, especially the one taking out Boudin. None of us saw a German shooter, none of us heard him, and where could he possibly have been?"

"Keep talking," Ashton said.

"It could only have been the person at the back of the line. Tex. And it was Captain Hangerland who made me wonder. He tried to tear strips off his parachute to sleep on, remember? So did you, Ben. Neither of you could do it, you had to cut the material. The cloth. And the cuts you made, they were just like the slice in Guerra's parachute. I saw it with my own eyes, it wasn't a tear, it was a clean cut. That parachute didn't just rip of its own accord."

"Don't you dare," Tex stammered. "He was my friend, my best friend."

I looked at him. "You were sitting behind him on the plane. You cut into his parachute and slashed it while we were in the air. It was dark and cramped, all you had to do was slice through. No way for anyone to see before he jumped."

"That's not proof enough," Ashton said.

"It's crazy, is what it is," Tex said. But next to him I could see that Ben Hardy had paled, and even Leo had shrunk away, watching us nervously from beside a low bush.

"And then there was the prayer you said over him."

"What are you talking about, prayer?" Tex asked.

"It didn't click at the time, not until I started suspecting you.

It was cover, right? I mean no one would suspect a good Christian of being a traitor."

"What does the prayer have to do with it?" Ashton asked.

"I heard him say, *For thine is the kingdom, the power and the glory, now and forever. Amen.* And then he crossed himself."

"Explain," Ashton said patiently.

"It's one or the other. I spent enough time with nuns, I know my prayers inside and out, and I know which version is Protestant and which is Catholic. Catholics don't add that last line, the doxology. But he said he was Catholic and crossed himself." I stared at Tex. "One or the other, not both."

"That's interesting," Ashton said. "So he's a shitty Christian or even a flat-out liar, maybe, but it's not proof he's a traitor."

"True. That particular proof is back at the barn. In the dirt." I pointed in that direction. "Right before we left to come here, you were sitting with your back to the wall and digging in the dirt with a stick. It was literally minutes before we all left, which you knew we were about to do. I thought at first you were just . . . digging for the sake of it, messing around. But you were digging a message." I looked back at Ashton. "That's where I was, that's where I went. I realized what he'd done so I went back to make sure I was right. And I was. He even knew where we were going so he dug the name Montclair into the soil, and wrote the number six."

"Which is how many we were at the time," Ashton said quietly.

"This is ridiculous!" Tex exploded. "How dare you accuse me!"

"Anything else?" Ashton was looking at me but his eyes kept moving to Tex, specifically his holster. "Keep talking."

"Things just added up, there's no one point of proof." I stared at Tex, who glowered at me. "But remember who put himself at the back of the line, behind us all and out of sight of all of us, including Boudin. And that sprained ankle sure healed fast, didn't it? One minute you could barely walk, the next you're sprinting along with the rest of us. And later, you sure hurried over to Hangerland's body, almost like you knew it was there."

"He's not strong enough to overpower Hangerland," Hardy interjected.

"He didn't have to be. Watch this." I put my hand out to Ashton. "Give me your bayonet, I'll show you." With one hand, he slid his bayonet from its scabbard and handed it to me. "There," I said. "It was as simple as that."

Hardy looked confused. "What do you mean? You didn't do anything."

"Yeah, I did. I disarmed Ashton of his bayonet, and armed myself at the same time. Think about it. Hangerland had no reason to suspect or mistrust Tex, no reason to be on his guard. And he'd have had no time to defend himself from one quick upward stab."

Fury burned in Tex's eyes. "Bullshit, this is all ridiculous bullshit."

"Then give me your pack," I said.

"Why?"

"I'm betting there's something in there that gives you away."

"He's a Boche?" Ashton asked.

I thought back to my train trip, to the wild-eyed, almost demented fervor of the man shot and thrown onto the tracks.

"More likely he's an anarchist. One of those loony, brainwashed foot soldiers that were sent over here to disrupt the war."

Ashton barked an order at Hardy. "Look in his pack."

Hardy scrambled over and started digging inside. "What am I looking for?"

"If it's in there, you'll know when you see it," I assured him.

A moment later, he pulled out a battered envelope, like the ones we all got from home. Well, everyone except me, I had no family to send me anything. Hardy pulled out a letter, scanned it, and his eyes widened. "Propaganda," he said quietly. "About . . . a free Europe, no government, no taxes. Oh my god, it says . . ." He looked up at Tex, his voice low and incredulous. "You're really an anarchist?"

"Specifically, a Pohl anarchist," I corrected. "He wants Germany to win, believes in some twisted way that Gustav Pohl will turn that country, and eventually all of Europe, into some kind of haven free from oppressive government and forced labor. Or some shit."

Finally, Tex raised his head and I was shocked at the hate in his eyes. Black and blazing at me like I was the devil, not him.

"You stupid little kid. You know-nothing little kid. I'm here in this stupid country risking my fucking life, and for what? Tell me, for what?" I didn't answer and Tex went on, spittle flying from his lips as he ranted. "Because some asshole generals in America decided they wanted to play war, and I'm their pawn. Their expendable, worthless, faceless pawn who can be used and sacrificed like I'm a painted wooden figurine. Like I'm nothing. And then some bastard politicians agreed, *Yeah, why not? Do you think their sons are over here dying in the mud?*"

"I have no idea," I said.

"Of course they're not. They're suckling from public funds in their cozy government jobs, taking bribes and slapping each other on the back about how clever they are. Meanwhile, we're here, all of us. And for what?"

He was right on that point, I couldn't begin to grasp the larger picture well enough to explain my role in it all. But then again, I also hadn't just murdered three comrades and betrayed my country. So I told him all that.

"Your country?" He shook his head in disgust. "You know what a country is? It's a landmass. It's a geographic area upon which you happened to be born. That's it. So are you telling me you have some death-worthy allegiance to a piece of real estate? If you'd been born in China or Italy or Russia, to idiots like you those places would have substituted in for France because you can't see that patriotism is your rulers' way of controlling you. What happens if the English, French, and Americans win this war, what do you personally get out of it?"

"A train ride home, I expect."

"You shouldn't be here in the first place. Randomly drawn borders make for countries that are as meaningless as the stupid flags people wave. Sure as hell not worth dying for."

"This is getting boring," I said. "Are you admitting you're a traitor?"

"I think he is," Ashton said, his grip tightening on his pistol.

"No, I'm a patriot, I am the most loyal person here!" Tex was almost shouting.

"You want to tell that to Guerra, Boudin, and Hangerland?" I snapped. "They may dispute that point."

"Because I'm not loyal to them. I'm loyal to humanity, to

the only idea that makes any sense. And dressing up in stupid uniforms to travel across the world to kill other human beings is not an idea that makes any sense at all."

"Your loyalty is to anarchism," I said.

"You say that like it's a disease, which tells me you don't understand it. Anarchism is freedom, freedom to live where and how you want. To not bend under the will of some government that owns you. Anarchists don't cold-bloodedly send innocent people to die in foreign wars."

"You sure?" I said. "You're pretty fucking comfortable with killing innocent people in cold blood."

"They were innocent?" He laughed. "They came here with guns and knives and have killed how many people? How many have you killed?"

I squared up to him. "I couldn't tell you, but I'm about to add to the total."

"Enough!" Ashton snapped. "You murdered them, and you are a traitor despite how you try to justify it."

We stood there staring at him, for ten long seconds. Finally, Ben Hardy asked what we were all thinking. "So, what do we do now?"

Tex surprised me by being the one to reply. "You have two simple choices," he said, his voice calm. "Join me, or kill me."

"Join you?" Ashton almost laughed. "Join with a cold-blooded, traitorous murderer?"

"The world is changing," Tex said. "In my favor. The Germans will win this war, they will take Europe, and Gustav Pohl will lead us all into a new way of living. Free of this killing, this stupid, pointless war."

"We're out of time," Ashton said. "And I'm out of patience with this bullshit." He raised his pistol and pointed it at Tex's chest. "Which means of the choices you gave me, I'm taking the second one."

I looked away as he pulled the trigger, but the bang echoed for an age, bouncing between the hardwood trees around us and rolling out and away across the meadow. The sound of Tex's body crumpling to the ground made me want to vomit, no matter how much he may have deserved his fate. And, instinctively, we all looked out toward the still-busy road a half mile away.

"You should have taken him into the trees," Hardy said matter-of-factly.

"They won't hear one shot, not above all those engines and horses." Ashton turned to me as he tucked his gun away. "You saved our lives."

"Yeah," Ben Hardy said. "You did, for sure."

"Not yet I haven't." I gestured to the packed road.

"For now is good enough," Ashton said.

Throughout my admittedly short life I'd not received many compliments or expressions of gratitude, and these made me uncomfortable. Especially since, as I'd pointed out, any reprieve from the grave was likely only temporary.

"Yeah, well, I guess you're welcome." My feet shuffled in the leaves and my eyes lingered on the dark stain in the front of Tex's jacket. "Just be sure and repay the favor, if it comes down to it."

"I will if I can," Ashton assured me. He went to Tex's body, bent over, and grabbed the dead man's ankles. Hardy and I watched as he dragged the body deeper into the woods, and

I was glad we wouldn't have to look at it while we waited for dark to come, or for the convoy to peter out. Whichever came first.

•   •   •

"He really shot him dead?" Mimi Bonaparte asked. "Executed him."

"Yeah, afraid so."

"I suppose his choices were limited. How did you feel about it?"

"That his choices were limited." I gave her a tight smile, and it was the truth.

"I think I told you this before," she said, her voice solemn, "but I see my great-grand uncle as a mass murderer. All those wars, all those needless deaths. So many killed that it's almost incomprehensible." She looked up at me, tears in her eyes. "But there are different kinds of killings, I know that. The murder of a brave man, like your Captain Hangerland, makes no sense, but the shooting of that Tex character. Much more understandable."

"Yes. I think so, too." I roused myself and looked at the clock. "Well, time goes by so fast when I'm in here. Good night, Mimi, I will see you tomorrow."

CHAPTER SIXTEEN

Friday, July 19, 1940

That annoyance who called himself Lawrence Clayton was lurking on rue Jacob when I stepped out of my building.

"I was right! You *do* have a brother!" The delight in his voice made me want to punch him. "At least, I'm ninety percent sure you did."

"Jesus wept," I said. "I've not even had coffee yet and you're giving birth to siblings for me."

"I'm serious," he said. He grabbed me by the arm. "I'm writing this story whether you like it or not, so you may as well cooperate."

"No, thanks. I have actual work to do." I pulled my arm free and turned to walk away, but stopped in my tracks at what he said next.

"I know what happened. I do. Almost all of it."

Fuck. I need to know what he knows, or thinks he knows, and for this I need coffee.

"Follow me," I snapped, and strode toward rue de Seine and a little café that I knew would give us privacy. He hurried after me and trailed me all the way there. I chose an inside table in the far corner, ordering two coffees as I passed Alejandro, the waiter. I sat with my back to the wall and stared at Clayton as he sat down.

"I was in the trenches with this guy, who I think was your brother." He was staring at me, shaking his head. "This is crazy, to see your face in the newspaper like that. And you don't just look like an older version of him, you walk and move like he did. The little shit never even told me he had a brother."

"You were friends with him?"

"Friends, no. I didn't get close to anyone back then." A hard look came into his eye. "I used to get more packages from home than most. People were always trying to take shit from me."

"And I'm guessing you're not much of a sharer."

"Fuck you." He said that in English, and I understood it perfectly well. "Why should I? It was every man for himself in the trenches, and what did he ever do for me?"

I shrugged. "I wouldn't know."

"Nothing, is what. At all. He was a kid, probably a homosexual, who mooched when he could and made jokes when he couldn't. *Il était un gars sage*," Clayton said, and he wasn't being complimentary. *He was a wise guy.*

"Your French is decent for an American," I said.

"I learned a little in the war. Liked how it sounded and it impressed the ladies back home so I learned more. Taught it in high school for three years until I became a reporter. Kept it up for the ladies."

"How utilitarian of you."

"Yep." He tapped his own chest. "I'm a real man, no homosexual here."

"Congratulations. Can we get to the point?"

"Yeah, sure." We both sat back as Alejandro dropped off our coffees. "So, yesterday and last night I made a lot of phone calls, and had two other reporters do the same. I'll tell you what I know, and you can confirm or deny it."

"Fire away."

"There are some gaps, of course, so I'd be grateful if you'd fill those in, if you can." He pulled a notebook and two pencils from his pocket and put them on the table. He thumbed through the notebook and settled on a page busy with scribble, but his writing was much worse than his French and I couldn't decipher any of it upside down. "You were born Henri Vincent Lefort, but your birth records are in Paris. You told me you're from the south, why does it show you were born here?"

"I told you where I grew up. You'd have to ask my mother about birth records, which would require a séance."

"Your mother, yeah, I saw she was dead. Your father, too." He watched me, as if for some reaction, but he wasn't going to get one. He may be the reporter but I was a murder detective and figured myself a little better at the game of information extraction. At least I hoped so. "But I'm guessing you never really knew what happened to your father."

Not true. "True. Why don't you tell me?"

"Did you know you had a brother?"

"No." *Another lie.*

"Then let's do this in order, shall we?" He was enjoying himself, like some kind of emotional sadist, showing off how much he knew about me while keeping the important stuff to himself. The more he talked the more I wanted to punch his little rat face, but I didn't have that option, I had to listen. For now.

"Whatever you say."

"You were born here, and when you were a baby your parents moved to America. New York City, to be precise. I assume your brother was born there, since I found nothing here." He looked at me again, and I actually wondered if there was a little sympathy in those hard eyes. "About a year later, your mother moved back here. With just you."

"And a sister was born soon after she got back."

"How much of this do you already know?"

"Some of it. This is pretty good investigative work." Flattery was a handy tool, especially for fools like Clayton.

"Yeah, I know." He sat back and stroked the handle of his espresso cup. "Lot of gaps, though, like I said. For example, I know your birth date but not your brother's."

"Why is that?"

"The records office burned down in 1901. So your information I know because of what was created and filed after your return from America. Your brother's information I got from New York sources. There's an information gap there." When I didn't offer to fill it in, he continued. "Next thing I know, it's 1903, and your father is out of the picture, missing or dead. Your brother gets taken in by a foster couple but I didn't see they formally adopted him, though they did change his name and collect the adoption fee the city paid back in those days."

"They sound lovely."

"I doubt it." There was that look again, one of curiosity and pleasure, like he knew something and was lording it over me. "Your brother didn't think so, I can tell you that."

"Why, did he talk about them?"

"Never. Not once. Not to me anyway."

My stomach tightened. "Then how do you know he didn't like them?"

"While researching your little brother, I found something unexpected. Very unexpected."

"Get on with it," I growled.

"An arrest warrant. Actually, two arrest warrants but they came out of the same incident." He sipped his coffee while staring over the rim at me. I still didn't say anything. He put his cup down gently. "Thing about arrest warrants is that they're like herpes. Can't get rid of them, they never go away. Unlike herpes, though, they're public record so easy for people like me to find. And read."

"Warrants for what?" I asked finally.

"Your brother joined the army in July of 1917. He was seventeen years old. And those warrants I keep mentioning? They weren't issued until early August, which I guess was lucky for him. Who knows, maybe the army would have been happy to have him anyway."

"Answer my question."

"I am. But I wondered to myself, why would a seventeen-year-old want to join what everyone knew was a messy, bloody war thousands of miles away? And what parent would let their kid do that?"

"I'm listening."

"Well, we've already concluded they were bad parents and that your brother didn't like them, right?"

"If you say so."

"It was how much he didn't like them that was a surprise." He cleared his throat and fixed his eyes on me, wanting, expecting a reaction. "Your brother killed them. Both of them."

"Bullshit."

"Strangled the foster mother, then bashed in his foster father's brains with an ashtray."

"No," I said. "I don't believe you."

He spread his arms wide. "I'm just telling you what those arrest affidavits say. They say that your little brother was a double murderer."

He let that sink in. For me, I just stared down into my little coffee cup, my mind processing his words, parsing out what he knew as fact and what conclusions he was making from those facts. My stomach was in knots because I didn't trust this little man to use whatever he knew, or thought he knew, in any kind of responsible way. He was after a headline, wanted his name on the front page, and whoever he had to trash to get there, I figured he wouldn't hesitate.

"Do you know what happened to him?" I asked.

"Do you?"

"No. I didn't know any of this." *A giant lie, but let him prove otherwise.*

"Well then." He grimaced, his version of sympathy maybe. "I suppose I'm sorry to be unloading all this on you now. But it's important."

"So, you do know. What happened to him?"

"I last saw him myself in the Ardennes, there one day and gone the next. I'm guessing one of two things happened—either those warrants caught up with him or he got pulled out to join some other unit. There was a lot of patching up going on, and our unit hadn't lost many people for a while so were better stocked with live bodies than most."

"You'd know if he was arrested, wouldn't you?"

"I think so. That's why I suspect he went to another unit and ended up like so many."

"Dead, you mean."

"Yes. Dead." He drained his cup. "I have a couple of feelers out to people who may know where he went, they're getting back to me today. But the story for me is how one brother is a hero, and one is a murderer. And a murderer I served beside. I had no clue, which makes him a stone-cold killer, if you ask me."

"Or innocent," I suggested.

He snorted. "Sure."

"Oh, yeah, that'd ruin the story, any sense of doubt or fair portrayal of a man who isn't around to defend himself. Isn't that slander, or libel?"

"You can't slander a dead man," he said, with a self-satisfied smirk that I wanted to wipe off his face with my fists.

"You don't really care, do you?"

"I read those reports. He was seen leaving the apartment with blood on him. He joined the army the same day. Are those the actions of an innocent man?"

"When are you running this story?"

"I have an appointment to speak to Princess Marie Bonaparte tomorrow afternoon. I'll get some quotes from her about your heroics and run it in the London *Sunday Times* the very next day. They know it's coming."

"Fast work."

"That's the business. People want a distraction these days. Read about something other than the Germans taking over the world."

"I suppose."

"You have anything you want to say?"

"Non. Rien." Nothing.

"Not about saving the princess, or having a murderer for a little brother?"

I thought quickly. "Maybe later. Tomorrow."

"Why then and not now?"

"Because I want something in exchange."

"I'm not paying you—"

"Not that. If you find out what happened to my brother, I want to know."

"Sounds reasonable." He flipped through the pages of his notebook. "I can tell you his name now though. His name was Michel."

I held his eye and repeated the name. "Michel. Michel Lefort."

"No. I'm talking about what they changed it to, his name growing up in America. Who he enlisted as, and who I knew him as. His name was Ashton. Mike Ashton."

CHAPTER SEVENTEEN

Any military commander will tell you that one way to win a battle, or even a minor skirmish, is to identify the enemy's weak point and hit there. Even though my little band of suspects weren't exactly the enemy, given what everyone had said about Nicolas Allard I knew he was my weak point.

I didn't want to go into the office and wait for Nicola to dig up an address, and I sure as hell had some thinking to do, so as soon as I left the café I took a long, slow walk to the Louvre. Once there, I forced myself to concentrate on the reason I was there, the case that would make or break me quite literally.

I paced back and forth near the rear entrance Florence Petit used. I'd made about six passes before I looked up and spotted Nicolas Allard at a table at a café forty yards from my path. He wasn't hard to recognize, with his large head and broad shoulders hunched over a cup of coffee. He wasn't fleshy, like the other giant, Babin, but much leaner (apart from those impressive shoulders). He looked to be by himself, so I went over and sat in the chair opposite him, the large head rising slowly to reveal an impressive set of cheekbones and small, sadly vacant, eyes. I'm sorry to say that he reminded me a little of Dr. Frankenstein's monster, just without the bolts and stitching. Nevertheless, I introduced myself warmly and he was unconcerned enough to shake my hand and smile nervously in greeting.

"Do you have a moment to talk about the poor man who died at the museum?"

He nodded and took a sip of coffee, but something happened in his eyes, a flicker of life, of recognition. "Walter Fischer."

"Yes. Did you know him well?"

"Well enough to know he wasn't a nice man." It was odd, that deep voice but the words of a child.

"In what way wasn't he nice?"

"He called me 'Nicolas *Lourdaud*' instead of Allard."

"*Lourdaud?* He called you a dullard? That's not very nice, you're right."

"But I didn't speak to him much. Florrie made sure of that."

"Florence Petit?"

"*Oui*. She treats me well."

"How do you know her?"

He hesitated for a moment before answering, as if remembering the circumstances wasn't easy for him. "After the last war, there was some kind of program for veterans, to help us get jobs. The museum employs some and I was told to work with her, and I have been ever since."

"I'm a veteran myself," I said. "I understand how hard it was to adjust. So what do you do there?"

He shifted in his seat and sipped his coffee again. "I think I am going to be late. It's not good to be late."

"Oh, please don't worry about that. I've already spoken with Florrie, she knows I need to chat with you about this." *True and true.* "I'm sure she won't mind in the least." *Less than true.*

He looked doubtful, stirring his half-empty espresso as he thought. "Well, if you think she won't be mad."

"Great, thank you, Nicolas. I just have a couple more questions anyway, then I'll leave you to your breakfast. You're not having anything to eat?"

"They're supposed to bring me some croissants." He jerked a finger toward the interior of the café. "They can be slow sometimes. Especially now, with the Boche . . . I mean, the Germans, here."

"No need to apologize. Call them Boche all you like, worse if you want."

"You don't like them? But you're a policeman."

"I'm a French policeman," I reminded him. "And I'm investigating the death of a man who, in my opinion, should've been shot the moment he set foot on French soil. At the very least, shot *at*."

Allard smiled. "In the old days, no way we'd have just let them walk into Paris."

"Damn right. We stopped them in their tracks, didn't we?"

"Yeah, we did." The memories seemed to make him sad, and I had a rush of affection for the man. He was large, yes, and there was something dark and brooding going on in that head. I knew it'd been put there during the last war, a wound from that conflict as unpleasant and permanent as any lost limb.

"So, what do you do at the museum?"

"I carry stuff. Help pack stuff." He shrugged those big shoulders. "Anything they want, really."

"What kind of stuff? I don't really understand what was happening in that part of the museum."

"Florrie told me that the German Fischer was sending things back to his country."

"Things like paintings and sculptures."

"Yeah, I suppose." He didn't seem very interested in the details.

"Makes sense. Where were you on Sunday afternoon, do you remember?"

"I was at home."

"And where is that?"

"Rue Dauphine."

"Do you live there by yourself?"

"No."

This is like pulling teeth with baby tweezers. "Who do you live with?"

"Her."

"I don't understand. I don't know who *her* is."

"Florrie. I live with Florrie. She's my sister." He gasped and his eyes widened with fright. "Oh, no. No! I'm not supposed to tell anyone that. Please, monsieur, you have to promise you won't tell her I told you that." The pain on his face and the desperation of his plea was a complete transformation from his previous guarded if helpful demeanor.

But all I could think was, *Well, well, well. What an interesting coincidence.*

•   •   •

She spotted us as I was paying Allard's bill, swerving from her route to the museum and marching over to us. Her face hardened and reddened with every step and I knew I was in for a blast, so just waited for the storm to come. Instead, when she reached us she ignored me and put a hand on Allard's arm.

"Nicolas, do hurry, you'll be late. Even now, we can't afford to be late, we have work to do."

"I told you," he mumbled to me, as if she weren't able to hear. For her part, Petit raised a delicate eyebrow and held it there until Allard had shuffled off toward the museum.

Finally she turned to me and her words dripped with anger. "What did I tell you about him?"

"I know. But you better sit down so we can talk some more."

"I have a job to do. And god knows what damage to mitigate."

"The truth isn't damage," I said firmly. "Now please, sit down."

The waiter who'd taken my money appeared in front of the table. "Oh, you're staying. Coffee, mademoiselle? Breakfast?"

"No, nothing for me. I won't be long."

"Me neither," I said.

The waiter harrumphed and said, "Excuse me but this is a place of business, you can't just—"

I silenced him with a flash of my badge. "I am investigating a murder so right now I can do what the hell I like, you understand?"

"*Oui*, monsieur, I didn't know, I'm sorry." He backed away like I'd pointed a gun at him, and left us in peace.

"You do that a lot? Bully people using your badge."

"Only if they don't cooperate."

"I cooperated fully. I answered every one of your questions."

"You did," I conceded. "But trying to block my access to a witness hardly merits use of the word *fully*, now does it?"

"He's not a witness, he's . . . vulnerable."

"I know. But I have to talk to everyone, whether they are vulnerable or not. And I gave you a chance, you were supposed to come see me about his alibi."

"I forgot," she said, but neither of us believed that. "So what did he tell you?"

"Not much. Nothing that gets me any closer to the killer." She said nothing, so I continued. "I happened to see you at Café Hugo last night."

She stiffened, almost imperceptibly. "I don't recall seeing you there."

"I saw you as I was leaving."

"And?"

"Who were you with?"

She laughed. "If you saw me, you know who I was with."

I smiled in return. "True. But why with them?"

"Tell me, Inspector. The Germans have been here less than a month. Are we already at a point where we have to declare our dinner companions in advance? Maybe get permission or register for a permit to eat together?"

"In all honesty, Mademoiselle Petit, I imagine we'll get to that point, given how things are going. However, no, we're not there just yet."

"Good. Then I shall pretend you didn't ask me that question."

"It's not that simple, I'm afraid. I have a list of suspects, and three of them were eating dinner at a time that would mean they'd be out after curfew. Not to mention they were eating with one of the most famous artists in Paris."

"A list of suspects? And what makes us suspects, exactly?"

"If you must know, I was asked to investigate this murder by an SS major. He provided me with the details of the case, including potential suspects."

Her eyes narrowed. "An SS major . . . what is his name?"

I didn't see the harm in telling her, especially if it might provoke a reaction. "It was Sturmbannführer Ludwig Vogel." She stared at me, but gave no other discernible reaction, so I asked, "Do you know him?"

"I do not." She sat back. "So am I to understand that the French police now take their orders from the SS, and investigate a murder based on a list of suspects handed to them by our jackbooted invaders?"

"You might want to be a little more circumspect in the expression of your distaste for our occupiers, mademoiselle. If history is any guide, once they get a handle on the practicalities of running a city they've conquered, paranoia sets in and those who speak unflatteringly of their new masters tend to go missing."

"Thank you for the warning, Inspector."

"Not a warning at all. I despise the pigs as much as you do. I just don't intend to get locked up for saying so."

"If you despise them, why are you doing their bidding like a well-trained sheepdog?"

I smiled at the image. "I am fairly certain that I'm not doing their bidding, since they have already told me who I should pin this on."

"Oh?" She looked distinctly worried at that, and I could understand since two of the suspects were her and her brother.

"Just someone they'd love to victimize."

"Then why don't you?"

"Because I see no reason why he'd commit murder. And, like it or not, a man is indeed dead."

"Ah, the noble policeman," she said mockingly. "And no matter the nature or name of the victim, justice must be served."

"That's right, as it happens."

"What if justice was served by the death of your so-called victim?"

"Maybe it was but that's my job, to find out. It's *not* my job to blame people the Germans tell me to blame, nor to let people obstruct my access to witnesses because it's in their best interests."

"And I understand that," she said, her voice suddenly quiet.

"Good. Then will you please tell me why you and Monsieur Allard were having dinner with the frame-maker and the painter."

"Yes, I will," she said, getting to her feet. "We were hungry."

•   •   •

I trudged to my office with my head down and a growing sense that the looming deadline for solving this case might crush me. Nicola tried to cheer me up with a cup of coffee she brought to my office but it just made me wonder whether, like in the last war, this simple pleasure might soon become a scarce and unaffordable luxury.

"And this came for you." She handed me a large envelope. "From that nice SS Sturmbannführer."

"He's sending me information three days before executing me for not solving his case?"

"Apparently. You should probably open it."

I did, and pulled out a report and a handwritten note from Vogel, which read: *Inspector. This should have been included with the original file. It did not come to me until today.* The note was dated July 18, the previous day.

"A charming apology for a possible lethal oversight on his part," I said, looking over the report. "Turns out there wasn't an autopsy, but the doctor who attended the scene felt compelled to scribble down what he did and saw."

"Typical doctor," she said. "All about the paperwork."

"And a German doctor to boot, I'm sure he was unable to help himself." Something in the report caught my attention and set a few wheels spinning in my head.

"I recognize that look," Nicola said. "Come on, spit it out."

"The doctor pulled the murder weapon out of the victim's head." I looked at the words on the page to make sure I was right. "He says that it was a frame-maker's chisel."

"Well, yes. We knew that already."

"Right, exactly." I sat back to think. "That's my point."

CHAPTER EIGHTEEN

I returned to the side door of the Louvre my artist suspects used, but paused by the bench to admire the building for a moment. The Louvre had always been one of my favorite places even though others, including Nicola, seemed to enjoy smaller and more intimate museums. The idea that a once-royal palace could be filled with works of art and opened to the public did something for the egalitarian in me. Additionally, I wasn't the art expert Nicola was so I also enjoyed the building itself, finding the ornate ceilings and broad hallways more appealing than some of the heavy, serious paintings they housed. The enormous Louvre museum was a place you could surround yourself with people, but feel wonderfully alone if you wanted.

I'd not been inside for a year and, now that I had a good

reason, I wasn't allowed in. That wouldn't have been so bad if I had someone on the inside willing to help me out, but none of those who had daily access seemed particularly cooperative. But then an idea struck me, and I walked straight up to the service door and banged on it. After my second banging, I was surprised when the door opened and Abraham Simon cracked it open. One sharp blue eye stared at me.

"Can I help you, Inspector?"

"Yes. I am here to view the crime scene."

He looked past me. "By yourself? By knocking on the side door?"

"Is there a door that's more convenient for you?" I was irritated and didn't mind showing it. "Open up, man, I need to come in."

He stood still for a moment but then opened the door and moved aside. "I'm no detective, but why wait until now to see the crime scene?"

"You're right."

He waited for me to go in, and followed me down a short hallway to an open room. "You said I'm right, about what?"

"That you're not a detective." I looked around the room, where trestle tables were piled high with framed paintings of all sizes, and pieces of sculpture crowded together precariously. Packing crates were strewn about the place, some open and some with lids nailed shut and, like Simon's workshop, the place smelled slightly of sawdust. I turned my attention to the art and saw styles I recognized and many I didn't, colorful scenes of Paris, the French countryside, and places farther afield I couldn't name. I walked up to one painting, which showed a tree-lined boulevard here in the city, with trees dabbed on with green and brown paint, the familiar stone apartment buildings overlooking it all.

"Camille Pissarro," Simon said. "One of our great Pointillists. This one is from 1897."

"Very nice, I'm sure." I looked around. "What is this room?"

"This is where we bring everything to sort through."

"I see. Who else is here today?"

"Florence Petit is here working."

"And Monsieur Allard?"

"He's here, helping Florence."

"How about the good Monsieur Babin?"

"Out running errands, I believe."

"Right." I nodded. "Can you tell me where the body was found, or should I ask someone else?"

We both turned at the sound of footsteps. Distinctly Germanic footsteps.

"What's going on here?" He rounded the corner from another room and stood with his hands on his hips, glaring at me. "You?"

Merde. "Sturmbannführer Vogel," I said with as much respect and charm as I could muster. "What a surprise."

"Considering I gave you explicit instructions not to be in the museum, it most certainly is!"

"Remind me, what was the reason for that again?"

"Do not be insolent! There is nothing to see here, and I am trying to make your precious museum available to the people of Paris. Having anyone wandering in whenever they choose does not help me achieve that goal."

"I'd hardly say that I was just wandering—"

"Enough! We have work to do here. Leave."

"I'm sorry, Sturmbannführer, I'm not clear on why *you're* here."

He took a stride toward me, eyes furious. "You do not question me. I am here because I have to replace Fischer, and I need to know what kind of replacement is required."

What kind of replacement. Like he was a table or a potted plant.

"Right, yes, of course." I gave him my most ingratiating smile. "Well, since I'm here, maybe I could have a quick peek at—"

"We have work to do," Vogel said, and gestured to Simon. "Show him out, the same way you showed him in."

Simon threw him a dirty look but started toward the hallway and I followed. When I thought the others were out of sight, I asked Simon a question in a quiet voice, something that I'd wondered about since I'd met him.

"Monsieur Abraham Simon. Why don't you wear the yellow star?"

"Ah, you've read about those. They are not here yet." A smile twitched at his lips. "Yet. And I won't wear one until someone has told me to my face I must. Probably not even then."

We reached the door. "Seems like you'd be taking a risk."

"We are all taking risks, all of the time." He turned on me and put his face close to mine. "I am told there is a dead man on your list of suspects, *n'est-ce pas?*"

"Well, yes, that's true. But I'm not about—"

"Do you consider yourself a patriot, Inspector?"

"I have a complicated relationship with that concept. And I don't see how it has anything—"

"In that case, I will give you the benefit of the doubt and assume that you are," he said, interrupting me again. "Therefore, you should blame the dead Frenchman. He did it. Blame him and then go close your file, so that you can save your own neck, and do your part for France."

And with that, he ushered me out of the door and, as I turned to ask for an explanation, he slammed it in my face.

● ● ●

I headed for the river, wanting to spend a moment lost in its swell and flow, to think about what Simon meant about being a patriot. I wanted to think, too, about what the reporter Clayton had told me, and what he was planning to write. More to the point, I wanted to figure out what, if anything, I was going to do about both situations. Time was definitely not on my side.

I started to cross Pont des Arts when I heard a cry from the other side, the quai de Conti. A woman was at the river's edge, flapping her arms and screaming at the water beneath her. She stooped as if to pick something out of it but she was far too high, and I realized that someone had gone in. I started to run but looked up to see two men shirking their jackets and kicking off their shoes. The one closer to the water finished first and jumped in without hesitating, and he started swimming madly toward the bobbing head that was being taken away by the current.

I kept running but by the time I reached the left bank and the cobbled promenade, the man had reached the boy, who looked to be no more than six or seven. The rescuer had him wrapped in one arm and was kicking toward the shore, slapping at the water with his other arm as his friend knelt on the edge of the bank, arms stretched out and down. I joined him and with a little trouble we managed to haul the boy out, and then the man.

The poor little fellow was white with fear and his teeth chattered with the cold, despite the fact his mother wrapped herself around him like a blanket, as she sobbed with relief. She let go for a moment and turned to her son's savior, and I think we all realized the same thing at the same moment because the soaking wet man who lay panting on the quai looked up at the patched-up clothes worn by mother and son, who in turn looked at the expensive clothes worn by the off-duty German soldiers. The starkest contrast, the most important one, was between the dark and curly hair of the boy and his mama, and the blond, blue-eyed soldiers. They all knew what was happening, here in Paris but more so elsewhere, and so none of them knew what to say or do.

Eventually, the mother nodded her head toward the young German. Then she turned and walked away.

The German, barely out of his teens himself, got slowly to his feet with the help of his friend, obviously disconcerted by the lack of gratitude. He started to put on his shoes but stopped mid-shoe and stared after them. His friend noticed me looking and said something in German, at which I shrugged. He switched to French.

"Why did she just walk away? He saved the life of her son!" I didn't reply, which didn't go down well. "What is wrong with her? With all of you? You look at us like . . . like we are animals. He saved that boy!"

I took a step closer, unable to control the anger rising inside me. "So what, he's a hero now? For saving one kid? You take over our city, you lock up and murder our people, and he wants a fucking medal for getting his nice suit wet?"

"He risked his own life to—"

"No," I interrupted, hot with anger. "Tell me this, Fritz. When the Gestapo goes knocking on that family's door will he step in and save them? Or maybe another Jewish family. Will he risk his life by stopping the Gestapo or the SS or just the Wehrmacht fucking army from taking away another entire family? It doesn't take a hero to save a drowning kid from the river, it just takes the ability to swim. If he wants to be a hero he's gonna have to do a lot more than that, and every single fucking day."

The sopping wet rescuer spoke, finally, and his voice was thick with emotion, his French more broken. "I am not a hero, you're right. But I'm not a monster, either. Not all of us believe that, what the Gestapo believes, not all of us want to do that, it's wrong and disgusting." He put a hand on his friend's shoulder. "Come on, Alfred, we should go." They turned and walked away from me, shoulder to shoulder, their heads down, but twenty yards away the rescuer turned, his shoes still in his hands, and shouted back at me. I could see that he was crying. "I can't. If I could stop it I would. But I can't." He waved a shoe at the river. "That is all I can do. I'm sorry."

• • •

I stayed there on the walkway beside the river, strolling along the line of barges that were tied to concrete bollards. I couldn't get the previous scene out of my head. Not so much the rescue, that happened several times a year, probably more. No, I couldn't shake the effect the encounter had on that German boy. Like every Parisian, I found it easy to despise the German war machine that had steamrollered through our country and

taken possession of its beautiful capital city. But a machine is
made up of many parts and not all of them are destructive. What
rattled me as I strolled along beside the Seine was the realization that in the same way not every criminal act is done by a
person who is rotten through and through, not every German
was a Jew-hating, child-stealing monster. If good people could
do bad things, and I knew that to be true for certain, I was going
to have to admit to myself that some of these goose-steppers
were probably decent people, as caught up in the war as we
were. Did that boy choose to join the German army? Did he
choose to wear its uniform and carry a gun? Even if he did,
did he choose to be here in Paris? Unlikely. Given the choice, I
was sure he'd ask to go home, go back to his parents' house or
farm or wherever they lived in Germany. He probably chose to
be here to the same degree I chose to hunt for Walter Fischer's
killer.

   I turned my attention away from the thoughts spoiling what
should have been a pleasant walk, and toward my surroundings.
I stopped beside a blue and red houseboat, trying not to look
obvious as I peered inside. I'd always thought it might be fun to
live on the river but never had the time or energy to explore it
as a real option. Did they unmoor and head downstream from
time to time? Did they pay for a space and live there permanently? I continued to wonder about it as I walked, and when I
neared the Pont du Carrousel I slowed again, but this time not
of my own accord. A crowd of people had gathered to watch in
disapproving silence as a dozen or more Wehrmacht soldiers
loaded crates onto a barge. I joined the crowd and exchanged
nods with a man in his late forties wearing a chest full of war
medals.

"What's going on?" I asked him.

"Germans looting our city, is what's going on. They steal that stuff, and from what I hear ship it to Rouen where they load it onto a train and take it to Germany."

"What's in the crates?"

"Art."

"Is that right?" I mumbled to myself. I looked at where the crates were coming from, following the trail of gray uniforms to my left, up the stone staircase to a line of four trucks parked along quai Voltaire. I blinked twice, unsure if I was right about a figure standing with his arms crossed and leaning against the lead truck. I made my way around the group and waited for a break in the line of worker ants before striding up the steps to the road. At the top I went to my right, and straight toward the man I recognized.

"*Bonjour*, Monsieur Babin. Out running errands, I see."

He threw me a look I couldn't interpret and our burgeoning chat was interrupted by a pair of soldiers who looked at me suspiciously and gestured to the back of the truck. He followed their lead, leaving me standing there wondering what in the world was going on.

CHAPTER NINETEEN

Time was ticking away, I knew that. I walked away from the riverfront but stopped at a newspaper kiosk to distract myself. The papers were full of news of Hitler's return the following Monday, each headline a reminder that I was standing knee-deep in a mess I was supposed to be clearing up. And yet there I was, lingering on the quai Voltaire at another bemusing twist in the case with no better idea than to buy a newspaper and watch Maurice Babin help the Germans steal our art.

Twenty minutes later, though, the trucks were empty. Babin got into the passenger side of the lead one, and they trundled off in a cloud of diesel fumes. When the convoy turned the corner, the quai fell quiet again, and I suddenly needed a drink. And maybe a moment or two to think sitting down. *May as well drink somewhere with a nice view*, I thought, picturing the waitress named Véra. I made my way back along the mostly empty riverfront to Café Hugo, where I saw a few people through the front window inside, and a couple of tables taken out front. What really caught my eye, though, was the yellow star affixed to the front of the premises. Véra saw me and came outside, her little tray tucked under one arm.

"*Bonjour,* Monsieur Henri, the policeman."

"How did you know?"

"These days it pays to know who is who. Or what."

"Speaking of that, what's with the star?"

"We put it up, and yes before we had to." She frowned. "Don't be angry with me, talk to our invaders. I'm expecting them to shut the place down altogether."

"They've been doing that," I said. "But in the meantime, I'll take a demi-carafe of your worst Bordeaux."

"Yes, sir," she said with a mock curtsy. "We have several to choose from, I'll pick the worst of all, just for you."

I laughed, the first time in months it felt like, and for a moment everything felt normal: an available table with a view toward the river, cheap wine for lunch, and flirting with a pretty waitress. Then I made the mistake of watching her sashay into the café, my eyes halting as they took in that revolting star marking the doorway. Then and there I resolved to shop only at places forced to exhibit it, as far as possible, anyway. A small and insignificant poke in the eye of our new watchdogs, but even more than that a vote of solidarity for my fellow citizens.

The rumble of a motor vehicle distracted me, and I turned to see a truck that belonged to the place where I sat, the words CAFÉ HUGO painted in jauntily sloping letters across the box siding. I was a little surprised, in truth, I'd thought most vehicles like that had been requisitioned for use by the Germans so I asked Véra about it when she showed up with the wine.

"I think it was a combination of things," she said, her voice lowered. "For one thing, the owner knows how to grease the wheels, if you know what I mean." She must have remembered who she was talking to. "Not in that way, I mean nothing illegal just . . . you know."

"It's fine, I don't care about that, not even a little bit. If it means I get my cheap wine, I actually approve."

"Sometimes I speak without thinking."

"Well, that you should probably work on," I conceded. "But not with me. Anyway you said there was another reason."

"Oh. We're trying something new, a catering business."

"Catering?"

"Yes, when someone's having a party or something like that, we show up and cook the food or bring prepared food."

"People have parties still?"

"*Oui.*" Her voice was soft and her head dropped, like she was embarrassed.

"Oh. The Germans."

"We have to make a living somehow."

"Of course," I said hurriedly. "Please, I'm not offended. Come to think of it, I'm working for them myself right now. Well, for one in particular."

"We do what we have to," she said with a sad smile.

"So your family owns the café?"

"Yes."

"Who drives the truck?"

"Someone who works for us, Nicolas."

"Nicolas Allard, by chance?"

"Yes." She was clearly surprised. "Do you know him?"

"I do, just a little," I said. "A useful man to have around, it seems."

She cocked her head, and was about to ask a question when a voice drifted out from the café.

"Véra! *Qu'est-ce que tu fais?*" Her father, I guessed. *What are you doing?*

"I'm coming, Papa, be right there. Do you want a lunch menu?"

"No, I'll get through this and go back to work. Thank you."

"*Bien.*" She gave me a wink and dashed inside, leaving me with a pleasant view and a vile carafe of wine. There was also a disconnect tugging at my mind, a handful of strands that dangled close to each other but didn't obviously tie together nice and neatly. I had an idea, though, and wanted to set Nicola to working on it as soon as possible so I quaffed the wine as fast as I could, dropped enough francs in the dish to cover it, and swayed quickly back to the Préfecture.

"You can find out who owns which business, right?" I asked when I got there, disheveled and out of breath. And maybe a little red of nose. "Don't we have some kind of directory?"

"Have you been drinking?"

"Just some wine with lunch," I said defensively.

"You mean some wine *for* lunch."

"Cheaper that way. Look, are you going to help me or not?"

"Of course." Her lips smiled but her eyes didn't. She looked worried. "Clock's ticking, right?"

"Right." I leaned over her desk and grabbed a piece of paper and a pencil. "And if you can, find out if the owner is Jewish."

"This about Abraham Simon?"

"You're such a smarty-pants." I handed the paper to her anyway.

"What does being Jewish have to do with anything? Is this request business or personal?"

"Sadly, I don't have time for personal."

"Good, because if you're sticking your neck out for someone, I want to know in advance."

"You will." I looked around the empty room. "Where is everyone?"

"No clue. Working?"

"This bunch?" I snorted. "Seems unlikely."

Our eyes locked and we both had the same thought at the same time. "*Merde.* You think it's another series of arrests?"

"They don't waste any time, do they?"

At the end of the previous week, we'd received orders to assist with a few arrests of a handful of people, who turned out to be Jews, in the Marais. Despite a few of us asking, no one could figure out what they'd done wrong but that didn't seem to matter to those in charge. French police, in uniform and out, had stood shoulder to shoulder with the black-suited SS and gone from house to house pulling out the residents and packing the Jewish ones into the backs of trucks. I'd been out on a case at the time and I like to think I'd have done what a couple of the other detectives did, which was figure out quickly what we were needed for, and slip away from the procession.

Then again, as I'd said to Véra, I was working for them anyway, wasn't I?

"So, what's happening with the case?" Nicola said, rousing herself. "Anything to talk about, or you just want me to get on with this little task?"

"I think that's it for now," I said. "Bang on my door if and when you find out something. Oh, and don't forget, we'll need a few more rations for dinner tonight."

"Ah, yes. Our large mouse."

I smiled at a memory. "You remember the last mouth we had to feed?"

Confusion knitted her brow for a moment, then she smiled, too. "It's been a long time, Henri. A very long time."

"I know." She was right, and when I pictured our last dog in my mind he was older and slightly plump, grizzled in the snout but still with that loyal look in his eye, and his endless patience. "But it's good to remember a friend from time to time, no matter how long they've been gone. I do miss him still." I sighed. "Well, back to work."

I retreated to my office as Nicola reached for the phone. I had no idea how she was going to get that information, but I was utterly sure she would, since she was the brightest and most charming woman I knew, and deviously resourceful when she needed to be. Which, obviously, was then and there.

In quiet moments on a serious case, I'd normally sit back, stick my feet up on my desk, and doodle on a notepad with a pencil, listing the suspects and putting them in order of likelihood. The problem, as I saw it, was that even though I could write six names on my pad, one of them was dead, one appeared to be a pro-German collaborator, and the other four were interchangeable. I basically had one live suspect, made up of four people: Nicolas Allard, Florence Petit, Abraham Simon, and Pablo Picasso. The only difference between any of them was that, as far as I knew, Picasso wasn't a regular at the Louvre, at least lately.

Which meant that either my killer was the shot-to-death Pascal Voclain, who some wanted me to blame but who I didn't see as very likely, the giant Maurice Babin, or one of my Louvre suspects. I squeezed out the thought that the killer could be some unknown person—Walter Fischer hadn't been here long enough to compile a long list of enemies, and since he was killed inside the locked Louvre it wasn't a random killing.

I wanted to rule Babin out, but I'd not satisfied myself that I knew all he knew and as much as anything I wanted to find out more about my victim. He'd been reluctant to talk before but since I'd seen him helping the Germans load French art onto the barges, or at least drive it there, I felt like I had a bit more leverage to get his tongue wagging.

With a little more hope and energy, I let Nicola know where I was going and said I'd pick up something to eat for us and our guest, assuming she'd be working late on getting the information I needed.

"And a bottle of wine," she threw in. "Each."

"Cutting down, are we?"

"Funny. Be home by eight, if not I'll start in on your schnapps."

"I'll be there. I need to talk to Mimi again anyway." I wanted to tell her that the sessions were over, that despite the fabulous wine and the relief of unburdening myself, I'd said too much. I'd put myself, and possibly my sister, in jeopardy with this self-indulgence, and so it needed to stop. I shook my head. *And I've not even told her the worst of it.*

The walk to Babin's home was another sobering, surreal, and almost lonely experience, as pretty much every walk in the city had been since the Boche had arrived. On rue Valette I found myself strolling behind two Germans in pressed shirts and slacks, a pair of visitors exploring the new city they owned. They paused in front of a wine shop but one of them pointed to the name over the door, AARON LOWENSTEIN. My blood sizzled in my veins and I strode up, right between them, and walked into the store.

The bespectacled owner, tall and thin, gave me a tired smile, which broadened considerably when I splashed out on three of his better bottles.

"People have been very kind," he said. "In some ways, business is better than before, it's like people are shopping here to make a point."

"I'm glad to hear that. But now more than ever the people of this city need a good bottle of wine."

"Ah, that is true," he said, shaking his head sadly.

"For someone whose business has picked up, you sure wear a long face."

"Because I know that it won't last. The kindness of my fellow citizens cannot match the cruelty of the Germans."

"Meaning?"

"Have you not been listening, reading about what's going on in other places?"

Here, too, I thought but didn't say. "Yes. Yes, I have."

"Then you'll know it's only a matter of time before they close the place down. And who knows what will happen to us then."

"You have a family?"

"Yes, but now they are in the south, the Pyrénées. I send them money when I can, they are with my wife's family."

"I'm glad they are safe."

"*Merci.*" He shrugged. "But I don't know who's safe, if

anyone is anywhere. It's only a matter of time before they come for me."

"Then you should leave, join your family."

"It's a question of timing. I will do it, but I don't know when." He smiled. "If I'd done it yesterday, you wouldn't have those bottles of wine."

"Maybe," I said, returning the smile. "Or maybe I just wouldn't have had to pay for them."

I shook his hand before gathering my wine and a sadness settled over me when I closed the door behind me. At moments like that it was hard to comprehend what was happening to my city but I reminded myself it was worse for a lot more people. I still had a job, a home, and the security of knowing my name wasn't on some jackbooted thug's hit list. I stopped at one of the grocery stores that was still open, and had things to sell, and picked up a few things for dinner, but my spirits were still wallowing at the bottom of the barrel by the time I banged on Babin's door. And they were quickly spiced with a dose of irritation when he made me wait on the stoop. I banged again and announced myself in a sufficiently authoritarian and officious voice, such that a couple of Wehrmacht soldiers passing by eyed me with trepidation. I rather enjoyed that moment.

When Babin still didn't rouse his lazy backside to come to the door, I tried the handle and leaned on it, surprising myself when it swung open. The bigger surprise was Maurice Babin himself, who sat in an armchair facing the door, eyes wide and staring at me. He didn't get up, or object to my invading his home, but then I didn't expect him to. The hole in his chest, the bloody shirt, and gray-yellow pallor of his skin let me know he didn't give a damn about me being there, and never would.

I put down my bags and made a cursory search of the place, aware that the way things had been going Vogel, or some other cabbage-pickler, would show up and arrest me for murder. I was hoping to find a key to the shiny padlock on the shed door, but I didn't see one, nor find one when I patted down Babin himself. He chose that moment, just my luck, for his guts to settle a little lower and expel a noxious odor that further encouraged me to grab my food and wine and make a hasty exit.

As I closed the front door behind me, I wondered about reporting the scene, but I was tired and just wanted to be home. Too tired to deal with any more paperwork, any more Germans, any more anything. I walked slowly away thinking I'd seen so many dead people, questioning why Babin's death seemed so great of a tragedy in that moment. Perhaps it was because I'd known the man, just a little, unlike the usual victim of crime, and unlike the scores of dead soldiers I'd seen twenty years before. Or perhaps it was the looming certainty that I had no handle on this case, no clue what was going on, which meant in turn that this slow trudge home might be one of my last.

CHAPTER TWENTY

A couple of baguettes, some pickled beets, cheese, and two ropelike sausages filled my bag, but I wondered how much longer I'd be able to eat like a normal person. Mimi had promised supplies, but we'd not seen any yet and, anyway, these days promises were like dreams—the good ones you enjoyed but recognized them for what they were: fleeting moments of hope and pleasure. Already everything was a day or two older than it should have been, except the fresh baguettes, which is why I'd not bought the too-soft pears that were melting into each other while on display inside the grocery store.

"About time," Nicola said when I closed our front door behind me.

I put the groceries on the kitchen counter and shook hands

with Grégoire Burton. "Thank you again for your kindness," he said earnestly.

"You come up with a plan for your future?" I asked. *Because I sure as hell haven't.*

"Not really, no. I'm sorry."

"Don't be, you can stay as long as you need to," I said. "Now, if you'll excuse me, I have to attend a meeting downstairs."

"A session before dinner, Henri?" Nicola asked.

"I'm not having a session. I've told her too much, I'm stopping this."

"Maybe you've said too much to stop."

"No such thing." I gave her a sad smile. "You know how many times a criminal has started blabbing and halfway through even I'm thinking, *Friend, you're digging this hole too deep.* I'm learning from their mistakes. This has gone too far." Before Nicola could protest, I turned on my heel and walked out, trotting down the stairs to Mimi's front door. She opened it immediately, as if she'd been waiting.

"Come in. The wine's decanted and I'm eager to hear more."

I opened my mouth to speak up but she didn't give me a chance to say anything, so I followed her into the makeshift study and we sat down.

"Look," I began, my voice resolute. "I can't do this anymore."

Her eyebrows rose in surprise. "Do what? Talk?"

"Yes. It may be just talk to you, but to me—"

"Henri, stop," she snapped. "Do not play games with me."

It was my turn to be surprised. "Games? I'm not playing games."

"Yes, you are." She reached over and poured a glass of wine.

"Did you think this would be like sitting around a campfire, telling stories to your kids? Or maybe like in the bad old days when you compared conquests with your comrades in arms?"

"No, I didn't really—"

"Because I told you this was important. I revealed some things about myself and we had a deal." She leaned forward, her eyes imploring. "Henri. I'm not doing this just for me. I have never met a single human being who has gone through psychotherapy and who's come out the other side worse off or regretting it."

"There's a first for everything," I grumbled, my own resolution creaking.

"Not for you. There is something eating at you and it's bad for your mind and your body. You have my word, Henri Lefort, you will not regret one minute you spend on that couch."

In truth, I didn't doubt her. I was scared though, because when a man holds on to a secret for so long, letting go of it is like letting go of a part of himself. I knew that she was right, telling her the truth, and the full truth, would change my mind and body. I just didn't have the confidence it would be for the better. I took a sip of wine and it rolled around my mouth with far more clarity and delight than the thoughts that rolled around in my head. What I'd told her so far mattered. What I'd left out, however, mattered considerably more.

"If we go on with this," I said finally. "There's something we need to talk about. Something I need to tell you."

"Go on."

"And you may not be happy about it."

"It's fine, Henri."

"In telling this story, I've . . . kept some things to myself. Big things."

"Henri, listen to me." She cocked her head sideways as she spoke, and she looked almost amused at my admission. "I can promise you that I have never had a client who didn't lie or try to mislead me at some point. It's part of the process, people take time to face their pasts, to deal with them, and so talking about them is hard. And, of course, it's the big things they want to keep hidden. People are not embarrassed or ashamed of the small things they've done, it's the big things."

"That makes sense."

"I'm just telling you that I'm here to listen, and to help if I can. So don't feel bad about withholding things, and definitely don't feel bad about revealing them."

I took a deep breath, and when the words came out of my mouth it was as if someone else was whispering them, not me. "He was my brother."

She blinked and stared at me for a moment. "Who was?"

I smiled. "Who do you think on that mission might have been my brother?"

"Playing games after all." But she was smiling, too, and her brow creased as she thought. "Oh, *mon Dieu*. Ashton. Mike Ashton."

I nodded. "We were brothers."

"Mon Dieu." She looked shocked, but when she spoke again her voice was gentle, friendly even. "Well, I wasn't expecting that." She thought for a moment more, then nodded slowly. "That makes more sense."

"What does?"

"You told me before you talked for two hours in the woods. It seemed odd at the time that two strangers would use their time like that, in the middle of the night and in the middle of nowhere."

"It was the first real chance we had."

"I need to digest this for a moment." I could see her thinking back about everything we'd talked about, looking for clues she'd missed, for meanings that had changed. Eventually, she spoke.

"Incredible. Just incredible. Tell me more."

I thought about how to do that. "There's a reporter from London. Actually, he's American, but he's freelance or something and he's working on a story."

"Yes, he dropped off a letter of introduction today. Clever fellow, figuring out where I live so quickly."

"He is that," I said. "You're going to meet with him?"

"I don't see why not. Why do you ask?"

I told her about my encounters with Lawrence Clayton, what he'd found out and what he was planning to write.

"That man would happily blow up my world for a headline and there's no deal to be made to change that—even if I had anything to offer him."

"Surely there must be something," she insisted.

"Even if there was, I trust him about as far as I could throw the Eiffel Tower."

We sat there in silence for a while, then she said, "Well if there's nothing to be done about that right now, why don't you finish your story? The mission. Knowing this changes everything, of course, but I need time to understand everything that happened to you, and to think about this Clayton character."

I nodded. "Obviously, us being on the mission together wasn't a coincidence."

"How did that happen?"

"My mother . . . our mother, died when I was a teenager."

"Wait, I have a question. And I'm sorry if this brings up bad feelings, but I'm just wondering something. Did your mother ever look for Michel? Or tell you that you had a brother?"

"She never told me, and she didn't look for him for the same reason. She thought he was dead."

"How do you know?"

"I was just getting to that. After her death, I went through her things and found letters, from America. From my father. He was on his deathbed and he was apologizing for the way he'd treated her. And us. From what I could piece together, he beat her and put her in the hospital one weekend. Then he took my brother out of state, but left me there with her. Why he took just one of us, I don't know. Anyway, one of those letters said Michel was dead."

"Why would he say that?" Mimi asked, shaking her head.

"Maybe he was ashamed of giving him up. Ashamed he couldn't be a father. I really don't know. But what I do know is, that while my mother was being treated in the hospital they discovered she was pregnant again. So she got out of that hospital as fast as she could. She thought he'd kill her or both of us when he came back and, even if he didn't, she couldn't put the baby at risk."

"So she moved back to France with you."

"Yes."

"How did you feel finding out you had a brother in America?"

"Shocked. And I knew I had to try and find him."

"How did you go about that?"

"With difficulty." I smiled. "To keep a long story short, from the money she left us I paid a private investigator, who was also a family friend. He was happy to help and told me what he could. It took a year, but the last piece of information was that my brother had joined the army. I got his regiment, all the details I could."

"And then you joined, too."

"Yes. I told my major I was looking for my long-lost brother, and he helped me track him down. Thing was, he was about to go on that mission I've been telling you about."

"So you volunteered for it, too?"

"I begged my major to assign me, so yes."

She thought about that for a moment. "How was it seeing him for the first time?"

"Pretty shocking, even though I knew it was coming, even though I was expecting to see him. It was at the briefing before the mission, I walked in and everyone did a double take because we looked so alike." I smiled at the memory. "Mike stared the most, so I told him as much as I could when I could. Luckily, he had longer hair and mine was short, and he had this little mustache, so those things blurred the similarity a little. Enough I guess. There was no time for personal questions anyway. But we couldn't let anyone else know, they'd never have allowed brothers to go on a mission like that together."

"Why not?"

"Because if something went wrong behind enemy lines, and even if it didn't, there'd be a risk our allegiance would be to each other, not the mission."

"Makes sense," Mimi said.

"You know, he didn't have any idea I even existed."

"No one ever told him he had a brother?"

"No one."

She shook her head. "Adults can be so cruel."

"I won't argue with that." I finally took a sip of wine, and with that little secret off my chest the Pétrus tasted even better than before. "Should I go on with the mission story?"

"Yes, please." Her eyes softened as she remembered where we were in the tale. "Mike Ashton, your brother, had just shot Tex."

"Yes. But he had to."

"Of course, and you were about to carry on with your mission to get the spy."

"Yeah, that was the plan," I said, settling back into my chair. I took another sip of that delicious, fruity wine. "But other than finding Mike, things never seemed to go to plan back then."

"If I may suggest something as you tell this story?" she proffered. "Call him *Ashton* as you've been doing. It'll put some distance between you and the telling, and make the remembering easier, I think."

I nodded. "I can try that."

•　•　•

When Ashton got back from dragging Tex's body deeper into the woods, Hardy and Leo disappeared to find a tree to piss on. Ashton took a long draft from his canteen, screwed the cap back on, and looked at me. "You know we're going to the village of Montclair. What you don't know is that it's no more than two miles away from here. We just need to cross that road and one or two more fields, there's a path to it."

"That's good. But do you think some of those soldiers will make a detour and fill the village?"

"That's what I'm afraid of, yes. They are obviously retreating and if some of them think there's food or rest or . . . *other* sustenance, then there's a very good chance they will head that way."

"Who exactly are we looking for?"

"His name is Hans Schneider. He's some kind of senior signalman, and he's been collecting plans and troop movements that he wants to pass on."

"Why? And aren't they all going to be out of date?"

"I don't know the answer to those questions, but I'm guessing that's why this mission was put together in a day or two. But yes, in a week those plans will be out of date, you're right."

"Or sooner." I waved an arm at the road in front of us, which was a little less busy than it had been an hour ago. "You think he even knows about this?"

"It looks organized, so he might."

"What's the name of the inn we're going to?"

"It's called la Magnanerie, one street back from the main road that runs through the town. It will be easy to find."

I frowned in thought. "La Magnanerie, got it."

"It used to be a place where they make silk. Not much need for that in war, more important to produce women and alcohol, which is what the place is used for now."

"Why does *he* get to be stationed there?" I asked, unable to hide my grin. Not a bad barracks, especially when I thought about where I'd spent the last year. The only thing worth taking my pants off for had been to comb myself for lice, and I'd still not tasted alcohol, just heard about its effects from my comrades.

"We'll have to ask him that." Ashton returned my grin. "Perhaps he's more senior than we think."

An idea struck me. "How are we supposed to get him back to our side? Or are we just getting the information?"

He didn't reply for a moment, and I suddenly wondered whether we were supposed to take the information and leave him . . . whether he wanted to be left or not.

"The orders say he knows a way."

"So we have to trust a traitor to get us safely home?"

"We do." We turned as we heard footsteps crunching through the woods and Leo trotted out toward us, heading back to his tree where he nestled himself against the trunk. "No need to share the information with Hardy. He seems all right but . . ."

"But then so did Tex," I finished for him. "Don't worry, I won't say anything."

We sat in silence as Hardy reappeared and took his place beside Leo. All three of us turned ourselves toward the south edge of the wood, and the road beyond it. We stayed like that for hours, shifting to stay comfortable, but otherwise not moving, passing the time the way experienced soldiers knew how to: wandering minds inside our still, patient bodies.

Eventually, most of the horse and motorized traffic tapered out, leaving behind a tired line of men on foot. The sun was low in the sky to our right and the Germans we could see were dark and faceless figures, stragglers drifting toward it and away from the battlefield.

"Sundown is close," Ashton said. "Another hour, maybe two, and we move."

We should have stayed alert with just an hour to go, but we didn't, and that's why two stray German soldiers strolled

out from the center of the wood, and why they saw us before we saw them. We caught a slight break because one was
still buttoning up his pants and they were both out of breath,
laughing, and their shoulders bumped gently together as they
walked. But they were obviously used to being alone and then
not because they sprang into action before we'd managed to
sit upright.

They pointed their rifles at us and shouted something unintelligible. We immediately put our hands in the air, all three
of us looking unsubtly in the direction of our own weapons.
Hardy had commandeered Hangerland's and it was half buried by leaves a good ten feet from him. Ashton's was propped
against a tree, a little closer, but not much. Mine was at my feet
and I nudged my toes into the ground, working them under
what I hoped would be the fulcrum point.

They approached slowly, stopping ten feet away. Ashton
was trying to talk to them, his voice calm but urgent, and the
Germans snapped angry replies back at him, their guns jabbing
in our direction as if daring us to make a move. The only one
who did was Leo, whose growling was now loud enough to get
their attention. They were both surprised enough to swing their
guns away from me and Ashton toward Hardy and his stray,
the former white with fear and the latter showing all his teeth
in anger, his thin little body drawn tight and rattling with rage.

I didn't think we'd get a better moment so I jammed my foot
farther under my rifle and flipped it up, at the same moment taking a step forward. I'd misjudged the balance of the gun and it
spun as it flew up in front of me, and I ended up grabbing the
barrel as I charged forward. The German nearest me saw but
was too slow to respond and my first full swing caught the side

of his head, sending his helmet into the trees and his instantly unconscious body toppled sideways to the ground.

Ashton had moved fast, too, and was midair when the second German swung his aim away from Leo and back toward us. My ears rang when he fired and I readied myself to take another swing, hoping desperately that he'd missed Ashton, but by the time I'd set my feet they were a tangle on the ground and I didn't have a clear target. I watched them writhe there for maybe five seconds before Ashton had the German's rifle pressed across its owner's throat. They stayed like that for another three or four seconds, until the American's weight became too much to bear, and eventually I looked away because the sounds told me everything I needed to know, told me that Ashton had crushed the man's windpipe and ended that fight forever. When it was done, he rolled off and lay on his back, panting, and his face covered in sweat.

I felt a swell of relief that he was all right, but worried about that gunshot. The trees would likely muffle some of the noise, and we were in the middle of a war, but there was a chance someone might come investigate. Ashton had other concerns.

"The other Kraut," he said between breaths.

I walked over and kicked the man I'd clubbed. Nothing. "He's out cold."

"Dead?"

"I don't know, but I hit him pretty hard."

"Not hard enough, if he's still breathing," Ashton said. Behind him, Hardy was on one knee with his arm around Leo, both of them watching with their tongues out like they couldn't quite grasp what had happened. "Put your bayonet between his ribs," Ashton said. "Make sure."

That was something I'd not done before. I'd seen it on several occasions but never managed to do it myself, finish someone off with my hands or cold steel. I looked around for a reason not to, and saw one in the shape of a bullet hole in Ashton's neck. The sight of it made my own blood run cold.

"*Merde*, you know you got shot?" I said, and went over to him.

"That's why my neck stings." He put a hand to the side of his throat and pulled it away, red with blood. "Take a look, see how bad it is."

Which, in any other circumstance, would be a stupid, ridiculous, bizarre comment. *I'm shot in the neck. See if it's bad.* But in this war, here in this place, it seemed like a normal, reasonable request.

I knelt beside him. "Looks like it took out some skin and flesh, and it's bleeding pretty badly." I cast around for something to use as a bandage and ended up pulling off the strangled German's boots to use his socks, which were clean and dry. Which was a first, in my book.

"There's a main artery," Hardy said, moving forward tentatively. He saw my quizzical look, and said, "Had some medical training. Two main blood vessels in the neck. It's not spurting like a fountain so the bullet missed them."

"My lucky day," Ashton said. He was trying to be funny but his face was pale and his eyes flickered around, like he was nervous. I'd seen that reaction a thousand times, the shock of being shot, and I knew that even a fairly minor wound could cause the body to react in odd and dramatic ways. Deep feelings of fear and sorrow welled up inside me, and right behind it the fear that I might lose my brother a matter of hours after meeting him.

"Keep the pressure on it, to stop the bleeding," Hardy was saying, so I did. Ashton winced, and winced several more times as Hardy and I took an armpit each and carefully dragged him into a sitting position with his back to an oak tree. I fed him some water and wondered what the hell I was supposed to do next.

He had an idea.

"I'll be weak and slow you down," he said. "You two, go to the village and find the German. Bring him back here. I'll be rested and ready to move by then. If not, you will leave me."

"I'm not leaving you." I said it reflexively, stating a fact not raising an argument.

"You have to. It's close, you'll be back soon and I'll be good to go by then." He put a hand on my arm and squeezed. "Come on, brother. We've come this far, we need to finish this." He smiled. "Then we can collect our medals for heroism, get out of these damned uniforms, and spend some time catching up."

"Heroes, eh?" I said, with a smile. "Except I'm the one going into the German-filled brothel to carry a spy out and across the fields on my shoulder."

"I'd do it if I could."

"I know. But I don't even know who I'm looking for, who the hell I'm supposed to be carrying out like a sack of potatoes."

Ashton grimaced, like he was trying to smile but it hurt too much. "He won't be heavy as you think. He's only got one arm. A redhead with one arm, even you won't be able to miss him."

"Are you serious?"

"Very."

"Great, I'll be toting a one-armed redhead across the fields. No one will notice that, I feel much better now."

"Hardy will help you." Ashton's eyes burned into mine. "Anyway, brother, do you have a better idea?"

•　　•　　•

"Did you?" Mimi asked, after I fell silent. "Have a better idea?"

"I wished to god that I had. But no." I sighed heavily and wondered, yet again, what the hell I was doing in this room, sipping fine wine and reliving hideous memories of death and murder. "All this is supposed to help me, right?"

"Yes, it is."

"Well, it's fucking stressful, if you'll excuse my language, and I still have an urge to shoot people chewing gum near me."

"This is your third session. You can't expect miracles, Henri."

"I suppose not," I said, grumpily.

"You're finding it hard to talk about?"

I looked at the floor for a few moments. "Yes."

"Henri, to tell me all this, it's very brave. You're doing great, although I have a feeling there's still something you're not telling me. It's in your eyes, it's in your little hesitations when you talk about Mike. You're either leaving it out or changing the story a little. Am I right?"

Extremely right, I thought, but didn't say. "I'm doing the best I can." To head off any further inquisition, I cleared my throat and asked, "Do you want to hear the rest of the story?"

She held my eye for a moment, as if challenging me, then relented. "Of course. *Absolument.*"

CHAPTER TWENTY-ONE

I lingered over another heavenly mouthful of wine, making Mimi wait as I gathered my thoughts, and continued with the story.

• • •

We gathered our packs and put them close to Ashton. We needed to travel light and fast, carrying just a canteen and a rifle each, the rest of our supplies staying in the wood with the American.

Hardy kept touching Leo's head and we both knew he'd have to stay, too. We had a job to do, one that needed our full attention and no hangers-on, not even friendly four-legged ones. In truth, when we walked out of the wood I felt bad about leaving him. Worse about leaving my brother, of course, but bad about the dog, too. I'd grown attached to that bag of bones and fur, with his soft, feltlike snout and trusting brown eyes.

Not to mention his timely growling that had probably saved all our lives. Not probably, certainly.

The sun was melting into the horizon to our right and its dying light projected our shadows long and thin as we headed south to the village of Montclair. Ben Hardy walked a step behind me, clearly unhappy.

"We'll be back before sunrise," I said, having no clue if this was true. "Leo will be fine."

"It's not just that," he grumbled. "I escaped from those bastards once already, now here I am walking right back toward them."

"You shoulda hitched a ride with a secret mission on our side of the front then."

"Very funny."

We reached the road ten minutes later and crouched behind the raised bank to see what lay ahead. Whatever that German convoy had been, retreat or repositioning, it looked to have passed by but my eyes strained in the darkness to make sure there were no stragglers who might take a potshot at us.

"Shit." I looked at Hardy.

"What?"

"The other German. The one I hit. He's still alive, right?"

"Yeah, he had a pulse," Hardy confirmed.

"What if he wakes up?"

"You mean when." Hardy looked over his shoulder, back at the wood. "Does Ashton have a pistol?"

"Yeah."

"Problem solved." Hardy turned to look up and down the road again.

"If he stays awake enough to use it. And has the strength. Maybe we should—"

"Look." Hardy stopped and glared at me, a look I'd not seen from the quiet, meek man. "I don't wanna be here. I want to be walking with my dog in the other fucking direction. I've done my time here, in this war. I've served my country and been beaten, starved, imprisoned and god knows what else. Honestly, I don't care how this mission goes. My sense of duty evaporated about the time I realized no one was coming to save me, and pretty much all I care about anymore is not getting killed. So let's get on with this, and get back to safety."

I had a sudden urge to punch him. Not because he was being unpatriotic and selfish, but because I felt precisely the same way—I was leaving my brother behind to walk, possibly, into a hornet's nest of angry Germans. Sure, getting this one Kraut and his information to our HQ might end our war with a medal, but lying there by the road my stronger inclinations matched those of Ben Hardy: stay alive right now.

"I get it, but no," I said.

"You know, we could pretend we went to find him," Hardy said. "Just lie here until dawn and then tell people the guy was gone. No one would know, we'd be safe, and as far as they're concerned we've done our duty."

He was right, of course, we could do precisely that. But that would mean lying to my newfound brother, which I had no desire to do. It meant the world to me, it meant everything, to have found him and be with him. No way I was going to do what Hardy suggested—not just because my brother might find out I was a liar, worse than that he might think I was a coward.

And in the back of my mind was the idea that maybe, *maybe*, this German spy did have information that would end the war a little earlier. For all of us.

"You can do what you want," I said. "I have to at least try."

"Why? Why risk getting killed for this two-faced German?"

"Because too many people have died in this war already. Hell, on this mission."

"And you really think getting information from that bastard will make any difference?"

"Maybe, maybe not." I stood slowly. "But someone somewhere thought all this was worth it, and they know more than I do."

He stared at me for a good ten seconds before pushing himself to his feet. He may have been calculating whether I'd turn him in, tell people he'd refused to help. And that made me wonder if, on the short walk to the village, I'd be better off having him in front of me than behind. As it was, he moped along beside me as if resigned to his role of unwilling helper.

It took us thirty minutes to get to the main road just outside Montclair. The sun had set by then and in the dark we took two wrong turns that first put us in front of the high brick wall of what looked like a factory, and then almost into someone's back garden. At the side of the road we paused, looking and listening. The village lay to our left, a dozen or more stone houses either side of the road, which tilted downhill away from us.

"This way," I whispered. We kept to the edge of the road, alert to any movement in or between the houses. But the place seemed deserted. I tried peering in the windows of some of the houses but either the curtains were pulled tight or every light in the village had been extinguished.

We passed the last of the houses and came to a stream, the road continuing over a wide wooden bridge. On the other side I could see the silhouettes of more buildings, houses maybe. The brothel, hopefully.

We crossed as quietly as we could and I heard the gentle sound of the water passing beneath our feet.

"We didn't check for trolls," I said, but Hardy either didn't hear or didn't care to answer.

The road sloped up a little on the other side of the bridge and I recognized on our right the redbrick building that was la Magnanerie. It, too, was covered in darkness with no suggestion of anyone inside.

"Maybe he's gone," Hardy said finally. "It looks like everyone else in the village has."

He was right, I'd never been so close to civilization yet been wrapped in such a profound silence. No animals, no people, nothing.

"One way to find out," I said. He followed as I walked up to the wooden double doors. I pushed and pulled, and then realized that I needed to turn the iron latch. It was unlocked, and the door gave the slightest of squeaks as I swung it out and open.

The place was dark and, it seemed, empty except for the odor of stale beer that hung in the air. We moved cautiously inside, rifles at the ready. My eyes slowly adjusted and I saw that we were in a large bar, with tables and chairs all around, and a long, curved counter ahead. For a second, I thought I heard movement above me but when I stopped and listened, the place was silent.

"The whole village is abandoned," said Hardy. He propped

his rifle against a table and started toward the counter. "Maybe
they left something behind for us." With an agility I'd not seen
in him before, he hopped across the bar and into the bartend-
er's area. I walked up, too, and saw that all the bottles behind
the counter were broken or missing, and the smell of spilled
alcohol was strong. Hardy was on his knees, scouring under the
counter for something to drink.

"Damn it," he said, and stood back up. "They drank it all or
took it with them."

"Who? The Germans or the French?" I wondered aloud.

"That doesn't matter. Fact is, there's none for us."

"He's supposed to be here," I said. "Let's find some stairs
and go look."

We stopped as a low, distant rumble reached us. "Thunder?"
Hardy asked.

"Maybe. The air did feel thick out there."

"Yeah." But he didn't look sure. "Let's look through this place
and then get out before it rains."

"We're better off here than the woods," I said.

"That's your opinion." He slid back across the counter and
walked over to his rifle. He picked it up and headed to the back
left of the room, a dark rectangle of an opening into another
part of the building. I followed and it turned out to be a large
but musty vestibule with wooden chairs circling the outside
of the space, and I wondered if this was where the customers
sat while the women paraded themselves to be chosen. I'd only
read about how these places worked in a crappy novel I'd gotten my hands on, so who knew if that was even real. But it got
my imagination working.

The main feature of the entryway was a staircase that led

to the second and third floors. It was wide enough for us to go up side by side, and creaky enough for a mouse to alert a deaf man it was on its way to steal his cheese. We stopped halfway to listen for someone else but silence settled around us, so after a moment we kept going.

The second floor was no more than a hallway with rooms off to each side, and finally there was light. Lamps glowed gently outside each doorway, and to begin with we cleared the rooms together, one of us throwing the door open and the other waving his rifle at an empty space. After about four of these, I quickly calculated the number of rooms left, including those I assumed were on the third floor, and suggested we each take a side.

They were mostly the same: a bed with brightly covered linens, a dresser with a metal or porcelain jug on top, and a wooden chair, occasionally a more comfortable armchair. The other thing they had in common was the mess of clothes strewn about the floor and furniture, the dresser drawers open and spewing their contents like the occupant of each room had fled in a hurry, leaving their lamps on.

The task was beginning to get monotonous, and then I opened a door near the end of the hallway. It was just like the others, except the bed was neatly made with light blue sheets and blankets, and the rest of the room was tidy, too. The most significant difference, though, was the woman lying on the bed in a short, white nightgown. She was around thirty, maybe a little older, but this war had aged everyone a decade or two, so I didn't spend time guessing. She was plump but very pretty, with pale skin that was unblemished but for a scar that ran down her right cheek, starting at the corner of her eye and dropping straight down to her chin. She just lay there, impervious to my presence, staring up at the ceiling.

Truth be told, I'd had two dalliances in my life, but never more than a kiss and clumsy fumble, and certainly not in the luxury of someone's bedroom, so I'd never seen a woman in this state of dress, or undress, before. I'd not seen a woman of the street in such genteel attire, either, though that would've been more likely than some fresh-faced girl my own age giving herself up to me.

But as I stood there looking at her, what struck me the most was that she was also the first dead woman I'd ever seen. In a year of ten thousand deaths, some more horrific than I could ever have imagined, I'd not seen a single woman killed.

This one had done it herself, if I had to guess. The gun was on the floor beside the bed and the bloody circle in the middle of her chest was as neat as the rest of the room. She'd not struggled, not fought to live, it seemed to me. For whatever reason she'd decided not to follow everyone else and run from this place, but chosen to lie down here and end it. And of all the deaths I'd seen, either before or after the fact, this was one of the saddest. I didn't know who she was or why she'd decided life wasn't worth living anymore, but I felt a touch of comfort that, even if she'd not lived a great life recently, she'd died with her dignity intact, in a place of her choosing, and on her terms. I walked over and closed her eyelids, the back of one hand brushing against her cold cheek as I stepped away, the back of my other hand brushing away the teardrop that rolled down my warm cheek. I took a deep breath and forced my mind back to the job at hand, and walked out of the room to find a spy, closing her door gently behind me to leave her alone in her rose-scented tomb. Alone but not unnoticed because, even if she would never know it, at least one other human being, albeit a battle-hardened and still teenage boy, had shed a tear for her passing.

With the second floor secure and devoid of spies, Ben Hardy and I took the ever-creaky stairs up to the third floor together. I'd expected another set of rooms for working girls, but the entire top floor was one open attic space with exposed rafters beneath a sloping roof. There was no light up here, but Hardy had found some candles and we each held one as we moved through the dusty attic. Best I could tell, it was a dumping ground for bicycles, boxes, broken glasses, and stacks and stacks of newspapers.

"There's not going to be anything up here for us," Hardy said when we were halfway across the attic. "We should go."

"Let's just check out the rest of the space, then we can head out."

I led the way forward, picking my way through and around the piles of junk, and we found him at the back of the attic, tied to a chair. We stopped in front of him, candles flickering in our hands, silent and staring.

"Jesus." Hardy grimaced. "That's him?"

"A one-armed redhead tortured to death. I'm going to hazard a guess it is." I knelt with my candle to take a closer look. "You know what, he was shot. And all this was done in a hurry, look."

"No thanks."

The man's fingers had been broken, one torn off, and there was no subtlety about any of the abuse he'd suffered. Uncharacteristic of German interrogators, from what I'd heard.

"They must have figured out he was a spy. Caught him hiding here with no good explanation." I held my candle up to look around and saw bedding, a couple of pillows, and two canteens. "Yeah, it must be. He was hiding up here and they found him."

"Right. And now he's dead, so we can go."

"Yes, we can." I stood. "After we look for his little secret."

"His what?"

"He had maps. Troop movements. That's what we're here for, and if the people who caught him were hurried he may not have confessed. It's possible they had no idea what to look for, if anything at all." I glanced back the way we'd come. "And he would've heard them coming, which meant he'd have hidden the maps then, if he hadn't already."

"It's dark. He could've hidden them anywhere." Hardy was exasperated. "We have to go before it gets light but we can't see properly until then."

He was right. Which meant that our dead spy had also been up here when it was pitch black and I'd not seen any candle stubs lying around. I moved in a circle around his little nest until I saw the lantern and lit it with my candle, swearing loudly when the hot wax coated and burned my fingertips.

"There you go," I said. The lantern lit maybe one-tenth of the large space, but that was still nine times better than our flickering candles.

"Where do we look?" Hardy asked.

He was beginning to annoy me, he was like a whiny child who just wanted to go home.

"Wherever the light falls, look there," I said, making the exasperation in my voice obvious.

He started picking up things in a half-hearted way, joining

in the search because I'd told him to, not because he wanted to find anything. I started poking around myself, and it wasn't until I straightened up and moved the lantern to a different part of the attic that I saw a dark object wedged unnaturally between a rafter and the roof. I stepped past Hardy and over several stacks of books and held up the lamp. It looked to be a canvas bag so I tugged it from its hiding place. I set the lamp on yet another stack of books and worked the bag's drawstring open.

"You find it?" Hardy asked.

"I found something. Come hold the light up over it, I can't see properly."

Hardy moved toward me, his candle flickering and dancing in his hand as he held it up in front of his face. He was eight feet away when he tripped and fell forward, and I realized a second too late that the lantern was in his pathway. I watched, rooted to the spot, as he slammed into the stack of books holding it, and when I finally jumped backward my foot caught on something I couldn't see and I fell onto what felt like a sack of nails. I arched my back in pain and dropped the canvas bag as I scrambled to get myself off whatever was torturing me.

A loud *whoomp* sound was quickly followed by an orange glow that filled the space, and a moment later Ben Hardy screamed in pain. I rolled over and got to my feet to see flames as tall as me spreading from a writhing Hardy all the way back to the rear of the room. I moved quickly to him and saw that his right hand was burned and full of glass shards. Heat from the fire rolled across my face and I felt my eyebrows singeing, so I grabbed him by the lapels and dragged him to his feet. I had to shout to be heard above the growing roar of the fire, above the snap and crack of wood and glass dissolving in the sudden but intense heat.

"Let's go, now!"

But he just stood there for a moment staring at his hand, which looked like a burnt cactus and must have hurt like hell. I pulled him so he was in front of me and then shoved him toward the staircase, picking our way through the piles of stored junk using the light of the angry fire behind me. It was only once we hit the first step that I remembered.

"Damn it!" I stopped and turned. "The bag. I have to get the bag."

The flames filled the back of the attic, a roiling red and orange inferno that put up a wall of heat between me and the bag, and I had to hope that it was still intact because from where I stood, I couldn't be sure. Almost as bad as the heat was the smell of charring flesh, a too-familiar stench that made me want to vomit.

I got control of my guts and glanced toward Hardy to tell him to get out of there, but he was already halfway down the stairs, his injured hand aloft as he stumbled away as fast as he could. I turned back to the burning room and my nostrils stung from the heat and smoke so I covered my mouth with one hand, took a deep breath, and pitched forward, crawling on elbows and knees beneath the black cloud that was rapidly filling the attic.

Halfway to my target my eyes started streaming and an already hazy world blurred completely. I tried wiping them with my sleeve but that seemed to just grind soot into them because they hurt even more. I used my hands to sweep the floor in front of me for the bag, and sharp objects that might stick me, but the heat was making the skin on the back of them crisp like bacon and I knew I had just a few seconds to find what I was looking for. I dropped to my stomach and tried opening my eyes and there, right in front of me, was the canvas bag, its string alight like a fuse. I grabbed it and shuttled backward toward the stairs, slithering over and scraping my shins on the top one when I got there. A sweeter pain I'd never felt.

Smoke poured out from the attic around me, moving like a fog down the staircase, and I bumped down that flight of stairs on my butt to keep myself from choking to death. At the second floor I thought of the woman so peacefully lying in death, and wondered for a second whether she'd be pleased at a belated cremation, but I didn't have time to linger with my thoughts and ran down the final flight to the main hall, coughing as much smoke out of my lungs as I could while I ran back into the bar. Behind me I could hear and feel the fire building on itself and I knew it was just a matter of time before the ceilings and roof started to collapse.

Which is why I was surprised to see Ben Hardy at the main doors, peering out into the night.

"How is your hand?" I asked, panting.

"Numb, but I feel like puking."

"I think that's normal." I shrugged. "Or maybe not, I don't know. But let's go, get away from here."

"Someone's coming."

"Maybe, but we can't stay here."

"I've been a prisoner once, it's not happening again." There was determination and more than a little resignation in his voice. "Not for anything."

"Have you seen anyone?" I looked past him into the street,

and the fresh air made me cough up the rest of the smoke I'd inhaled. When the tears finally left my eyes, I saw that we had two options: left would take us the way we'd come, and right led to places unknown.

"I heard engines," Hardy said.

"Which way?"

"I couldn't tell."

Very helpful. "We have to take a chance and just go. If we stay here we'll burn or be discovered." And it only made sense, to me, to pick the direction we'd come from. "Follow me."

I stuffed the canvas bag inside my jacket and pushed past him, basically dragging him with me, and we moved quickly and quietly along the edge of the road. I could hear it, too, the low growl and rumble of motor vehicles, and it sounded like they were coming right toward us.

"We need to hide," Hardy said, and for once I agreed with him.

"Yeah, why don't we—"

We froze on the spot as a voice close by shouted, *"Halt!"* I gripped my rifle tighter and looked toward where the voice had come from, but I couldn't see anyone. *"Lassen Sie Ihre Gewehre fallen!" Drop your rifles, now!*

Ben Hardy did.

Then he turned and ran. For a split second, I thought about following him but the pointlessness of it struck me just as quickly, so I stayed put. I heard another shout and felt the bullet zip past me, it was that close, and it nailed Hardy in the back, sending him face-first into the street. With proof these guys were serious, I dropped my rifle and raised my hands. A few seconds later, two soldiers appeared from an alleyway I'd not noticed before and marched across the street, rifles trained on me. The fire was sending sparks over the road now, the heat pulsing out from the burning building, and it sounded like the floors inside were collapsing.

"Fuck," I said, as they stepped into the light. I slowly lowered my hands, and said: "You're Americans."

They closed in on me, and lowered their guns. "You are, too?"

"Yes, special mission."

"Fuck," one of them said, and trotted over to Hardy. I followed, but as soon as we rolled him over it was clear he was dead. The soldier was young, looked younger than me even, and he was clearly distressed. "Shit, I'm sorry, man. I'm so sorry."

I wanted to say something, to scream at him for killing one of our own, or maybe tell him it wasn't his fault, but the words were jumbled in my head and my heart ached for another life lost, wasted, by this damn war.

The young soldier's comrade joined us. "Shit, sorry. It happens, we didn't know who you guys were. No way we coulda known."

"He shouldn't have run," the young one said, shaking his head. He looked at me. "Why did he run?"

"He'd been a prisoner," I said, my voice almost a whisper. "He wasn't part of the mission, he escaped and we found him. He didn't want to be a prisoner again, at any cost. He said the Germans treated them very badly."

"Can't blame him for that," the older soldier said. He pointed to the raging fire behind us. "What happened with the building? You do that?"

"Not on purpose, but yeah."

"I heard it was a brothel."

"Used to be, it was empty when we went in."

He smirked. "Sounds like a fun mission."

"Not as much as you'd think," I said. "Most of us didn't make it."

"Wait, how many of you . . . ?"

"Two left." I thought of my brother in the woods and a pang of worry punched me in the gut. "Maybe one by now, I'm not sure."

The older soldier cocked his head. "Meaning?"

"Meaning I have a man down nearby. You have medics close?"

"We're the advance team, but not by much. So yeah, we'll have medics somewhere nearby."

"Coming down the main road? He's in some woods near to it."

"Yeah. You want me to come with you?" He looked down at Hardy's body. "We don't want that happening again."

"Good idea. Thanks."

"Gary, wait here with him," he said, and stuck out a hand. "Corporal Jason Wells, First Battalion, 160th Infantry."

But I'd already started walking, I knew Ashton needed medical attention quickly and the niceties of introductions could wait. Wells trotted to catch up with me and we fell into a fast stride. As we took the shortcut across the field I could see a line of traffic again on the road, our guys this time, and I picked up the pace.

"Why are you traveling at night?" I asked.

"Because the Krauts don't expect us to," Wells said. "Or

maybe someone read an order wrong, who the hell knows anymore."

When we got close to the road, several soldiers on horseback spotted us and raised their rifles, watching us as we got closer to make sure we were friendly, not trusting our voiced assurances. I figured striding in the open field rather than skulking along the hedgerow gave them confidence because they didn't shoot, instead lowering their weapons and waving when we were close enough to identify.

We scurried across the road between a backfiring truck and a horse-drawn cart, the latter making better time than the former. My stomach tightened as we started across the field and the dark silhouette of the wood loomed directly ahead, and I wondered what we'd find. Who. I also wondered why the hell I'd left a live German with Ashton, even if the latter had a gun and the Kraut didn't.

At the edge of the wood, I gestured to Jason Wells that we were close and we approached with our rifles waist high, but ready to fire. I recognized a pair of bushes that stood near the path that led to our lair and beckoned Wells to follow me. My eyes took a moment to adjust to the greater darkness inside the wood, but we managed to pick our way forward, mostly silent, slowing as we got close to the site.

I saw the clearing and went down on one knee, and Wells followed suit. A gentle breeze blew between the trees, making the movements of the leaves and branches seem almost human, and confusing my eyes. I tried to focus more on what I could hear, which turned out to be nothing at all. After a full minute, I crept forward with every sense on high alert, and when I stepped into the clearing I saw three men lying on the ground: the German that Ashton had killed, the one I'd knocked out, and Ashton himself. I trained my rifle on the German I'd whacked, but he didn't look like he was going to pose a threat, he was completely still.

As was Mike Ashton. I pointed to the German, the only one who was a potential danger, and said to Wells: "Cover him, while I see to my . . . buddy." I then knelt and looked into that familiar face, now pale and his eyes closed. "Hey, brother, how're you doing?" I put a hand on his wrist and my heart almost stopped at how cold he was. I looked up at Wells who shook his head and pointed to the German.

"This one is dead. Shot in the face."

"Shot?" *He must have woken up and attacked.*

"Yeah. What about your friend?"

My heart started racing out of pure fear as I moved my hand up to Ashton's neck and touched it with my fingertips. I found no pulse, just dried blood. I moved my fingers, thinking I had the wrong spot, but still no pulse. I tried again and again, but nothing. I put my hands on his shoulders and shook him, but the coldness of his skin and the stiffness of his body told me what I already knew, that he was dead, and had been for an hour at least. A desperate sadness washed through me like never before, and I raised my face to the sky and didn't even try to hide the tears that poured down my face.

●　　●　　●

"My goodness," Mimi said, her voice a whisper. "That's one of the most awful things I've ever heard. I'm so sorry, Henri."

"In a war of awful things, it was the worst." My eyes were blurred by tears all over again at the memory of losing my brother. "I should have killed that Boche when I had the chance, like he said to."

"Have you blamed yourself ever since?"

"Of course. If I'd killed him, I'd have a brother still."

"You didn't kill him because you didn't want to kill a man in cold blood, am I right?"

"Didn't want to, or couldn't. It comes to the same thing."

She nodded. "I take the position that people should not blame themselves when they do the right thing, even if something bad happens as a result. The person who is to blame for killing your brother is that German. No one else."

I grimaced at the words. "You have no idea how many victims of crime I've said that to. People blaming themselves for getting robbed or mugged."

"Then you know."

"Yes." But the empty pit in my stomach swallowed up and digested any logic, and continued to gnaw at my insides. "Yes, I know."

"You've given me a lot to think about, Henri," she said, her voice quiet. "You should go back home. Drink more wine and get some rest."

"Good idea." I stood. "I have a plate waiting for me upstairs. Until tomorrow . . ." I gave her a polite bow and showed myself out.

CHAPTER TWENTY-TWO

When I got back to my apartment, Nicola and Grégoire were talking. I was parched from doing the same thing, and hungry, too. They both got up and joined me in the kitchen, and I handed Grégoire a bottle. "Open this, would you?"

"Of course." He reached for the corkscrew.

"But don't expect good wine *every* night. Wine, yes, but not good wine."

He inspected the bottle. "I didn't drink this well *before* the invasion."

"Well, don't just admire it, open it."

He worked on the cork as I laid out the food on the table and Nicola provided the plates and cutlery. "So how did it go with Mimi?"

"Fine."

She glanced at me. "You tell her everything?"

"No, not yet."

"Do you plan to?"

"I trust her," I said.

"So do I." She smiled. "How about your visit with Monsieur Babin?"

"Ah, that did not go so well."

"He wasn't talkative?"

"Even less than last time." I pulled out a chair and sat down. Burton poured us all a glass of wine and they joined me. Nicola tore off the end of one of the baguettes and I told them what I'd found.

"Suicide?" Burton asked.

"Looked like it. Or was made to look like it, maybe."

"Who would want him dead?" Nicola asked. "Poor man, life was hard enough for him, being that way."

"What way?" Burton looked back and forth between us.

"Let's just say he was a man's man, not a lady's man," I said.

"Oh. That would've put him on the same list I was on for being Black. But the Germans don't normally do things that way, and by that I mean straight-up murder."

"Right," I agreed. "Not enough humiliation and suffering."

"So why else would someone want him dead?" Nicola pressed.

"He was helping the Germans not an hour or two before that."

"Helping them how?" Burton asked.

"They were loading crates from the museum onto barges, he was there with them."

"A traitor," Burton said.

"I imagine a lot of people would be less than happy with him for doing that," I pointed out.

"Unhappy enough to kill him?"

We all looked at each other, and while I couldn't speak for our new friend I knew that Nicola had seen and heard about the same things I had. The underground leaflets and the graffiti still happened, but levels of dissent had been increasing. Small demonstrations, acts of vandalism, and the anger of a conquered people turning not just on the Germans but on each other. Citizens drawing lines, and if their neighbor crossed one by helping or consorting with the enemy, well, if it hadn't happened in this case with Babin then it was just a matter of time before someone got himself labeled as a traitor to France, and killed.

"The question remains," Nicola began, looking at me, "with just the weekend left what're you going to do?"

"Wait, what do you mean just a weekend?" Burton looked confused. "You have a deadline to solve this?"

"I do. Monday morning." I tried to make a joke of it. "The Germans are famous for being efficient, they even have deadlines for their murder investigations." No one found it very amusing, so I turned to Nicola. "Did you find out that information?"

"Oh, yes, I'm so sorry. No one connected to the place is Jewish. At all."

I sat back in my chair, the wheels turning. Nicola knew to let me think but Burton seemed to want to fill the silence, with action if not words. He reached for the wine bottle, charged Nicola's glass, and then went for mine. I covered it with my hand.

"I think we'll save that for later."

"Later?" he asked.

"I have somewhere I need to go."

"But it's almost dark," he said. "The curfew."

"I have a gun and a badge. And if those don't work, I'm a pretty decent middle-distance runner. I also know Paris better than they do."

"Where are you going?" Nicola asked.

"Better you don't know."

Burton crammed a chunk of bread and sausage into his mouth, but it didn't stop him speaking. "I'm going with you."

"You don't have a gun or a badge," I reminded him.

"No, but I'm faster than you, believe it or not. Plus, as you noticed, I'm pretty good at hiding in the shadows."

I wasn't sure I needed backup where I was going, but these days who knew anything anymore?

"How long since you fired a gun?" I asked. "And, just to be clear, we'll be trying very hard not to."

"I took a couple of decades off, away from firearms," he said. "But more recently there was a need to pick one up. And if it makes you feel better, I only fired because I had to, and I didn't miss."

• • •

We stood in the doorway to our building and looked both ways. The street was dark and soundless. It seemed impossible that a man could stand on any given street in the middle of the most vibrant city in the world and be blanketed by silence, but there we were. If a rat scuttled across rue Jacob we would have heard it.

"Follow me, and stay to the side of the street. If we run into anyone, let me do the talking."

"I was planning to do both of those things, so thanks."

I grunted acknowledgment. "Sorry, stating the obvious is one of my strengths. It's not far, we should be fine."

In fact, it was not even a half mile but the walk felt like it took forever. Our footfalls were as light as we could make them but they seemed to echo mockingly off the stone buildings around us, to roll forward and around down the narrow streets like lures for the Germans. We both listened intently, every little sound making us freeze, our eyes scanning the street.

But when we rounded the corner into rue des Grands-Augustins there was nowhere to hide from the two men striding toward us.

"*Merde,*" I said, and pulled out my gun as subtly as I could.

"We can fight them, we don't have to shoot them," Burton hissed.

"I've no intention of shooting them." I pointed my gun at him. "Put your hands behind your back."

"What the—?"

"Just do it!"

His eyes filled with uncertainty, but he did as he was told, facing away from me with his hands clasped behind his back. One of my greater gifts as a street *flic* was the ability to handcuff someone with one hand while the other pointed a gun. In less than ten seconds, I had the giant Burton cuffed, just in time for the two-man patrol to spot us. They leveled their rifles and shouted something in German.

"Police!" I said, holding up my badge. "Paris police!"

"You speak German?" The shorter of the two men asked.

"A little."

"What are you doing here?" he demanded.

"I saw this man out of my window. It's past curfew so I arrested him."

Both rifles swung a few inches to point at Burton's belly. "Why didn't you just shoot him?"

"I had no reason to, he didn't resist or try to fight me."

"He's a Negro out after curfew," the taller man sneered. "That's all the reason you need."

"It's your curfew not mine, and it's you guys that object to the color of his skin. Not me."

"Then we will shoot him!" The tall soldier raised his rifle.

"Wait!" I said.

"What for?" His eyes narrowed with suspicion.

"I just want to get my handcuffs back first. He's a big bastard and if he falls on his back it'll be work to get them off." I moved behind Burton, put the key in the lock, and said loudly, "Just let me get out of the way before you fire, please. I promise it's a lot more paperwork if you kill a policeman than just a Negro."

One of them laughed, I couldn't see which one, and I didn't much care. My attention was on getting the cuffs off my prisoner and slipping the gun from his waistband into his hand. I switched to French and muttered, "You take the one on the right. Don't fucking miss. Ready?"

"Ready," he said. "Very ready."

"What are you telling him?" the short German demanded.

"To say his prayers," I said in German, then switched back to French. "As soon as I step out of the way."

He grunted, so I took that large step and fired my pistol without aiming, and in that same second Burton fired, too. His German dropped to the ground but mine was still standing there, mouth agape. I raised my gun and fired again, and his head snapped back before he dropped like a rock.

"Head shot, nice," Burton said, uncommonly cool.

"I was aiming for his chest," I said. "We better go, someone will come check out the gunshots." I didn't wait for him, just started running down rue des Grands-Augustins toward the river. Before the end of the street, I cut left into an alley. Burton was right about his speed, I felt like if I stopped suddenly he'd squish me, so I held up a hand to slow him down. "Here."

We were at the back of Café Hugo, the service entrance. I looked up at the apartment above the café but either the windows were blacked out or the place was empty. I tried the back door and was surprised to find it open.

"I hear engines," Burton said, and I took a moment to listen and heard them, too. Coming our way.

"Quick, inside." I yanked the door all the way open and he followed me into a dark room that smelled pleasantly of raw vegetables and cheese. I closed the door quietly behind us and whispered, "We'll hide out here."

Our eyes adjusted to the dark quickly and we each found a wooden crate to sit on, Burton testing his before settling down, elbows on his knees as if waiting for a train. That was when we heard the voices.

"Well, listen to that," I said. "There's someone here."

"*Merde.* Downstairs, I think," he whispered.

"Interesting." My head was spinning with ideas, but I felt a sense of vindication.

"Not the word I was going to use. Where were we headed, anyway?"

"As a matter of fact." I flashed a smile at him, with no idea if he could see it. "Right here."

CHAPTER TWENTY-THREE

Burton stared at me for a moment, then I saw those enormous shoulders shrug and he said, "Well, I guess that's good, then."

"Maybe. That might depend on who's downstairs."

"You want to find out?"

We both stood, weapons in hand. "Let's go. But seriously, no shooting unless we absolutely have to."

"Again." I heard him chuckle in the darkness.

"Right. Again." I led the way, moving slowly through the kitchen to the swing doors that opened into the main dining area. It was dark and empty but I paused to listen. The voices were low and urgent, but I couldn't identify any of them. And then she spoke.

"Please, there's no need for this. You're mistaken."

I gestured to Burton and we moved toward the stairs at the

back of the dining room. At the top of the iron spiral staircase I turned to him and indicated for him to wait. He hesitated for a moment, then nodded. I wasn't wild about going down there, descending into a strange dark place, one that emanated a sense of danger as loud to me as an air-raid siren. But I thought I knew what was going on and, if I happened to be right, the people down there needed my help very badly.

Slowly, crouching so I could see as much as possible, I started down, hoping I was protected from making sound by the solid iron stairs, and from the sight of those below by the darkness. There was a glow of light down there, though, I just hoped it didn't extend to the foot of the stairs.

Hoped in vain.

The second my right foot hit the floor, I felt cold steel pressing into the back of my neck.

"Give me the gun, very slowly," a familiar voice said. I did. "Now move to the table and sit with your friends."

"Technically, they're not really friends." Sometimes I can't help myself, and I received a swipe of gun barrel across the back of my head, which burned and sent me stumbling forward. Nicolas Allard caught me and steered me into an empty chair. When the tears had left my eyes, I saw that the other seats were filled by, in addition to Allard, Abraham Simon, Florence Petit, and Pablo Picasso. They all sat with their hands flat on the table, which bore three large flickering candles and an oil lantern. It looked like a séance, apart from the gun-toting German standing over us.

At his insistence, I put my hands flat on the table, too, and looked up at my captor. "Sturmbannführer Vogel, what an unpleasant surprise."

"For me, also," Vogel said with a sneer. "What are you doing here?"

"My job. Looking for a murderer." I glanced around the table, swapping looks with Mademoiselle Petit. Unfortunately, I couldn't read the look in her eye. Picasso seemed slightly amused, and Allard utterly confused.

"Is that so?" Vogel said. "I thought we decided, Maurice Babin killed Herr Fischer."

"You decided that. I would prefer to identify the *actual* killer."

"Of course you would. And have you done that?"

I looked around the table again to find everyone staring at me. Behind Vogel the staircase was wrapped in darkness and I hoped that Burton, if he decided to come down it, would make less noise than I apparently had.

"You know, Sturmbannführer, sitting here a few things have clicked into place."

"Is that so?"

"Yes. But would you mind me asking, why are you here with these good people?"

"If you're so smart, Inspector, why don't you have a guess?" His eyes glittered in the candlelight.

"It will be something of a guess," I said. "Complicated by my finding the body of Maurice Babin in his home this evening. Shot to death."

Vogel was the only one to show any surprise, everyone at the table remaining frozen in place.

"One less degenerate. And now I insist," Vogel said, his voice firm. "That you tell me what you have discovered, what you think is happening here."

"Be happy to try." I cleared my throat, wanting to make any and all noises to cover any movement Burton might be trying. "I would have to say that you are conducting an audit of your art redistribution protocols."

"Meaning?"

"I have to assume that these fine people here were part of your plan to syphon off certain works of art for yourself from the Louvre."

"It's a little more complicated than that," Vogel said. "Or so it has turned out."

I looked up and opened my mouth to ask a question, but froze as a figure came out of the shadows and loomed behind Vogel. He started to turn and Burton hit him, hard. Vogel collapsed to the floor and I threw myself onto the arm holding the weapon. I needn't have bothered because the German was out cold.

"Who are you?" Allard demanded, half rising from his chair but his hands still on the table.

"He's with me," I said quickly. "Everyone stay calm, we need to make some decisions."

But Greg Burton didn't know any of these people and didn't seem eager to put away his gun. "Henri, please tell me what's going on?"

I took Vogel's pistol, put it in my jacket pocket, and stood. I gave him a kick in the ribs to make sure he was still out, and turned to the table.

"One of you want to explain to my friend what's happening?" They all looked at each other, but no one said a word. "Well then," I said. "I'll take a stab at it. I'm guessing that Vogel was helping himself to some of the better, and probably smaller, art. Using his position to line his own pockets. And you fine people were in on his little plan."

"Wait," Burton interrupted. He was staring at Picasso. "Aren't you . . . ? You are." He switched his gaze to me. "Are you saying these people are traitors? That Pablo Picasso is a traitor?"

"Not at all," I reassured him. "In fact, quite the opposite."

Picasso smiled. "I told them you'd figure it out. I know intelligence when I see it."

"Thank you," I said.

"But I'd love to know how," the artist said.

"Several things. Small things."

"Such as?"

"Such as the voluntarily posted yellow star on the door upstairs. Also the Germans being the only ones with food poisoning, and the time Monsieur Simon 'disappeared' inside the café. Oh, and the truck you use to make deliveries." No one spoke so I continued. "All that interested me, so I checked and found out that no one associated with Café Hugo is Jewish. That made sense to me because if the owner had been, there's no way in the world his truck would not have been requisitioned. Almost every truck, Jewish or not, in Paris is now being driven by a German, which told me that you knew someone, managed to pull a string or two."

"And the yellow star?" Picasso was smiling now.

"The same reason you gave those soldiers the trots. To keep the Germans out of the café. Nice touches."

"You said they were helping this pig," Burton interjected. "I still don't understand."

"Not quite," I said. "I said they knew about his scheme. Tell me if I'm wrong, but here's how I think it worked. He would get lists of art from Walter Fischer, which I assume included some kind of designation as to rarity or worth."

"That's correct," Florence Petit said, but her voice was cautious and she offered nothing more.

"Vogel here would then choose one or two pieces for himself."

"And they would help him?" Burton said, incredulous.

"No." I looked at Picasso. "This is where you come in, right?"

"Keep talking," he said, an enigmatic smile on his lips.

"The truck is used to bring paintings here from the Louvre, where they are hidden until you take them after dark to your studio. You make a copy of the piece he wants, then get it back to the museum and Vogel gets a worthless painting from you instead of the priceless art he thinks."

"I'd like to think that *none* of my work is worthless," Picasso said mildly.

"Of course, my apologies." I turned to Abraham Simon. "And you, sir, assist with the technical practicalities. I assume you either make a new frame or put Monsieur Picasso's work into the old frame."

He nodded. "The latter, unless the frame itself is of value and then I make a new one on the spot."

"It helps, I assume, that Vogel has no eye for art."

They all laughed a little, and Picasso said, "That would be an understatement."

"What else gave us away?" Florence Petit asked.

"I saw a piece at Monsieur Picasso's studio, on my brief visit." I turned to Picasso. "You claimed it as a work of your own and I accepted that as a fact, unable at the time to distinguish the difference between your signature and that of Claude Pissarro. But then I remembered what my colleague had told me, and saw no reason in the world why you'd have another man's art in your studio."

"I was telling the truth," Picasso said. "I did paint that."

"Sturmbannführer Vogel has a thing for Pointillism." Simon spoke up. "Pablo's version was destined for his little collection."

Burton finally lowered his gun, but kept it in his hand. "So, who killed Walter Fischer? One of you?"

They all looked at each other for a moment, and I couldn't help but chuckle.

"No," I said. "None of these good people did. Fischer was murdered by Sturmbannführer Ludwig Vogel."

CHAPTER TWENTY-FOUR

Saturday, July 20, 1940

I awoke at seven the next morning and was hit by a moment of panic, as I had been every morning for the past week. But it washed quickly away when I remembered the events of the previous evening—case solved, pressure off. That one jolt of adrenaline left me wide awake so I made coffee and sat with my thoughts, wondering about that other major thread in my life, and how best to tie it off.

You need to tell Mimi the rest of the story, I thought as I drained my cup. *The entire truth, too. All of it.*

I sincerely believed I could trust her, despite the enormous potential risk to both myself and Nicola. I'd been a *flic* long enough to know who to trust and who not to, and I'd spent enough time with Mimi to feel like I knew her to be honest, trustworthy, and reliable. And if, for some reason, she did reveal my little secret I would just have to deny everything, and hope that I'd covered my tracks well enough that even if people doubted me, that's as far as it would go.

Lawrence Clayton was another matter. I didn't begin to trust him, and I had no idea what more he was dredging up. Hopefully not all of it, but I couldn't rely on mere hope. I needed to think of something, some way to mine him for what he knew, and some way to control what he wrote. Nicola was smart enough to figure something out but I wasn't sure she'd be ruthless enough, so I thought it better to leave her out of this particular equation.

Mimi, on the other hand, had a love of all things criminal and given her determination to help me, I was sure that she'd help me marshal Clayton. To help, though, she had to know the whole truth. All of it.

"Henri, what a surprise." She wore a long gray dress and her hair was perfectly coiffed.

"I have to go make my report on the Louvre case in a couple of hours, but wondered if you had an hour for me."

"Now?"

"Yes."

"Come in." I followed her to the study and we took our usual seats. "Was there something in particular?"

"I haven't told you everything, and I changed the story to maintain a lie I have been telling for many years. I hope this won't upset you, but I think you'll understand when you hear the truth."

She gave me a small smile. "I'm intrigued. But you'll forgive me if I don't pour you a glass of wine, I don't encourage drinking before noon."

"I should wait until after my meeting with the Germans anyway."

"Yes, of course."

"I need to tell you I'm also concerned about the story this journalist Clayton is writing."

"Why?"

"Because he knows about me having a brother and wants to paint me as a hero and him as a murderer."

"Because of what happened in New York?"

"Yes. But I'm concerned because it wouldn't be the truth, he didn't murder those people."

"Is that what he told you?"

"He didn't have to." I shook my head and smiled. *I'm all in now.*

"What do you mean?"

I waited a moment and watched as understanding rolled through her like a wave.

"Oh my god," she said. "I was going to ask how you knew that. And it came to me, what you said when we first talked. I asked who you lost in the war and you said 'myself.'" She stared intently at me. "This makes sense now. Your accent, your worry about the journalist. He wasn't just your brother. He was your twin."

I nodded. "Not identical, not in the technical sense. We were fraternal twins but still looked a lot alike."

"And that night in the wood. When he died." She was processing my story, unwinding it and looking at it from a new angle. "You . . . you . . ."

I spoke softly, as if my tone could soften the hard truth of the next words I spoke. "I was born Michel Pierre Lefort. When I was a small child, I was given an American name. Michael Ashton."

"So, you're Mike Ash . . ." Her hand hovered over her mouth, and her eyes were wide. "And that means it was Henri who died in the woods."

"It was. Except . . . I became Henri that night. I had to."

"Had to?" It wasn't a challenge, just a question.

"Remember, I was wanted for murder. If I went back as Mike, even though I survived the mission, it was over for me. I had to."

•   •   •

It had hit me like a cold wave, chilling me but also waking me up. I'd survived a mission no one else had. Survived and succeeded, in fact. And my reward was going to be a pat on the back and a shove into the brig, followed by a long and uncomfortable ride back to the States where a cop and his handcuffs would be waiting for me. And at the end of a long line of lawyers, judges, and jailers, there would be a prison cell, and maybe even an executioner. All for two murders I hadn't committed.

Behind me, Corporal Jason Wells had given me time and space, but was now getting antsy.

"He was a good friend?" he asked.

"Yes. The best."

"Fuck, I'm sorry. What was his name?" Wells's voice was soft, sympathetic. "Come to that, I still don't know yours."

That's right, I never told you my name.

I knelt there in the wood, surrounded by old trees and the

night's slowly fading darkness, one hand on the neck of a dead man who looked just like me, a man I barely knew but who was my twin brother. A man who, in death, could do something for me that I know I would have done for him. And so my voice was thick with emotion as I turned to Corporal Wells and finally introduced my dead comrade, and then myself.

"This man is Mike Ashton, 165th Regiment, Sixty-Ninth New York, Infantry. He was from New York City." I paused, my throat tight with emotion, and maybe a little fear. "My name is Henri Lefort."

•　　•　　•

When I'd finished that part of the story, she sat quietly for a moment. Then she asked, "So what really happened to his . . . to *your* foster parents?"

"Jerry and Alice were their names. She was nice enough to me, I suppose. Cooked and did laundry until she taught me how to. And I was a useful buffer for his Friday night rampages."

"He hit you?"

"Seemed like he took turns. Me and then her, then me again. You could set your watch by him."

Her face darkened with anger, and she said, "I'm sorry, that must have been awful to live with."

"Most of the week was fine, he was too tired to do much more than yell. And eat with his mouth full, chomping like a pig that hadn't eaten for days." She raised an eyebrow at that and I knew she was thinking what I was, that maybe my little surges of rage at those kinds of noises sprang from sitting across the kitchen table from him. "He could only afford to drink at the end of the week, so it was just Fridays we had to watch out for."

"How horrible," she said.

"One Friday evening Jerry came stumbling in around midnight. Something was different that night because he went straight for me, I've never seen anyone look so mad." I shook my head at the memory. "I swear, I didn't even have time to do one little thing to piss him off. Well, maybe he saw my bicycle in the hallway and that was enough. Anyway. I managed to shove him away and ran into my room, barricaded the door. He banged on it for a while then must've realized his other punching bag was available. He left me alone and headed for the kitchen where Alice was trying to make him a sandwich. Peace offering, I guess."

"But it didn't work."

"No. Although things got real quiet so I thought it had, and I eventually went out. I walked into the kitchen and she was on the floor, he was sitting on top of her with his hands around her throat. I remember, her legs and feet were kicking and she was scratching at him. But they were both quiet, and I knew that he was going to kill her. Just knew it." I took a deep breath to calm myself. "He had a big glass ashtray for the stinking little cigars he smoked. Alice had washed it for him, and it was just sitting there on the sink. I grabbed it and hit him in the head, good and hard."

Mimi nodded. "What happened next?"

"Nothing. I mean, I didn't do anything else. I hit him that one time, watched him fall off of her, and then walked out of the apartment. I spent the night in a nearby park and the next morning I was first in line at the recruiting office."

"So *he* killed her."

"And, it turns out, I killed him."

It was true, of course, that I'd not killed anyone intention-
ally, not committed murder. I'd laid an ashtray across my foster
father's ugly mug and, if pressed, I'd be slow to show remorse
for his passing. But I'd not meant to kill him.

"I believe you . . . Henri."

"I've been Henri for more than twenty years. I'm Henri."

She shook her head, no doubt in wonderment at the story.
"What did you do when you left the wood that night?"

I smiled. "There's a happier ending to that part."

"Tell me."

●　　●　　●

Corporal Jason Wells and I were halfway across the field when
I stopped in my tracks and said, "I forgot something."

"Forgot . . . Oh, shit, you're right. His dog tags. We need to
get his tags for his family."

"You mind if I go back alone?"

"No, man, not at all." He squinted as he appraised me. "You
know, it was dark in there but you guys sure seemed to look
alike."

"Yeah, we do," I said. "But I didn't know him for long, just
the mission."

He nodded. "Sure, go ahead. There ain't any Germans
around but just be careful when you come back to the convoy.
Make a lot of noise and keep your hands up."

"Thanks, I will." I gave him a parting wave and set off, back
for the wood. It wasn't dog tags I was going back for, I'd already
palmed them and switched them out for mine.

No, I was going back for an actual dog.

I slogged back into the woods, cutting a wide circle around

the clearing where my brother, and possibly now my savior, lay dead, calling Leo's name and whistling for him. I had no idea if he'd bolted, if he'd been hurt, or if he was just done with trusting humans to look after him. But he and I were the lone survivors of this mission and if I didn't at least try to find him, I knew I would regret it.

He was there still, cowering in the bushes barely a stick's throw from the bodies of Henri and the German. He growled as I approached but when I called his name he crept forward, his head bobbing and his tail wagging so hard I thought he might dislocate his own hips. I ruffled his head and held him close to me, feeling his rough tongue licking my neck and face. I held him closer when, like the idiot I was, I explained what had happened to his best friend, Ben Hardy, the man who'd taken him in. He may have cared if he could've understood, I'm sure he would have, but in that moment, Leo just seemed very happy that someone had come back for him, and grateful enough to lick the tears from my face as I sobbed and apologized for losing *his* friend and savior. He was quick to forgive that one, because he stuck close to my side as we walked back out of the wood, and stayed there as we headed for safety, for that long line of cars, trucks, and horses that meant a hot meal and maybe, god willing, a night's sleep somewhere comfortable.

• • •

Mimi's eyes lit up. "The picture of the dog I saw upstairs. That was Leo?"

"It was. Is."

"You managed to bring him to Paris." She clapped her hands together. "For some reason that makes me so happy."

"You like dogs. It's not so unusual."

She nodded. "I had several when I was a child. They kept disappearing."

"Disappearing?"

"I didn't realize it at the time, but my father didn't want me to have one. So every time I got one, it disappeared. Ran away, he said."

"That's awful."

"Yes, but this isn't about me. So, you and Leo came back to Paris. Did you try and find your family?"

"My mother was already dead."

"What about your other sibling?" I didn't reply, I just looked at her and smiled, then glanced exaggeratedly toward the ceiling and watched as a second wave of understanding dawned on her. "Oh, my goodness. Nicola. She's your sister."

• • •

She'd not been hard to find. I went to the Préfecture to see if they'd somehow have an address for her. I knew her full name from a letter I collected from my brother's belongings, she must have married because she was now Nicola Prehn. The name sounded German, which wasn't ideal, but one of the old *flics* in the reception area corrected my pronunciation, saying it was pronounced *Preen* not *Pren*. He knew that because she worked at the Préfecture, so he headed upstairs to get her.

Neither of us was ready for that moment. I'd not rehearsed what to say, and she didn't even listen the first three times I said it. She just hugged me so tight I thought I might burst. Eventually I led her outside and we sat beside the Seine, our legs dangling over the concrete bank as I talked and she, finally, listened.

I told it as simply as I could and watched her face as confusion turned into disbelief, then into understanding and, finally, into numbed acceptance. When I'd finished, she wiped her eyes with the back of her sleeve, and I did the same. "I once found an envelope in my mother's things," she said. "I was a child, just playing, I think I was trying to find her clothes to wear." She laughed and sniffled. "I found a box and it had letters in it. From America. She'd not opened any of them but I was too scared to ask her why. Anyway, also in that box was an envelope with locks of hair in it."

"Yours and Henri's," I said.

"Yes." Her blue eyes twinkled as she smiled. "And one other. Now I know who it belonged to."

"She kept a lock of my hair?"

"She did." Nicola took my hand. "This is going to be . . . difficult. Calling you Henri."

"For me, too."

"Your French needs some work, too. You'll need to read for an hour every night. And tell people you're from the southwest, to cover your accent. We'll pick a place in the Pyrénées."

"I'll work hard at it, and do more listening than talking for a few months." I looked at her, my sister, for a moment. "So, you are married? That could make things difficult."

She grimaced. "I was. For three whole months. He was killed soon after the war."

"I'm sorry," I said quietly. "Do you want to tell me about him?"

"Not right now. Another time."

"Of course." I smiled. "So how long have you worked at the Préfecture?"

"Almost ten months. After my . . . our mother died and our brother signed up for the war, I did odd jobs here and there. Met a friendly *flic* one night, and he told me about the job opening."

I smiled. "How friendly?"

She feigned shock and elbowed me, as if we'd been best friends for years. "Not like that! He was older. I wonder if he sensed I wasn't on a great path. Anyway, he was the fatherly type and if you've grown up without one, well, let's just say I respond better to that than to men my own age telling me what to do."

"It must have been hard, being by yourself in those years."

"It was." She reached out and gave my elbow a squeeze. "Easier than being in the trenches though."

"Even so." I brought us back to the present with a worry that had been nagging at me. "Do you have any idea how I can find a place to live?"

"I already did."

"What? But we only just—"

"You're staying with me."

"Are you sure? You have room for me? I'll get my own place as soon as I'm on my feet, I promise."

"Absolutely not." She shook her head. "I lost a brother, then found another one. I'm not letting him go anywhere. You're not just staying with me, you're living with me."

I walked her back to the Préfecture, and she paused before going inside. She reached into her bag and took out a set of keys, which she handed to me.

"If I tell you the address, will you remember?"

"Unlikely. I'm not from around here."

She laughed and dug in her purse again, finding a pencil and scrap of paper. She wrote down the address and directions, and gave it to me. Then she pointed back the way we came. "Head that way."

"Thank you." I wanted to say more but didn't know what, exactly.

"I'm glad about one thing," she said, peering up at me. "I'm really happy you met him. And that he met you."

"Me, too." I smiled. "I think about that every day."

•   •   •

"How did I not realize she was your sister?" Mimi laughed.

"Because we've spent a long time hiding it. But she saves my hide on a daily basis." I thought back to the moment in Picasso's studio when the painter referred to the story of François Ravaillac, clearly a significant person in French history but one whom I'd not gotten around to reading about. (And this, obviously, was why I read for an hour or two every day—to firm up my language skills and also teach myself things I would have learned in school, had I grown up in France.) Nicola patched over the holes in my cultural ignorance whenever she was around, and while there were fewer than there used to be, they still existed.

"I'm glad to hear it," Mimi said. She looked over at the clock. "You know, that Clayton man will be here soon. Are you concerned he will find out more? The whole truth, as you put it?"

"I am. If he does, even if he can't prove it, it'll be enough to end my career and probably land me in a German prison camp for not being the hero they want me to be. Or perhaps a French prison for stealing my own brother's identity. Or maybe an American one for two murders I didn't commit." I shrugged. "Maybe they'll let me choose."

"I doubt it." Mimi stood up. "So you did know him. In the trenches."

"Yes."

"How was he?"

"Like he is now. A bully when he can be, a whiner when he can't."

"He bullied you?"

"Yes." Truth was, he was more than a bully. He was a callous, selfish opportunist. The worst of us out there, after a skirmish, would loot the pockets of the dead enemy. I'd seen Clayton empty the pockets of dead Americans. I'd never said anything because I was a kid and a little scared of him, scared of the sneer and the dead look in his eyes when he saw something, or someone, he didn't like. But now, I smiled at Mimi. "But I fought back at him in my own way."

"How?" She glanced at her watch. "Actually, hang on to that story for a moment, I need to make a quick telephone call."

"You have a working telephone? We barely have those at the Préfecture."

"One of the perks of being me. I had one installed yesterday."

I waited for no more than five minutes, and then she was back.

"Is everything all right?" I asked.

"I just needed to see if some friends were available to help me with something today."

"That's vague."

"Better it remain that way," she said. At that moment someone knocked on her door, three loud raps. "Our journalist friend, I imagine."

I followed her out of the study, through the main room and

to the door. When she opened it, Lawrence Clayton's eyes went wide with surprise on seeing me.

"You. You lied to me about who you are. I put all the pieces together and I know the truth." He looked at Mimi Bonaparte. "He's not who he says he is. He's an impostor." He stood as tall as he was able, which wasn't very. "This will be the scoop of the decade. I know about the mission you went on, about your brother. And I know who you are! I bet he hasn't told you, has he?"

"I cannot divulge anything my patient may or may not have told me," Mimi said, her voice neutral.

"Patient?" Clayton looked back and forth between us. "That's a good one. I remember when he was a little pip-squeak on the front lines. I made him fetch me water from No-Man's Land once, you remember that, Monsieur Lefort? Or should I call you—"

"Why don't you come in," Mimi interrupted, but politely. "No one likes people talking out on the landings." She ushered Clayton in and turned to me. "I have two friends running over right now, if you see them outside could you let them into the building? Their names are Giles and Horace."

"Giles and—?" Then I remembered. The two entertainers who'd posed in compromising positions with the man who'd tried to blackmail Mimi. Beaujolais and sedatives, I recalled her saying. I stifled a laugh, more than ever appreciating the wily and somewhat ruthless side of my royal friend.

"Meanwhile, I shall have a nice talk with Monsieur Clayton." She smiled graciously at him. "Can I offer you a glass of wine, perhaps?"

"I'm not finished talking to him." Clayton pointed at me.

"Later. You're here now and he has to go to work, so how about that glass?"

He looked at her for a moment, then relented. "It's a little early but yes, thank you."

"My pleasure. I think I have a nice Beaujolais I can open for you."

She nodded and, as she showed me out, gave me a wider smile and a wink to go with it. As the door closed behind me, I heard her saying, "I must bring out my camera equipment. As a newspaper man you can advise as to whether I should think about upgrading. . . ."

CHAPTER TWENTY-FIVE

Major Herman Jung sat behind his desk shaking his head and tutting. "This is outrageous. How can you be so sure?"

I was at 82 avenue Foch, in the Sixteenth Arrondissement, and the import of location was not lost on me. Number eighty-four, next door, was the headquarters of the SS and contained the offices of the man I was denouncing as a murderer. It was at that address next door that, I knew, many men, and even women, suspected of being spies were at that very moment being held and tortured. I was grateful for the thick walls between the buildings, but the imagined screams still found their way into my head. I'd felt a chill as I walked into the building and right now my blood was crystalizing into ice as a skeptical Major Jung watched me with narrowed eyes.

"Actually, it was the murder weapon that tipped me off."

Trying to look casual, and not let him see my quivering knees, I helped myself to the luxurious chair opposite him. "You were there when he told me about the case. Told me that it was an ice pick that was used."

"Yes, but what does that have to do with it?"

"Vogel said he got there after the doctor had already re-moved the murder weapon, taken it away. Right?"

"Yes, that's correct. So what?"

"I got the report later from the doctor, and he correctly iden-tified it as a chisel. One of Abraham Simon's, the frame-maker. Vogel was ignorant when it came to art, but he'd seen the thin chisel and it was understandable that he didn't know what it was. He assumed that someone had left an ice pick lying around for some reason."

"Which means he saw it with his own eyes," Jung said. "And would not have had cause to pay attention to it, to know it was there . . ."

"Unless he used it," I finished for him. "The staff at the Louvre confirmed for me that Vogel was purloining pieces for himself, and that's consistent with not wanting a policeman poking around in there, looking at paintings and paperwork. I assume it was Vogel and not you who insisted I not go into the museum?"

"Well, yes, now that you say that, it was his idea."

"As was, I would wager, the one-week deadline and severe consequences should I fail."

"Yes, and it makes sense why now."

"Of course it does," I said. "He banked on me fingering the first good suspect that popped up, and if I ignored his sug-gested perpetrators or somehow suspected him, well, he could declare it a failed investigation and use that nice shiny bullet he had waiting for me."

"Indeed." Jung's brow furrowed. "But why did he kill Fischer?"

"I can only imagine that the poor fellow found out that Vogel was lining his own pockets with stolen art and, like the good German he was, confronted his superior officer."

It was equally possible that Vogel had caught Fischer taking artwork for himself, like he did the Picasso drawing. But getting that part of the story right, whichever way it went, would just complicate matters. Most people, I assumed especially the clean, efficient Germans, liked their murders with as few loose ends as possible. Not only was Fischer's theft of the drawing a potential loose end, it was one in the possession of my sister.

"Good heavens, a German officer of his standing stealing like a common thief." He frowned. "Then again, his type are . . . well, let's just say that men like Vogel and his colleagues have a certain disdain for the norms most people value."

"Like human life," I said. "I'd noticed, what with mine being on the line."

"I spoke to him about his threats to you, they were not appropriate. But, as I said, he has a certain disdain for norms."

"And you have a certain disdain for him," I suggested gently. Suggested openly, and hoped inwardly.

The corners of his mouth twitched upward, but that was the only sign I was right. "Yes, well, I suppose this all makes sense to me. Thank you for your good work, is he in custody here?"

"Ah, no." I shifted in my seat. "I wouldn't say that exactly."

This was the part that could go very badly wrong for me, if Jung didn't see the situation the way I did. I swallowed, and said, "Unfortunately, Herr Vogel was less than compliant at the scene of the arrest."

He leaned forward. "Meaning?"

"It was necessary for me to use force." I cleared my throat. "To be more specific, deadly force."

He stared at me, expressionless. "You shot and killed a Waffen SS Sturmbannführer."

This did not seem to be going well, but I persisted. "I did. Although from my point of view, I shot and killed a murderous art thief who was resisting arrest."

"*Mein Gott.*" He sat back and closed his eyes. "And where is his body?"

I thought for a moment, and when I spoke there was meaning behind my words. "Where would you like it to be?"

"Excuse me?"

"Major Jung, he was stealing from the Third Reich, he murdered a German officer, and he tried to unbalance the fragile peace we have here by causing the investigation to fail and me to become another victim." I held his stare. "None of this is good for you. The man was basically a . . ." I let him fill in the blank, which he did, albeit in a whisper.

"A traitor to the Reich." His gaze fell to his desk and I could see the cogs turning. Eventually he looked up and spoke, his voice deliberate now. "I think, speaking hypothetically, that should a senior officer from the Fatherland have committed one or more traitorous acts, ones that amounted to stealing from and shaming the Führer himself, the best outcome would be for that officer to go somewhere very private and do the honorable thing with his sidearm."

"Understood, Major. Even better, and speaking hypothetically still, maybe he chooses a quiet stretch of the River Seine, downriver from the city, to make sure that he is never to be seen or heard from again. That would seem like the noble way out, don't you think?"

"Yes." Jung nodded solemnly. "As unpleasant as all this is, I do think that would be preferable under the circumstances. Especially so close to a visit from our esteemed leader."

"Well then, Major." I stood. "If you will excuse me, I have work to do."

Major Jung stood, too, and extended his hand over his desk. "Thank you, Inspector. For your hard work, and for your . . . discretion."

"You are welcome, sir. But if I may make a request?"

"Of course."

"If you have any more of your officers murdered, would you please choose a different detective to investigate? Especially if there are deadlines involved. They are distinctly bad for my health."

Major Jung smiled. "I will take your request into consideration. However, you've proved yourself very capable so I will make no promises."

I let myself out of his office, and the building, marching stiffly away from avenue Foch until the adrenaline washed itself from my limbs, and headed to the café where Nicola waited for me. It was a little busier than most places had been lately, perhaps because it was Saturday, and my spirits were much lighter than they'd been for some time. To be precise, a week.

"Wine or coffee?" she asked. "After being in that building . . ."

"At least it was number eighty-two, not eighty-four." I shuddered at the thought. "Let's start with coffee. I feel like I should wait until noon to drink wine."

"But we're celebrating."

"We'll celebrate at noon."

Nicola hailed a passing waiter, not hard with those big blue eyes, and ordered two coffees. Then she turned to me. "So he was fine with everything?"

"He was. A reasonable man, thank god."

"Well, it's in his interest to make this little incident disappear into thin air."

"I agree. He was smart enough to see that we'd tied off this potential gusher of a wound for him. Solved a murder and saved face at the same time."

"Did he ask about Babin?"

"No. I don't even know if he has any idea who Babin is, let alone know that he's dead."

"So you still have an open murder case. Or do you think Vogel killed him, too?"

"Between us, I doubt it. He hated him for being homosexual, but I doubt enough to go over and kill him. And he had no other reason to, not that I know of."

"So who did?"

"Any one of our artist friends. Some other Resistance fighter, I don't know."

We sat quietly as the waiter dropped off two espressos. Then Nicola leaned forward and said, "Are you serious? Do you really think one of the others, the ones we know, might have done it?"

I did think so. A war was raging around us, even though it was relatively placid in Paris, and I knew full well what people did to survive, to win. I remembered a moment twenty years ago when I lay beside a crumbling well and considered making a decision that I'd thought about many times since. I don't even know why that moment lingered in my mind. Perhaps because it was the worst thing I'd done up to then. Well, the worst thing I'd had control over, the worst *choice* I'd made up to that point. I'd done worse before and after, but until that evening by the well they'd been out of necessity. One that, given how he was trying to ruin my new life, I felt fairly sure I could finally rinse from the cracked and grimy crevices of my mind.

What I was absolutely sure about, though, was that I was in no place to judge acts of desperation. Life and decency were cheapened by war, and if a group of patriots had killed a traitor, either to help France through this war or just so they could survive another day, I was able to leave it at that.

I said to Nicola, "Remember that Maurice Babin was a senior curator at the museum. He had access to everything and everyone, and maybe he found out about the switching out of the art by our French friends. Maybe he threatened them, after all he *was* working with the Germans." My mind went to the shed in his back garden, and the shiny new lock on the door. I made a mental note to pry it off and take a peek, just to satisfy my own curiosity.

"'Collaborating' is the word being used now," Nicola said.

"Collaborating, then. So maybe he threatened to use that information somehow. To tell Vogel. Or maybe he blackmailed one or more of our Louvre friends, or wanted some kind of cut."

"And you're going to let them get away with it?"

"You know, I think I am." I took a sip. "Seems to me, each one of those people risked his or her life to make sure Vogel didn't steal priceless French art. He'd have killed any and all of them if he'd discovered what they were doing. Hell, I'd bet he was about to do just that at the café. I can't believe that if one of them killed Babin, it was done out of anything but patriotism."

"Proulx will have someone investigate it, right? Maybe even you."

"Possibly. I'm thinking it'll pretty quickly be tagged a suicide, and if not there's Vogel waiting to hold the bag."

"And you feel all right looking the other way?"

"I'm not." I smiled. "I'm looking right at it. Call this my little act of patriotism. And come to think of it, I rather like the irony."

"What do you mean?"

"Vogel wanted me to blame an innocent man, because it was easy and convenient to do so. On this one matter, I shall do as Vogel wanted and blame Babin's murder on a dead man."

Nicola smiled. "That is ironic."

We sat quietly for a moment, then I asked, "Do we need to get extra supplies in for dinner, or was our guest picked up?"

"You get your bedroom back to yourself," she said. "In fact, they drove right past here ten minutes ago."

"I hope he didn't wave."

"I'm sure he did from inside."

"Véra was driving?"

"She was, which is why I'm surprised you didn't notice her go by."

"Hush." I kicked her under the table, but smiled. "So, my future bride isn't just beautiful, she's brave."

"And too smart for the likes of you."

Véra had volunteered to drive Grégoire Burton to the city of Amboise in the café's truck, more than two hours southwest of Paris. They'd not shared the details, but I assumed there was a safe house there for him. I did know he'd decided to try and go back to America, where the discrimination was as real as ever but hopefully not as lethal as here. He'd shaken my hand that morning and thanked me with tears in his eyes, promising to make it back once the war was over. I'd smiled at his optimism that an end to the war meant Paris returning to the people of France, but that didn't seem like the time or place to argue the point.

I reached for the little pot of sugar on the table. "We should do that more often," I said, almost to myself.

Nicola cocked her head. "Do what more often?"

"Help people."

She eyed me over her coffee. "Yes," she said finally. "I think that maybe we should. We definitely should." She looked up and smiled. "But in the meantime, I need your help with something a little closer to home."

"And what's that?"

"I have a drawing I need to hang somewhere, and I was going to let you pick out the frame."

• • •

Despite what I'd said to Nicola, and despite meaning every word, Babin's role and his murder plagued my mind. Proulx gave me the day off so I slipped away from the Préfecture and made for his small house. I made short work of the lock that kept people out of his back garden, but knew I'd be a little more stymied by the heavy padlock on his shed. As I approached the outbuilding, I wondered if I'd have to shoot it off, but this wasn't an official visit and I didn't want to turn it into one by making a ruckus.

As it turned out I did draw my weapon, not because the padlock was too hard to open, but because it was gone. I stayed low, keeping out of view from the shed's small window, and crept to the door to listen. Someone was definitely inside and moving around.

Who the hell is that? I wondered, my stomach tight with nerves. I couldn't tell if there was a light on inside, so decided to wait rather than bust in and silhouette myself against the door. Too many guns around these days, and I was by myself, to boot. I backed up a little and noticed a two-person bench facing the doorway, about fifteen yards from it. I took a seat, my gun in hand.

Two minutes later, no more than that, the shed door swung open and I stood up, gun leveled at the man coming out. He saw me and froze, half in and half out of the doorway. Those already large black eyes opened wider than normal but, it seemed to me, with surprise and not fear. He had a painting wrapped in brown paper in his left hand, and his right rested on the handle of the shed's door.

"Detective. What a surprise." His eyes shifted to my gun and then back to my face. "Is that thing really necessary?"

"I hope not, Monsieur Picasso. What are you doing here?"

"I have the same question for you."

"I am a policeman. Working. You?"

"There is no case, though, you solved it." He gave me a slight bow. "Congratulations for that. But since there is no case, it seems you have no official business on private property."

"You are as good with words as pictures, monsieur," I said with a smile.

He shrugged, then stepped out of the doorway and closed it behind him. He leaned the painting against it. "Words and pictures are essentially the same thing."

This didn't seem like the time and place for a philosophical discussion about art, but the odds of me ever sitting down with Pablo Picasso to have such a discussion over a glass of wine seemed remote, so I lowered my gun and took the bait.

"Meaning?"

"I am not a writer and admire greatly those who can set down ideas and stories on paper. Just as many writers have told me they admire my work, partly for the ideas and images, but partly as something they cannot do themselves."

"I'm not following . . ."

"Writers and painters and poets and, I suppose, some actors. We all do the same thing. We open the mind and challenge perspective. We entertain, we amuse, and sometimes we shock." He waved his arms as he spoke, his voice deep and thoughtful. "But we do more than create, Detective, we also interpret."

"The world."

"That. And other people's work. We can bring it to life, and I'm thinking of an actor's role now because they are often seen as lesser artists." He snapped his fingers. "Photographers, too, how could I forget that brigade of marvelous geniuses?"

I swapped my gun for a packet of Gauloises and stepped forward to offer Picasso one, then lit it for him.

"*Merci,*" he said. He took a deep inhale, then jerked his

thumb at the shed behind him. "Do you know what else we do, as artists?"

"Steal?" I suggested, with a straight face.

He chuckled. "You are an interesting man, Henri Lefort. And I have said before that lesser artists copy, great artists steal. I mean, tell me, is any idea completely original?"

"Some of yours seem to be. *Guernica,* for example. I'm not an art critic but I've never seen anything like it. And your images of people, some of those are . . . original."

"I draw and paint objects as I think them, not as I see them. That is all of the difference." He took another draw of his cigarette and blinked as the smoke rose in front of him. "No, the answer to my question was that artists also preserve."

I pointed my own cigarette at the painting leaning against the shed door. "Is that another word for stealing?"

"If necessary, yes. If you grant the conceit that art is valuable and that artists have worth through their work, it's hardly a great leap to say that great art should be preserved if necessary. Maybe that's by a painstaking restoration project, or maybe it's by hiding a Monet in a shed for a week."

"That's a Monet?"

"Perhaps. Would it make a difference if it were a great work by an artist you've never heard of?"

"Probably not," I conceded.

"So, then. Here we are." He spread his arms wide and stared intently at me. "I am making myself busy preserving works of art, and you are . . . ?"

I took a last drag of my cigarette and dropped it into the grass, grinding it under my heel as I thought.

"Who killed Maurice Babin?" I asked.

"If it's a confession you want, Detective, I am sorry to disappoint. It was not me."

"But you know who it was."

"I have my suspicions."

"Would you care to share them?"

He smiled broadly and surprised me when he said, "Of course. But this is only guesswork on my part, you understand."

"I'll take what I can get."

"First of all," he said, holding up one finger, "it was not one of us. I wonder if that's what you're thinking but you can rest assured it was not."

"Because you're artists and you don't kill people?"

"Maybe."

"Breaking the law is easier once you've done it a few times, no? And your little cadre has been working subversively for France for a few weeks now. If you'd steal for her, maybe you would kill for her."

He smiled. "Again, some of us, maybe. But we had no cause to. Maurice had done us no harm, presented no threat. I'd like to think artists, as much as anyone, recognize the value of human life and so why kill someone for no cause?"

"Perhaps he was stealing, too. I know his dead German friend Walter Fischer was helping himself to a few works here and there. Including yours."

"And Maurice was keeping tabs on that for us. We let that German keep a few things, not even a handful, but anything valuable he wanted, Maurice would talk him out of it."

"So what's your theory?"

"I suspect that Major Vogel confronted Maurice here, either

about Fischer stealing pieces, or maybe about their relationship."

"But Fischer was dead by then, why would Vogel care too much about either of those matters?"

Picasso raised an eyebrow. "You met the man on several occasions, did you not? Finding reasons to hurt people seemed to me his driving ambition."

I thought back to the glee with which he gave me what he thought was an impossible case to solve. The glee coming not just from my failing, but from the thought of what he could do to me for failing.

"I can't argue with you on that."

Picasso sighed and looked over at the empty house. "He did not commit suicide, I can tell you that. He was a good man and valued life, including his own." Picasso looked back at me. "Whatever happened, I can see no other culprit than Vogel. And, thanks to you, he has been painted out of the picture."

I couldn't help smiling. "I'm an artist now?"

"There is an art to detective work, *non*? Surely it's more than traipsing from obvious clue to obvious clue? That would ruin my image of you entirely, Detective."

"I suppose you're right, there is an art to it." I thought about Mimi's theory about *aspect association*, which was as much about art as it was science.

"There we go then." He turned and picked up the wrapped painting, then nodded at me and walked away through the grass to the still-open gate. When he got there he turned and pointed to the painting under his arm. "Not Monet, but a work called *Young Woman Sewing*. It's by Mary Cassatt, perhaps you've heard of her?"

"Mary *Stevenson* Cassatt," I said.

"I'm impressed, Detective. Then you'll know that she was an American, but did her best work after she moved here to France."

"That can happen," I muttered, and watched as Pablo Picasso gave me a final wave, then turned and walked away.

EPILOGUE

France, the Western Front, Friday, July 12, 1918, around sundown

The bricks at the top of the well had mostly crumbled and fallen away, and I'd probably never have found the damn thing if I'd not fallen into it.

The well's existence was a rumor, one we all wished was true, and the stories put it near an oak tree in No-Man's Land. So, there I was, ankle-deep in mud and running half-tilt for a blackened stump that might once have been an oak tree, and what was certainly the only cover for a hundred yards. I felt a rush of relief as I got close, a rising elation that maybe I'd slide into safety before German eyes or bullets picked me out against the darkening horizon.

And then I disappeared completely into the ground.

I dropped straight down, like a bird falling from the sky, and my nose burned as it scored a vertical line down the brick interior until my mud-encrusted boots hit the waterline (which was almost immediately) and dragged me down. I was so surprised I automatically held my breath, which turned out to be a fine idea since there I was, kitted out in full battle uniform and ankle-deep in sludge at the bottom of a distressingly narrow, and very full, well. It flashed across my mind that I was finally getting a bath, but I didn't have time for any further thoughts because my burning lungs sent hot flames of panic licking up my spine to my brain and forced me into action over contemplation, and so I went from stationary shock to flailing panic.

Fueled by the pain in my lungs, and drawn by a circle of relative light fifteen feet above my head, I jammed my fingers and battered boots into the bricks, pressed my back against the other side of the well, and slithered and scrambled out of there like a rat with a piranha on its tail. I abandoned my rifle, which I knew would make Sergeant Peterman curse a blue streak, but I knew I'd come across one soon enough to replace it. There was always some poor sap lying around in the mud, eyes staring at the moon, no longer caring about his rifle. Or anything else.

Always.

I hauled myself over the rim and collapsed in a sodden heap, panting like a dog but reassured I could at least fulfill tonight's mission: bring Larry Clayton a canteen full of water.

I stayed there for a full minute, catching my breath and willing the gathering clouds overhead to cover up the silver disk that was rising over the horizon, rising and shining what was as good as a spotlight out here. The gray and fluffy lumps were moving in the right direction, but not very fast. That's the way things went around here, either at full tilt so that you didn't have time to wipe the snot from your nose, or so slowly you wondered if someone had finally put a bullet in your skull and stopped the world.

I waited. I looked around, and admired the night's scenery of splintered trees that were as black in the day as they were now at sunset. My gaze roamed over the dark mounds of human and horse remains that a week ago were happily (well maybe not happily) alive; one chowing down on hay, the other on hash meat (ironically, and most likely, made of horse), and both trying to grab some shut-eye on straw beds, smelling a lot like each other.

I looked past the well, my eyes straining to see any movement from the Germans who were no doubt scouring this patch of No-Man's Land in case of a dusk attack. No one made those anymore, but war brought out our childhood fears and the coming of darkness heightened the sense of danger. Ironic, then, that the moments of actual peace, of real respite, in this awful blood-soaked war would come at sundown, both sides tired of raining bombs and bullets on each other all day, grateful for that still beautiful moment when the blood stopped flowing and the only red we saw spread itself across the horizon as a signal that we'd managed to live a little longer.

Ironic, too, then that all four of my good friends managed to die around sundown. One by a German sniper who clearly didn't know the no-shooting-at-dusk rule, one from the flu, one shot himself while cleaning his pistol, and one just shot himself. So yeah, that streak of red in the sky meant a little more to me than most, and something a little different.

Eventually the clouds closed around the moon and snuffed it out. I sat up but immediately flattened out again as a bullet zipped past my head, and I waited for the barrage that would surely follow. But it turned out to be a speculative shot, maybe even an accidental one, and silence refilled the night as I lay still and let the mud creep into my nostrils. Eventually, when no one else took a shot at me, I rolled right up to the edge of the well with Clayton's canteen in one hand, mine in the other.

Yesterday, I had been covetously eyeing Clayton as he smoked a fresh cigarette, while not offering me one from the pack, when he showed me the rest of the care package he'd received from his family in Westchester, or wherever they were from. A comb, some playing cards, gum, and soap. I would have loved to have the gum, just so I didn't have to listen to his weaselly mouth chomping and smacking on it. But he'd figured out that drove me insane and kept every stick for himself, eating them one by one whenever I was around. I did have a chance at the dozen cookies he'd been sent, though, and I sure wanted some of those cookies.

Clayton knew it, of course, and we struck a deal because the one thing we both needed was water, despite the rain that soaked us every few days. Everyone's canteens were empty and the sappers were working double time trying to repair the catchment tanks. Some new officer had decided to move them close together to save carrying time, a bright idea until a single German shell landed amidst them. The blast had shredded the canvas siding of every single one, emptying all our drinking water into French soil in minutes to leave us parched, and considerably less receptive to new officers and their bright ideas.

For that reason, Clayton's and my negotiations were carried out dry-mouthed, our voices hoarse and scratchy. Clayton
had twelve delicious bargaining chips and I had just one, and
I had to play mine because those cookies, even though they
were probably hard as nails, represented one of the few things
I missed from back home. Even if they were as dry as a Death
Valley rattler, I just knew if I could hold one in my mouth for long
enough it'd soften up like butter.

"That's if you can generate saliva," Clayton said, when I suggested the technique.

"Or a taste of water," I suggested. "That'd do it."

"I'm out." Clayton held up his empty canteen and shook it.
"How about you?"

"Same." And then, for the fiftieth time that month, we spec-
ulated about the well in No-Man's Land. He offered me two
cookies to find it and bring him some water.

"Two?" I said, outraged. "I'm not risking my life for two
cookies. Eight."

"Three."

"Six."

We settled on four and, as I lay in the mud by that well
we'd all dreamed of, the softly smothered moon above me was
round like a cookie, and reminded me of my reward. I smiled
as I looked up at the clouds, at that faint silver circle. I'd done
some dumb shit as a kid but nothing like this; I mean, here I
was, not quite dumb enough to risk my life for two cookies, but
absolutely dumb enough to risk it for four.

Well, I told myself, *you're only eighteen, so you're still a
kid, and doing dumb shit is what we do.* Plus, since I'd now
found the well, the hard part was done.

I dropped my arm over the rim and shuffled closer, straining to reach down to the water. I let my fingers trail in its soft coolness, but then they caressed something solid, and I swore at the damn tree that had gotten itself shot or blown up a little more and plopped a gnarled limb into my water source.

Never mind, a little charred bark will add flavor. I reasoned, too, that after six months of eating ground oats, ground horsemeat, and ground mud, Clayton's taste buds might relish some freshly barbecued tree. It'd provide some of the vegetables he'd been missing—vegetable, vegetation, with diets like ours such distinctions didn't seem significant.

That said, I had my own canteen and I've always been more of a purist when it comes to my water, so I fished around for the branch. My fingers swished through the cold water and, two seconds later, they closed around the softness of another man's hand. Bile flashed in my guts and I let go with a squeal, snapping my hand out of the water and lying there panting as I tried not to puke. The image of gray, rotting, and waterlogged flesh hung in my mind like a ghastly tapestry, slowly rippling in the breeze like something alive.

I gathered myself and considered the options. Night was settling around me now, a chill moving in with the darkness, and I didn't want to be there anymore. Not by the well, not in this fucking field, and not in France.

Yet there I was, like it or not. And no way was I going to miss out on those sugar- and chocolate-laced cookies, no way in hell. I took a deep breath and reached tentatively back into the water and immediately my fingers brushed against the sodden but distinctive wool sleeve. I grabbed it and held my breath, then yanked the thing out of the water and hurled it as far into the night as I could manage. As it whipped past my face, I thought I felt cold fingers brush across my cheek, and I spent the next two minutes trying not to puke, telling myself that I was wrong, that I'd felt drops of water on my face and not human fingers, not human flesh at all, absolutely not.

I briefly wondered where the rest of the body was—not in the well, surely I'd have seen or felt it. Surely. I looked quickly into the dark hole, but couldn't see anything at all. I swished my arms around, but didn't feel anything else to spark further terror in my brain so I dipped Clayton's canteen into the well and waited as it filled, listening to the slow gurgle in the otherwise silent evening. I left mine empty and, while sending up a quick prayer for rain, slung both of them over my shoulder, rolled over onto my front, and sent up a second prayer for myself.

Then, with the darkness settling around me, I pushed my sodden self to my feet and ran like hell for our trench.

•   •   •

"That's disgusting," Nicola said, but her eyes twinkled with merriment. We were in our usual armchairs, and Mimi sat on the sofa between us. On the coffee table was one empty and one full bottle of that nectar called Pétrus.

"Did he drink it?" Mimi asked.

"I don't know, but I got my four cookies."

"How were they?" Nicola asked.

"Dry, sweet, and tinged with guilt." I shook my head as I remembered. "You know, it was the very next day that I was yanked from the front line by Major Armitage for the mission."

We sat quietly for a moment, then Mimi said, "He really stole things from dead comrades?"

"Yes. Is that clinically meaningful?" I asked. "After all, I stole something from my dead brother."

"Stop it," Nicola said, and I knew that sharp tone well enough to obey.

"She's right," Mimi said. "Those things are not the same. You do know that?"

"I do." I nodded. "Just a little residual guilt."

"I think it's remarkable," Mimi said. "How you two have built, or rebuilt, lives for yourselves here. You should be proud, not ashamed or guilty."

"Fine, but can you stop that, please?" I glared at her hands because for the past minute she'd been tapping one fingernail on the stem of her wineglass. Mildly annoying for others, I imagined, but for me it was like she'd broken the bottle and was poking shards into my brain stem. "You of all people should know better."

"Oh, I do." She smiled broadly. "I've been doing that off and on for about ten minutes. Poor Nicola here has said nothing, but I know she noticed."

"Ten minutes?" I was surprised.

"Indeed. Now, you're not cured, not by a long shot," she said. "But it's curious to note that a heightened state of anxiety may contribute to your condition. Just as a state of greater relaxation, as you're in right now, appears to suppress it a little."

"I do so enjoy being your lab rat," I said, but couldn't help but be a little impressed.

Mimi snapped her fingers. "We need a name for it."

"It's common enough to warrant a name?" Nicola asked.

"That's another reason I wanted to work with your brother," Mimi said. "I've seen it four times before, all in women. I found it interesting a man would have the condition and going forward intend to take note of the gender of my patients with . . . Let's think. You dislike certain sounds. . . ."

"Dislike? I *hate* them. With a passion."

"There it is, then. Misophonia. From the Greek, literally means a hatred of sounds. How is that?"

"Fine by me," I said, reaching for the bottle. I looked at Nicola and she nodded her agreement.

"Then we'll call it that," Mimi said, plucking the bottle from my hand and leaning over to refill Nicola's glass, then her own. "Now, I suggest one of you pull out that recipe book I gave you because, unless I'm much mistaken, your first large box of supplies will be arriving within the next hour." She turned to look at me, her eyes sparkling with humor. "And you can probably throw away that dusty, unused book that it's sitting next to in the kitchen. It seems to me you're doing just fine without your French-English dictionary, Henri."

ACKNOWLEDGMENTS

I usually save her for last, but I want to elevate my wonderful agent, Ann Collette, to the head of the thank-you pack. Ann, you worked almost as hard on this book as I did, somehow convincing me to completely rewrite and restructure the original story. Thank you for making it a much better book, and for all that you do for me.

Two friends I've known for almost as long as I've known Ann: Terry Shames and Jim Ziskin—I trusted you with this manuscript because you are brilliant writers and supremely honest people, so I thank you for your feedback, support, and friendship.

My love and thanks to McKenna Jordan (and my other friends at Murder By The Book in Houston!), without whom this book would not be in your hands. I am so, so grateful to you.

And, as ever, I'm also thankful for my other favorite booksellers and good friends, Scott Montgomery at BookPeople in Austin and Barbara Peters at The Poisoned Pen in Scottsdale. I've missed seeing you in person; I hope that's changed by now.

Thank you to old Joe Wallace, gone for forty years now, but your stories from the Great War touched me and stayed with me lo these many years, such that I used two in this novel.

An enormous thank-you to my editor, Leslie Gelbman, for bringing Henri Lefort into her fold and for guiding me through this new experience. You, too, made this book so much better, and I am so grateful for your experience, your kindness, and your wisdom. I feel truly honored that I get to work with you.

My thanks, too, to Lisa Bonvissuto for always being available, responsive, and encouraging. You are an absolute delight to work with, so thank you. And much gratitude to my eagle-eyed copyeditor, Justine Gardner. To all the crew at Minotaur, thank you for everything you do for your writers.

A word of thanks to some folks who inspired the title of this novel, and the next, the brilliant band Kings of Leon. You don't know me, but your music has accompanied me from first word to last, so thank you.

Last but never least, my love and thanks to my family. Of course, to the real Nicola and Henry for starring in the book, and also to Sarah and Blake for their love, patience, and unwavering support of my writing career.